HEAD OF THE FORCE

Assistant Commissioner Hicks knew that he was in for a troublesome morning—he had an appointment with the Commissioner, and was running late—but nobody could have been prepared for the sight that confronted him when he nervously opened the door to the office of the most powerful man in Scotland Yard. The Commissioner was on time: he was also indisputably, and spectacularly, dead.

Was this murder an act of revenge or part of a terrorist plot? How did it tie in with the death of a young revolutionary, who happened to be the son of one of the Deputy Assistant Commissioners?

Owen Smith, Detective Chief Superintendent, C.I. Murder Squad, was a "chancer", better known for his perseverance than for diplomacy. And he was determined—determined to untangle the web of murder and deception, only to find himself trapped in a world where subversion takes many and sinister shapes.

JAMES BARNETT

HEAD OF THE FORCE

HERON BOOKS

Published by Edito-Service S.A., Geneva,
by arrangement with Martin Secker & Warburg Limited

© *1978, James Barnett*
© *1982, Illustration, Edito-Service S.A., Geneva*

ISBN 2-8302-0260-0

Chapter I

It was late October, a still-born day. Dead before it had life. Trees, mouldering in damp torn rags of mist, haunted the roadside, dim apparitions in a heavy grey veil of rain. Visceral clay evacuated from some distant site glistened wetly on the back of a dumper truck and occasional clods dropped from the vehicle to spatter, flatten and spread under the wheels of following traffic. The trees died away in the passing. Grey factories rose and tombstoned both sides of the road.

The approach to Chiswick flyover was slow as the dumper truck ground up the slope. A huge freightliner broken down in the fast lane reduced all that moved to a centipedal crawl, a tail drawn up to an unmoving head, until the head itself began to move hesitantly forward only to stop and articulate the tail into tight, fuming, and cramped seizure.

Hicks cursed the irritating thump of badly adjusted windscreen wipers and sharply told his driver to get them fixed. He also cursed his own indecision in failing to respond to the driver's suggestion to take the Ealing turn-off until they were past, and it was too late. He sat moodily listening to the Force radio, his knuckled left forefinger in his mouth, chewing lightly on the bone. He had given up smoking six months ago. The Commissioner didn't like smokers.

He was going to be at least half an hour late by the time they arrived at New Scotland Yard and it was a Monday morning with all the week-end crime to assimilate and digest before his morning report to the Commissioner, and the Commissioner expected his report by 10 a.m.

9

He tried reading his newspaper. The lead story was on yet another of the Britain First movement's marches and the inevitable clash with left-wing counter-demonstrators. Sixteen policemen seriously hurt. Forty-three arrests. The General deploring yet another breakdown in law and order. Hicks consoled himself with the thought that at least public order was not within his area of responsibility, apart from the fact it was always down to the C.I.D. to sort out the mess afterwards. There might be a prolonged debriefing for the Commissioner's benefit. It would probably put back his own report. But the jerky stop –start rolling motion of the car induced a slight queasiness in his stomach, and the thought occasioned him no relief.

Hicks turned off the repetitive calls on the Force network to robberies, rapes, burglaries, arson, loitering suspects and indecent exhibitionists, and switched to the B.B.C. channel.

It was the General again.

He promised not Strength through Joy, but Freedom and Responsibility. He was not against immigrants, but against immigration. Those who were here could stay, but no more were coming in. 'Your colour, your creed and your culture are your own. But in Britain you must be of Britain and above everything put Britain First.' To the unions he promised fifty per cent worker participation on all Boards of Directors. The nationalized industries would be de-nationalized on that basis. 'Nationalization of industry does not mean the removal of industry from capital into the hands of labour. It means its removal into the hands of party potentates and civil servants, sleek, silent and sinister civil servants.' The general had a strong run of alliteration. A future Britain was promised with everyone owning a house facing the village green where the sun shone above a cricket match with the home team always winning.

Hicks thought a lot of Lieutenant-General Mulqueen.

As the traffic jerked and crawled towards Hogarth roundabout, Hicks listened intently to the radio interview. '. . . and it is being said, General, that Britain First is a nationalist organization formed with the sole object to set up a right-wing dictatorship in this country.'

The general's voice was attractive to the ear. Tuned, but not dominated by his Irish origins. 'There is nothing new in that. I can only give the answer I have given many times. Certainly the Britain First movement is a nationalist movement and proud of it. It is nationalist in the sense that it contains the finest qualities of the four nations that make up this wonderful country of ours, rightly called Great Britain. It is nationalist in the sense that our main objective is to preserve and enhance those qualities of British greatness and above all, to give opportunity for the great men to once again emerge from the morass of mediocrity in which the existing government has thrown the people of our country.'

'Who do you mean by great men, General?'

'Those men who I am sure are present amongst us at all levels of society. But whose skills, qualities and greatness are submerged in the humdrum mediocrity under which this nation is now obliged, nay forced, to live.'

The interviewer became aggressive. 'I must press you to answer the accusation levelled at your party, of an intention to establish an extreme right-wing dictatorship.'

The general sounded bored, 'Oh dear, I do wish you fellows would come up with something new. I am getting a little tired, and I am sure the nation is getting tired of this. From the pompous pontifications of the Conservatives, the squeals of anguish from the Socialists and Liberals, down to the malignant mouthings of the Marxists, Maoists, Anarchists and Syndicalists, and all the other "ists" and "isms". That's where the danger to democracy lies. Not with Britain First. We have won two by-elections. We are putting up five hundred and eighteen candidates at the General Election. We will win and we will attain power through the democratic process, not by violence in the streets as shown by the left-wing scum that attacked our perfectly peaceful march yesterday afternoon.'

The interviewer went in with a heavy doom-laden voice, 'General, Hitler came to power in the first instance through the democratic process.'

The general was suitably indignant in reply, 'You go too far, sir, I am not a Hitler and the people of this country who support the Britain First movement are not Nazis. You may call me what you will but you grossly and unjustly affront the British people who support our great movement. Most of them from what you would no doubt contemptuously call the working class so callously

11

deprived of work by the criminal inefficiency of the present so-called Government.'

The interviewer, unabashed, offered a qualified apology, 'No insult was intended, General, to you or your supporters, but I do feel the question has validity.'

'Then let me answer it. Whilst I blame the downfall of our country upon Conservative and Socialist traditionalists and bureaucrats, I apportion most of the blame upon those political, industrial, and philosophical agitators and subversives who, working within and without the political, industrial and educational systems of our nation, have nearly succeeded in bringing it down to the level of a mendicant. A beggar, no, a prostitute, whose body is being solicited through the banking houses of the world to support their mad dreams of universal mediocrity.'

The general repressed a note of fervour in his voice and adopted quiet but forceful sincerity, 'To eradicate and overcome the accumulative effect of subversion, to subdue the present horrifying increase in crime, is an intention we will rigorously pursue. National stability can only be achieved from a position of strong national morality. If that is extremist and reactionary policy, then I make no apology.'

As his car pulled up outside the Broadway entrance to New Scotland Yard, Hicks was firm in his resolution to vote for the Britain First candidate.

Chapter II

Roger Fernclough Hicks, O.B.E., Assistant Commissioner for Crime, Metropolitan Police, waited for the lift on the fifth floor, the fingers on his left hand snapping in exasperation at the delay. He had been thirty minutes late arriving at his office on that floor, to find a note on his desk saying the Commissioner wished to see him 'immediate upon arrival'. The note was timed 9.05 a.m. He looked at his watch and accentuated his annoyance with a curse. The damned lifts were always slow. He thought of taking the stairs and decided against it. A pronounced pot belly, a full but hurried breakfast, would have meant an arrival on the eighth floor flustered and out of breath. Hicks took considerable trouble to maintain an impression of the urbane, imperturbable and efficient administrator. But ever since they had stuck him into the post of A.C. 'C' four months ago, the pressures and aggravations of the hottest seat in the Yard had badly scratched the veneer. ('If you are hoping to succeed Hammertoe as Deputy Commissioner, Hicks, we had better add the necessary third dimension to your professional profile. You have never been in Crime and with McLean retiring I want a fresh mind in there. You know my views on the C.I.D. Do you think you can keep these detectives under control?' Thus the Commissioner had addressed him when he was A.C. 'D' in charge of personnel and training. A post wherein his ability to delegate responsibility could be fully exercised. Without in any way displaying the reluctance he felt, Hicks had thanked the Commissioner for the confidence he had shown in him, and firmly accepted the challenge.)

13

Hicks glanced again at his watch as he got into the lift. The Commissioner was a punctilious 9 a.m. arriver and, without ever saying so, conveyed to his senior staff that the same or better was expected from them.

The fact that Hicks was well in the running for the soon-to-be-vacant post of Deputy Commissioner increased his annoyance at his lateness. He knew his chances were greater than those of his immediate colleagues. At just under forty-eight, age was on his side. All immediate rivals were well into their fifties. There was always a chance the Home Secretary would go for some provincial Chief Constable, 'New blood you know, new ideas. Some of your provincial colleagues are coming up with wonderful ideas on progressive policing.' 'They've got damn all else to do.'

The thoughts and anxieties rolling across Hicks' mind vanished in the secretarial annexe of the Commissioner's suite. 'Morning, Miss Poole,' he gave the secretary a slow smile. 'I hope I haven't kept the Commissioner waiting?' he asked, exploringly. 'The Chiswick flyover is getting worse and worse.' The secretary looked puzzled. 'I was not aware the Commissioner had asked to see you, sir.' The voice was arch, with the superiority of minor people who closely serve superior men. 'In fact he must have arrived rather early. I haven't seen him myself yet.' She nodded towards the door of the Commissioner's office. The 'CONFERENCE DO NOT DISTURB' sign hung on the handle.

'Damn, Damn, Damn.' The word hammered in Hicks' skull. 'It must be really something!' He hesitated before the sign but considered the note imperative. 'I'd better go in,' he said hesitantly, seeking reassurance from Miss Poole.

'Will you enquire if he wants coffee now,' she said from behind her desk.

Hicks knocked and opened the door. Twenty-eight years of carefully acquired polish and aplomb fled from him in a second. 'Gawd fucking hell,' he said in the voice of a police constable.

An awareness that the shrill screams of Miss Poole had subsided in choking sobs came slowly to Hicks. He turned from the sight before him and looked at her. She sat on the floor crouched

14

beside the door, now making low howling noises with each exhalation of breath. Hicks wondered hopefully if it wasn't really happening. He had had a nervous breakdown and was hallucinating. He turned again, reluctantly. It was all too real.

Sir Maxwell Charles Steype, Q.P.M., LL.B., Commissioner of Police of the Metropolis, sat in full uniform behind his desk. All except his head.

That was impaled by the neck upon the spike of a ceremonial dress helmet of the now defunct Glamorgan Constabulary, the force he had joined thirty-two years ago as an ambitious law graduate. The helmet, without its present burden, had decorated a corner of his wide desk since he took office. It was there as a silent reminder to sometimes truculent representatives of the Police Federation, that he, the Commissioner, had done it too and knew what life at the bottom was all about.

Holding one arm clutched across his belly, the other hand to his mouth, Hicks forced his attention on the obscenity before him. The neck had been severed high on the front at a slight descending angle towards the back. In three places a thin line of blood ran down to the stiff starched white collar the Commissioner favoured when in uniform. The torso was held upright in the high-backed swivel chair by a black canvas belt.

Hicks found himself drawn round the desk closer to the body. An irresistable compulsion made him reach out a tentative hand and gently prod a shoulder of the headless corpse. The smooth bearings swung the body round to face him, but there was no face. Hicks stood back a pace, his hands falling helplessly to his sides. He looked to where there should be an out-thrust chin and upward enquiring eyes. There was nothing.

'Jesus Christ Almighty!' There was a roar from behind. Hicks started and quivered guiltily as though caught in some act of perversion. It was Hammertoe, the Deputy Commissioner. 'Jesus Christ Almighty,' he repeated in a quieter tone. 'What the hell has happened?'

'I just came in.' Hicks noticed he was wringing his hands, 'I just came in and found him like this.' 'How long ago?' queried Hammertoe. 'It must have been –' Hicks was going to say hours ago when he realized less than a minute had elapsed. 'Just now, I had just entered. I found him – just as he is. I haven't touched him.'

Hicks was now acutely aware he was wringing his hands and wondered why he denied touching the body. Hammertoe looked at him speculatively and went across to the drinks cabinet. He poured Hicks a stiff whisky and handed it to him. He placed the bottle back in the cabinet, shrugged, pulled it back and poured one for himself. Hicks stood looking dully at the contents of his glass. His awareness was returning. He knew something was demanded of him, but quite what he did not know.

'I don't think I'll need it – althought I must admit it was a bit unnerving finding the Commissioner like this.' He glanced over his shoulder. 'Well, Arthur.' He gave what he hoped was a confident smile and put his glass down untouched. 'Or perhaps I should call you Commissioner?' Hicks realized his effort at self-control sounded artificial but it was all he could muster.

Hammertoe looked at him over the top of his whisky glass and wiped his lips. Stony-faced. 'Whether we like it or not,' Hicks went on, 'we've got a bloody murder on our hands. The Commissioner of Police decapitated in his own office in the heart of Scotland Yard. The media will have a field day. Do you want me to handle that side of it, by the way?'

'You are already talking in headlines. Bugger the bloody media.' Hammertoe was now acutely aware of the sobbing Miss Poole still crouched by the door. 'For Christ sake, get rid of that blubbering woman.'

They held an immediate conference at the large table in the Commissioner's office. Hammertoe, Hicks and his two Deputy Assistant Commissioners 'Crime'. The severed head of the late Commissioner looked benignly across at them from its helmeted mount.

D.A.C. Angus Craddock was the only man in the room with previous murder investigation experience. His colleague, Cyril Fairchild, was a Fraud Squad man. Astute, perceptive and with perhaps the widest-ranging mind in the building. But the nearest he had been to a murder enquiry was twenty years ago as a detective-sergeant running the admin on a domestic murder resolved within twenty-four hours, when the husband heaved himself from the parapet of Southwark Bridge, leaving a full confession.

Hammertoe, shrewd, cunning and bluntly articulate. A

truncheon-and-fist copper of the old school, whose polish was the hard glaze acquired by years in the furnace of operational police life. An acknowledged expert in the common-sense psychology of public order. His mere presence at past industrial disputes or political demonstrations had often been enough to secure their quietude. He had been in post as Deputy for eight years. Sir Maxwell Steype was the second Commissioner appointed over his head.

Hammertoe returned the dull gaze of his late chief with a fascinated smile as a small globule of blood gathered at the root of the severed neck and splashed redly on to the shining helmet badge.

Craddock was the first to speak, and addressed himself to Hammertoe. They knew each other very well. 'I suggest, sir, we carry on this discussion in the outer office.'

'I didn't realize you were so sensitive, Angus,' Hicks interrupted smoothly. This was to be a committee meeting and Hicks could handle committees.

'It is the scene of a crime. It should be preserved. Look at it, glasses all over the place,' Craddock cast his eyes over the room. 'What phone did you use to get us up here?'

Hicks' reply was smoothly composed. 'The Commissioner's extension, of course.' Craddock bared his lips angrily to speak. Hicks held up a placating hand. 'I, of course, picked it up with my handkerchief.' Craddock held himself in check. You fucking idiot, he said to himself, you fucking T.V. detective. The words were written on his face. Hammertoe intervened, 'All right, we'll be guided by you, Angus. At least in the preliminary stages.' They moved to the secretarial annexe.

'Has anyone called a doctor to certify death?' asked Craddock.

'I would have thought the death of our Commissioner was all too apparent.' The pitch in Hicks' voice was still too high to make the flippancy sound convincing.

'It's a legal requirement,' said Craddock wearily. He wished he hadn't taken so deeply to the bottle on Saturday night. That was two nights ago. I am getting old, he thought. Christ, was it only four years ago he had gone nearly fifty hours without sleep on the Richmond child murders and then worked a sixteen-hour day for the succeeding seven weeks?

17

'We'll get the Chief Medical Officer across to certify death,' said Hammertoe.

'And we had better get hold of Professor Simonson for the post-mortem,' said Craddock. Fairchild left to make these arrangements. Hammertoe went back into the Commissioner's office and came out with the whisky bottle and some glasses. Craddock sighed, not at the sight of the whisky but at the treatment given to the crime scene.

After he had filled their glasses, Hammertoe said, 'Now as to the enquiry. It goes without saying it will be down to you, Angus.' He looked at Hicks, who indicated there would be no dissent from that quarter.

'No.' Craddock was surprised at the loudness of his voice. Hammertoe looked at him, puzzled. Craddock went on, quietly this time, 'I have been considering early retirement. I've made plans to go at the beginning of next year, in just over two months. This job is going to be a sticker. I cannot see it being finished by the time I go.'

'Oh, come on now,' Hammertoe was firmly persuasive, 'You'll finish this one in no time. It's down to somebody in the building. It could be somebody round this bloody table, but the answer is in the building.' He was looking straight at Hicks, who coloured defensively. Hammertoe laughed. 'Come on Angus. What was it you used to say, it will be a dawdle.'

'Not necessarily.' Craddock surveyed the palms of his hands. There was an enquiring silence. 'I mean, it is not necessarily down to someone at the Yard.' They waited for him to go on. 'There's not enough blood.'

'All right Angus, a nice dramatic touch,' Hicks was not smiling. 'Now let's have the explanation, we are but seekers after knowledge.'

'There's not enough blood.' Craddock paused. He detested having to explain the professionally obvious. 'If you cut somebody's head off when they are alive you get gouts of blood all over the place. Even if you do it when they are recently dead, you will still get a fair amount. You saw it in there.' He waved his hand to the closed door. 'Apart from a few spots on the carpet, dribbles from the head and a few drops that welled up from natural tissue contraction, there is nothing. Whoever chopped off the Commissioner's fu –' He checked himself, not quite quickly enough. 'Whoever was responsible,' he went on slowly, 'the act, the cutting off of the head, it did not happen in the Commissioner's office.'

Craddock was aware of an attentive audience. Fairchild had returned and quietly sat down.

'That,' Craddock searched for words, 'in there, it's a set-up, a stage prop, the body and head were brought in and stuck up like that for effect.'

'I think we all realized there was a dramatic effect, Angus,' said Hicks. 'Whatever we may lack in the finer aspects of murder investigation, the intended effect of finding the body is patently obvious. However,' he went on with an air of condescension, 'we take your point about the blood.'

He turned to Hammertoe and with grave formality said, 'Sir, it is nearly an hour since the er, ah, matter was brought to our attention. Do you think the Home Secretary should be informed?'

Hammertoe scowled, 'She'll keep for a few minutes. I want to be in a position to tell her an investigation is under way.' He transferred his scowl to Craddock, 'And who is going to do the investigating?' Craddock solemnly re-examined the palms of his hands. He said nothing.

'Angus, I don't want to threaten. You can do another two years before your age limit. You may have difficulty in getting authority to go before then in any case. I feel you should consider your position.' He paused for effect. 'I will clearly have to take an extension of service myself.' Hammertoe could not conceal the satisfaction in his voice, and he noted Hicks' pursed mouth with inner pleasure.

'Angus, you are the only man with the rank and experience to do the job.' Hammertoe fed out a low trump. 'I'll guarantee you will go out with an O.B.E. to hang in front of your Queen's Police Medal, and besides,' he laughed, 'think what you'll get for your memoirs. The *News of the World* will pay a fortune, why, with this one cleared up, it could be the *Sunday Times*.' All except Craddock joined in the laughter.

'It's nae use, nae use a'tall,' Thirty-four years in London had not eradicated Craddock's slow Fifeshire accent. He frequently used it in more pronounced form as a means of defence and sometimes as a method of seemingly innocent attack. 'Ah've had thurty-fower years in the job. Thurty-fower years of eighty, ninety, aye and hundred hour weeks, cancelled leaves. Months awa' in the provinces and overseas. Ah've a son who was a junkie living in a bloody commune because Ah couldn't bring him up the right way. All Ah ever had time for was to belt him into submission 'til he finally panicked and ran.' He looked around at them, 'I've got a dying wife.' Hammertoe took out a ball-point pen and to lessen the silence gently stabbed the point at the desk top, allowing the end to fall over, tapping, tapping.

Hammertoe had never taken his eyes from him. 'You still owe it to the service, Angus.'

'Aye,' said Craddock, his accent thickening again, 'Aye, Ah do that, but what does the service owe me? What does it owe ma wife and son?'

Fairchild spoke for the first time in an attempt to break the impasse, 'Would the answer not be for Angus, during the remaining months of his service, to nominally head the enquiry? He will in any case be heading a fairly strong team of detectives with a Detective Chief Superintendent at least as his deputy. The D.C.S. would be doing the donkey-work under the direction of Angus. I could let him have Creech from the Fraud Squad. I agree he has not a great deal of murder-squad experience, but I think even Angus will agree he is one of the ablest investigators in the Force.'

'It's an excellent idea.' Hicks smiled gratefully at Fairchild. Hammertoe was looking softly at Craddock. He reached out and grasped the top of Craddock's shoulder with a huge hand. 'What do you say, Angus?' He shook Craddock gently. 'Eh, Angus what do you say?'

'Not Creech.' Craddock felt it stirring in his belly like a stiffening erection. The hunter's urge, a controlled rape, an orgasm anticipated but delayed until all obstruction and rejection has been cleared and penetrated, until the quarry embraced him with an exhausted sigh. 'Not Creech,' he repeated.

'If you say so, Angus.' Hammertoe was reeling him in gently.

'But he is a very able man.' Hicks jerked on the line. 'A Bramshill scholarship resulting in a First in Sociology. One of the most impressive products of the senior command course, and as

Fairchild says, a very able investigator.' The line held and Craddock bit deeper into the hook.

'All detectives are investigators, Mr Hicks, but not all investigators are detectives. The investigator needs a trail of investigative factors leading to further investigative factors and to a successful conclusion of his enquiry. But if there are no investigative factors, he is finished. That's where a detective comes in, a man who can paint a landscape he has never seen from inside a darkened room. It's the difference between the craft and the art.'

'That's about the most pompous statement I've ever heard,' Hicks objected stuffily. Craddock smiled at him, quite pleasantly.

'Who do you bloody well want then?' Hammertoe was his usual brusque self.

'Smith.'

'Which Smith is that?'

Hicks came in. 'There is only one Smith as far as Angus is concerned. Owen Smith on the murder squad. The fellow that's caused all that trouble in the Caribbean. We sent him out there at the request of the Foreign and Commonwealth Office to make discreet enquiries, with the accent on discreet, into a series of political murders. He winds up arresting the island's Attorney General and about to arrest the Financial Secretary, when they throw him into an aeroplane and deport him.'

Hammertoe took off his spectacles and threw them on the desk. 'Oh Angus, for Christ sake, the Commissioner is still seeing the Foreign Office over that mess.' He swept the spectacles back to his face, 'Or at least he was.'

Craddock was firm, 'You know it, everybody knows it. They wanted to hang a few mug punters to save their own skins and Smith wouldn't wear it. He got right into the top team and they threw him out because the local Administrator wanted them in anyway. And the people down the road in Whitehall wanted them in.'

'That may be.' Hicks leaned back in his chair and clasped his hands behind his neck. 'As you say Angus, all investigators may not be detectives, but all detectives are certainly not diplomats.' He stretched his arms with fingers still entwined above his head.

'Mr Hicks.' Hammertoe did not conceal his impatience, 'Please make your point.'

'I was merely thinking,' said Hicks, adding 'sir' after deliberate hesitation, 'that diplomacy may be more important in this – ah – investigation,' he smiled at Craddock, 'than detective ability.'

'It wull be Smith and ma self,' Craddock was grinning now, 'or ye can find your ain wains.'

'So be it.' Hammertoe rose sharply to his feet. 'I shall now inform the Home Secretary of what has happened. I shall use the phone in my own office.' He looked malevolently at Hicks. 'I shall also inform the good lady I am prepared to soldier on as Acting Commissioner until she decides to recommend a new Commissioner to the Monarch.' He was smiling at Hicks but the malevolence was still there. 'And who knows, who knows.' He hesitated in the doorway.

'By the way, Roger,' he said amiably over his shoulder, 'by all means take charge of feeding the meat to the media.'

Hicks, still sitting in his chair, did not reply. Hammertoe closed the door softly. Hicks looked up at the solemn, composed face of Craddock. 'Go and piss up your kilt, Angus.'

Chapter III

Owen Smith, Detective Chief Superintendent, C.1. Murder Squad, was in his Commander's office on the second floor. He stood by the window looking moodily into the dull drizzle. He had just lost an argument with Commander Bastwick, who had knocked eighty pounds off his claim for incidental expenses incurred during the Caribbean enquiry.

'Owen, for Christ's sake be reasonable, you just can't claim eighty pounds for paying somebody to screw the suspect's house to find out what kind of gun he had,' Bastwick had said.

'I was paying for information. I didn't tell him to screw Esperanza's house. All I wanted was information about the make and calibre of his gun. The informant said he could find out. How he would do it wasn't mentioned.' Smith's reply had been straight-faced.

'I know you too well, you bugger,' Bastwick replied without insult. 'He did screw the house, didn't he, and was caught, and said you told him to do it?'

'That was two days later, after his fingers were broken and his three-piece suite kicked to pieces. All right, forget it.' Smith felt anger and recognized it as the anger of frustration and resentment. The recognition increased his anger.

The phone rang; Bastwick had returned to his desk and taken up papers with a finality that said the subject was closed.

'Commander,' he snapped into the mouthpiece. 'Oh yes sir –' he was immediately subservient '– He is with me now as a matter of fact.' Bastwick nodded into the phone. 'Right away, sir. Can I enquire as to the reason, sir?' The answer was obviously abrupt and rude.

'Craddock,' he indicated the phone. 'He wants you up in the Commissioner's office. Right away.'

Smith felt his collar was too tight. He eased a finger into the neckband. 'I take it he didn't –'

'No he didn't,' Bastwick waved his expenses claim. 'Bloody obvious isn't it.'

Smith did not relish the encounter. He had only met the Commissioner once before. Everything about him was brilliant and hard. His logic was the logic of the rigid administrator who, if he understood the need for resilience and elasticity in the operational demand, never openly recognised or acknowledged that need. The rough-hewn cog of improvised operational police work had to fit the precisely engineered gear of administrative policy. Any grinding noise emanating from a failure of cog and gear to mesh was decidedly unpleasant.

Smith felt a little better when he found Peter Wingate, head of C.3. photographic section, with his chief, Commander Claude Rissington, fat, genial, and in police circles, world-renowned fingerprint expert. The clutter of tripods, boxes and brushes indicated they were there on business. They waited in the secretarial suite looking expectantly at the closed door of the Commissioner's office.

'What's going on, Claude?' Smith cast a glance at Wingate to include him in the question.

'Haven't the foggiest,' Rissington was amiably uninterested, 'but I sincerely hope it is not another demonstration of Scotland Yard methods for a visiting dignitary.' He leaned across Smith to look at Detective Chief Inspector Dewlip, who ran the Scenes of Crime liaison section at the police laboratory and stood knocking tentatively on the open door.

'Come in son, and join the party.' Dewlip heaved his equipment across the threshold. 'Good morning, gentlemen.' He blinked nervously behind heavy black-rimmed glasses. 'I hope I am not late. First time I've been to the Commissioner's office, for some reason I assumed it to be on the top floor. I've been up and down the lifts . . .' His voice trailed away; he was sweating quite heavily. 'Mr Craddock insisted I came alone. These boxes are very heavy . . .'

Craddock opened the door of the Commissioner's office just

wide enough to allow him to slip through. Dewlip stumbled in confusion amongst his equipment blocking the door to the corridor. 'Shut that bloody door, Mr Dewlip.' They waited whilst Dewlip sorted himself out and closed the door.

They gathered round Craddock, standing with his back to the Commissioner's door. Craddock was smiling, the smile of secret knowledge about to be revealed. Smith knew Craddock. The smile did not necessarily mean it would be pleasant.

'Gentlemen,' said Craddock in a voice of exaggerated solemnity and respect, 'the Commissioner of Police, Sir Maxwell Steype.' He threw the door wide open.

Craddock was pleased with the effect of his presentation. The audience responded with open-mouthed astonishment and exhaled epithets. The Lord's name was blasphemously invoked many times. But all were case-hardened professionals and it was the person and place of the victim and scene that caused astonishment, not the nature of the crime.

Within a few moments they were in the office looking, examing and assessing, but only with their eyes. They touched nothing, moved nothing and having established a position stood there with only head and eyes in silent motion. Craddock watched approvingly.

'All right,' he broke the concentration. 'Peter,' he turned to the photographer, 'you know what's wanted. First set in black and white and a further set in colour. Mr Dewlip,' (he always addressed people of junior rank whom he did not know closely in a formal manner) 'you give him a hand and take care of the forensic side at the same time. Claude, Owen, we'll leave them to it.'

He ushered them out of the office. 'By the way, Peter,' he said to Wingate, 'three sets of prints only at this stage,' a harshness in his voice brooked of no misunderstanding, 'you will hand them to me personally and to no one else irrespective of rank. You will seal the negatives in an envelope in my presence and they will be kept in my safe. That applies to the later post-mortem examination photographs and any others taken in the course of the enquiry. Understood?' Wingate nodded.

Craddock moved into the anteroom with Smith and Rissington. He noticed he was glad to sit down. 'Shut that bloody door,' he muttered as Wingate's flash-gun stabbed his eyes. He leaned back and surveyed the bright dots dancing across his unfocused vision.

Smith thought how old and tired Craddock looked as he sat in the chair gently massaging his eyes between finger and thumb.

'Well now,' Craddock inhaled air and expelled it noisily. The act seemed to enliven him. 'Let's see what we've got.'

'There's one thing we haven't got,' said Rissington, 'and that's a Commissioner. God Almighty, this is going to upset a few apple-carts,' Rissington was looking forward to seeing one or two faces when the news broke.

'Make the most of it Claude,' Craddock was not being sarcastic, 'but we've got a murder and it's a murder that's got to be cleared up quickly, efficiently and' – he looked meaningfully at Smith – 'in the right way.' He paused. 'I want you on this one, Owen, you are cool and you are methodical. You've got the gift. But you are colour-blind to red light. You don't know when to back off. You're good but you're a fucking chancer, Owen. Don't take any chances with this one. If you do I don't want to know and I don't want to know you. Got it?'

Smith's voice was equally firm in reply. 'I never take unnecessary chances and I never take chances without anticipating the consequences. If things go boss-eyed it has never been down to anyone but me.' There was no defiance, only quiet respect when he added, 'And you know it, Guv'nor.'

Craddock waved a weary hand, not wanting argument. 'It will be apparent to you both that Steype was not killed in his office. He was killed elsewhere and his head removed elsewhere. I doubt if it was even in the building but we will have every floor, every office, store and cupboard searched anyway. Assume for the moment he was done outside. The last sighting of him alive so far established was about 3 p.m. yesterday afternoon at the Britain First march. You know his habit of sniffing round on his own in plain clothes at these Sunday demos to be sure no stupid copper goes putting the boot in when they cut up rough. Particularly when the T.V. cameras are about.

'He was seen in several places around the fringes of the march. He was on his own as usual, although he had spoken to D.A.C. Ormerod from "A" department, who was in charge of policing.

'Now the demonstrators marched from Hyde Park, down

Oxford Street, Regent Street and Haymarket to Trafalgar Square where they planned to rally, sing the National Anthem and dismiss. Now, the left-wing mob had a counter-demonstration at Trafalgar Square that was permitted on the understanding it broke up thirty minutes before the Britain Firsters arrived at the square. Much to Ormerod's pleasant surprise, it did break up as agreed. He thought he was in for a nice peaceful day. However, most of them just spread out in St James's Park, there were others around Charing Cross and still more in Pall Mall.

'Everybody thought they were loose and unco-ordinated, but as the Britain First crowd entered Haymarket, whistles started blowing and the mob re-assembled at the run, broke the police cordons on the square, and piled into the Britain Firsters. As usual, the coppers were middled and took the worst of it.

'The point is, if the Commissioner was caught in that melee he could have been swagged away down a side street, into a vehicle of some kind and off.'

'Why didn't his wife call in when he failed to show at home that night?' asked Smith. 'And what about his driver. Didn't he report him missing?'

'He never used his official car on Sundays, you know what he was like on overtime. He wouldn't bring his driver out. Hicks has spoken to Lady Steype and broken it to her. I believe she has taken it very well.'

Craddock searched for words to bring him back to the subject in hand. 'That's beside the point. She says, and it is known, it was not uncommon for him to spend the night at his club when he came out on a Sunday. She assumed this to be the case last night, particularly,' Craddock need not have paused; he had their attention, 'particularly when he told her he was meeting someone around eleven.' He met their enquiring eyes and went on, 'Over a matter of grave national importance.'

The trite phrase was an anti-climax, thought Smith. He knew at least ten nutters a day called at New Scotland Yard on matters of grave national importance.

Craddock went on, 'She doesn't know who he was going to meet or where and he didn't say what was of national importance.'

It was all too leisurely for Smith. 'Sir, I'd like to get every

27

coppet on that demo interviewed for sightings of the Commissioner as a starter. Then we will have to identify and trace the participants on both sides.'

'Yes, all right,' Craddock agreed. 'Who have you got to run the office?'

As Smith picked up the phone he said, 'Detective Inspector George O'Brien.' He looked at Craddock and asked, 'Can I tell what it's about at this stage?'

'Might as well,' said Craddock grumpily, 'I have no doubt at this moment Mr Hicks is changing into a powder-blue shirt and his college tie and otherwise preparing to be his usual calm, articulate and determined self at a Press conference. But for his ears only and I'll have his ears on a plate if it leaks further.'

'George,' said Smith into the phone, 'we've got a heavy one. The Commissioner been found decapitated in his office.'

They all heard the disbelieving laughter crackling through the phone. 'Is that some new kind of perversion, Guv. I always fancied him to be a bit –'

Smith cut in, 'Don't act the fool George. This is serious. Open up an action book and get this down.'

He waited whilst O'Brien found a book. 'Head it "Murder of Sir Maxwell Steype, etc." Body found at –' He looked enquiringly at Craddock who rose and took the phone.

'Craddock here.' It was a threat rather than an identification of the speaker. A nervous 'Yes, sir' sounded at the other end. 'Body found at 9.38 a.m. today by Mr Hicks, A.C.C. in the presence of Miss Poole, Commissioner's secretary, who is at present in Westminster Hospital being treated for shock and hysteria. She is to be seen as soon as she has recovered and a statement obtained. Almost immediately on scene, Mr Hammertoe, Deputy Commissioner. Mr Hicks and Mr Hammertoe will supply statements personally.'

He put his hand over the mouthpiece and said with grim anticipation, 'And further statements will be taken from them by me to fill in half the essential detail they in their bloody ignorance will leave out.'

He resumed speaking to O'Brien. 'You got that? Right.' He went on to list the sequence of events at the scene. 'You will get the names of every single police officer and support unit engaged in yesterday's demo from "A" Department. You will tell the

Commander concerned from me, politely and firmly, every man on duty, there will probably be around two thousand of them if I know "A" department's tendency to over-police every demonstration involving more than three men and a dog.' Craddock had never been a fully integrated police officer. 'Every one of them is to be warned to attend the Yard at intervals of one hour per hundred men, starting,' he looked at his watch, 'at 3 p.m.

'They can start with inner divisions and work outwards. This procedure will continue without stop until every man has been interviewed. It can be done by questionnaire, the relevant question being "Did you see the Commissioner at any time during the demo?" If any of them did, they are to be subject of full statements. The object is to see if the Commissioner was swagged away by anyone during the demo. Build up the questionnaire along these lines. I leave that to you.

'Next you will contact every Commander C.I.D. in the building. I want a total of eighty experienced C.I.D. officers, and tell them I mean experienced, not wankers and bag-carriers. Have them stand by in the fifth-floor briefing room. You will again be polite but firm with the Commanders concerned and let them be in no doubt these orders come from me and I don't want moans about manpower shortage and current commitments.

'When you've done that set up a murder room in the large conference room and refer any bleating about that to me as well. Got it all?' A series of 'Yes, sirs' replied.

Smith doubted it O'Brien had got it all but O'Brien had been with him on enough murder cases to start appropriate action on the briefest résumé of the facts.

Wingate came out of the Commissioner's office. 'All finished. Dewlip's got a few bits and pieces, mainly blood samples and fibres. Nothing that looks significant at the moment. Claude –' He hesitated at the familiar in Craddock's presence as Rissington outranked him, '– Mr Rissington has made a start. I'll let you have the prints as soon as they are developed.'

'And the negatives,' said Craddock. 'Oh and Wingate, I want them this afternoon.' Wingate was about to protest but changed his mind, 'I will do my best, sir.' Craddock gave him a dead, glacial smile.

*   *   *

Smith and Craddock went into the Commissioner's office, not so much to watch Rissington working in a controlled flurry of mercuric powder with quick delicate brush strokes, but just to stand looking at the spiked head. Wondering, with the subconscious hope of every murder investigator who is up against it, if the victim's mouth will open and just say a few words.

'I have heard there were a few hatchet jobs taking place along the corridors of police power, but isn't this going a bit far?'

The voice was interestingly cold and precise with no hint of the cynicism the words conveyed. The speaker was a tall man with high sunken cheeks. A wide thin-lipped mouth like a scar lay between an upturned wide-nostrilled snout nose and the blunt prow of a dark-blue chin.

Craddock was cautiously respectful, 'Thank you for coming over so promptly, Professor.'

'My dear man, when Fairchild told me what had happened, I dropped everything.' Something approaching warmth and enthusiasm entered his voice as he surveyed the corpse.

Simon Simonson, Professor of Forensic Medicine at St Peter's Hospital, was without doubt, including his own, the most eminent medico-legal expert in Europe.

His nose hovered like the barrels of a sawn-off shotgun at the side of the stumped neck. He probed round the edges with skeletal fingers then tried to flex a rigid arm. He pressed a calf muscle. 'Rigor seems fairly advanced. There will be little point in taking the body temperature but we might as well do it anyway.' He opened his bag and took out a long anal thermometer.

'This place will be as good as the other I suppose and a damned sight more convenient.' He thrust the thermometer down the oesophagus. 'I presume some medic has pronounced life extinct?' He looked up enquiringly.

'Doctor Finbien came along earlier,' said Craddock.

'Did he have any difficulty in reaching a decision?' Simonson seemed almost interested in the answer. Craddock said, 'One look was enough.'

Simonson turned his attention to the mounted head. He stood before it, contemplative, elbow cupped in hand, fingers drumming on his heavy jaw. 'Not really one for the National Portrait Gallery, but the Tate could do something with it – Hmm.' He looked at his audience but this time received no response.

'Any idea on a time of death, Professor?' asked Smith.

Simonson looked at him from lowered brows. 'Oh, Smith, you know better than that. The human body does not carry a concealed clock that stops with its hands fixed precisely at the time of death. Find out when he had his last meal and when we see what he has in his gut we might be more precise. In the meantime we have the rigor, and you do know about rigor, don't you?' There was no condescension in the question, only in the thin smile that accompanied it.

Smith knew about rigor ever since he attended his first C.I.D. course, but he couldn't help the sequences running through his mind. Onset in face and jaw muscles in about four hours, stiffening progresses downwards through the body, with complete stiffening in about twelve hours. This could be hastened in warm conditions or delayed in cold. Stiffness will last for about a further twelve hours, and gradually disappear upwards leaving complete muscular limpness after thirty-four to seventy hours, dependent upon temperature.

Smith considered the air-conditioning and said, 'About nine hours ago.' Simonson shrugged disinterested shoulders and said, 'I'd give yourself a couple of hours either way.' He hitched up the knees of slightly flared trousers and dropped on one leg beside the Commissioner's chair. 'Yes, I thought so,' he said without emphasis. Craddock eased stiff joints down beside him.

Simonson pointed to purpling weals around both ankles. Despite the correctness of every other detail of clothing, the Commissioner was not wearing socks or shoes.

'Yes,' said Craddock, placing a hand on the desk to help regain his feet. He looked apologetically at Rissington. 'There was nothing there,' the latter said assuringly.

Craddock came back to Simonson, 'Well, Professor, it's not surprising to find he was tied up at some stage.'

Simonson sighed. 'Not only tied up, my dear Angus, strung up. Did you not see how deep the pressure marks were above the front of the ankles and running with less pressure to the lower heel. Your Commissioner, Angus, was strung up by the ankles and bled like a ...' He reached for another, more delicate, metaphor.

'Stuck pig?' said Smith blandly.

31

'I thought sacrificial ram might be more appropriate.'

'Do you mean he was suspended in the air and they hacked his head off?' Craddock could not keep the revulsion from his voice.

Simonson had by now removed the uniform cap with its diced band from the spiked head, and was examining the sparse grey hair. 'They certainly cut his throat whilst he was suspended. Although the head has been washed there is still quite a bit of blood in and around the hair at the side of his head.' He turned to Smith. 'No need to draw little pictures?'

'No sir,' said Smith politely. 'Are we to understand, sir,' he went on 'that more than one stroke was made in severing the head?'

'It was certainly not done on a guillotine or by an immigrant Chinese executioner. Although I think they simply do it with a bullet in the back of the neck these days.' Simonson pondered the latter point.

'But I am digressing, am I not. Yes, Mr Smith, certainly more than one stroke. Come here, can you not see the clean incised cut across the left side of the neck, and a further deep incision across the frontal aspect above the larynx, and a third stroke extending to the right side of the neck where use of a very sharp instrument tapers out and a heavier implement used to disarticulate the head.' Simonson paused to reflect. 'No, that is too precise and surgical a term to use – shall we say, to hack through the spinal column.'

Craddock was making strokes with each hand in turn at the root of the Commissioner's neck. He seemed to favour the left hand as he repeated the gestures several times. 'A left-handed man?' he enquired of Simonson.

'Don't forget he was upside-down, Angus,' said Simonson, 'and even I cannot specify gender.' Craddock decided to change the subject.

'Well, we can assume two implements were used?'

'No, Angus, we know two implements were used, I have said so.'

'Something like a razor and an axe or a butcher's cleaver,' Craddock went doggedly on.

'Indeed a razor would be admirable. An old-fashioned and very appropriately named cut-throat razor, and more likely a cleaver than an axe. The hacking has been done pretty consistently in the same area, indicating fairly precise control. Better than you could expect with an axe, even a small one.'

Simonson withdrew his thermometer from the neck. 'Eighty-one degrees,' he said, looking round for something to wipe the glass rod. Smith gave him a paper tissue from the desk. With an exaggerated 'Tha-a-a-nk you!' Simonson went on, 'Your time of death looks all right so far, but don't expect me to give you more than an hour either side. Not even if you have a witness who heard Big Ben strike the hour when death occurred.

'And by the way, before you bother to ask, let me assure you no medical knowledge or skill was required to effect this butchery.' The nostrils pouted, 'Butchery, that any common butcher would find professionally abhorrent.

'Well now, is there anything else I can do for you at this stage?' Simonson looked at them enquiringly. There was no response.

'Then I take it you have not observed a further obvious point?' His glance at the three men was accusatory.

'Look here.' He withdrew a gold pencil from his waistcoat pocket and standing behind the chaired body indicated a point between the collar and the gaping root.

Craddock put on his spectacles and examined the place thus shown. Just visible above the collar were two small incisions, one slightly above and in front of the other.

Craddock's breath hissed through bared, grimacing teeth. 'Jesus Christ.' He looked up at Simonson, 'Tentative cuts?'

'Possibly, my dear Angus, possibly.' The scar that was Simonson's mouth slanted into a lop-sided grin. 'I am glad to see you have retained some forensic knowledge after all these years. The tentative cuts an intending throat-cutting suicide makes whilst gathering . . .' he hesitated, 'shall we say strength for the final irrevocable slash that resolves all his problems.'

Simonson glanced from spiked head to headless body, 'And the man did have his problems, did he not?' He picked up his hat and rolled umbrella.

'So, gentlemen, what we have to decide is this. Have we a suicide that is being made to look like murder? A grandiose and imposing murder as befits a Commissioner of Police?'

Simonson lifted his umbrella and aimed along the rifling of its tight immaculate folds. 'Or have you instead a hesitant, re-luctant murderer who scratches for his courage to kill and having found it begins to take pride in his work.' Simonson was one of those people who manage to speak in facetious terms with all the severity of a hanging judge.

He shouldered his umbrella and said, 'I shall have lunch before conducting the post-mortem. I prefer viscera as a digestif rather than as an aperitif. Shall we say Westminster Mortuary at three?'

The tip of his umbrella scratched across the lintel of the door as he went out.

Chapter IV

The Commissioner's body with helmet-mounted head had been discreetly moved out of the building and across to the mortuary in Horseferry Road.

Craddock and Smith were lunching on cheese sandwiches and canned beer in the former's office. They listened to the radio interview with A.C.C. Hicks.

'Mr Hicks, is it not an indictment of Scotland Yard's supposed efficiency when the Commissioner of Police himself is murdered in the most brutal fashion in his own office?'

'In the first place,' Hicks was calm, polite and even-voiced; he had studied interview techniques, 'I am satisfied from enquiries made under my direction and from forensic indications we noticed on discovery of the body, that the Commissioner was not murdered in his office or indeed, as far as we can at present ascertain, within the Scotland Yard building.'

'Thanks for the "we",' Craddock grunted.

'Is it not, then, a grave reflection on internal security at Scotland Yard that some person or persons conveyed the body into the building, placed it in the commissioner's office, and escaped undetected?'

Hicks knew when to make an admission.

'To an extent this is true. However,' – he also knew to qualify an admission – 'it must be remembered the body was brought in during the early hours of Monday morning, when only a skeleton staff was on duty. At normal times, the building is the place of work for many hundreds of people, both police and civil staff, and although only one entrance is in common use, there are many other entrances and exits for emergency use and service facilities. Our manpower shortage is such, they cannot all be covered.'

'It is obvious there must be inside knowledge and assistance directly or indirectly connected with the crime?' The interviewer went into his confidential just-between-ourselves attitude.

Hicks chose to nibble the bait but refused the hook. 'Naturally that is a hypothesis we have considered and are looking at most closely, but other than the facts already known, we have not, so far, found evidence to support this proposition. You must bear in mind we have a large turnover of civil staff in the administrative, catering and maintenance departments, and indeed outside visitors, all of whom have a greater or lesser knowledge of the geography of the building.'

'Bullshit.' Craddock's remark was addressed to the pomposity, rather than at the accuracy of Hicks' statement.

The interviewer saved his plum for dessert. 'Now, Mr Hicks, I have been told the Commissioner was found with his head severed from his body. Is this true?'

'Fuck it.' Craddock swore savagely.

Hicks was up to it. 'It would considerably impede our enquiries if, at this stage, I made any comment upon the manner or detail of this crime, and I have no intention of doing so.'

The interviewer was satisfied, the point had been made. 'Thank you, Mr Hicks.' The sarcasm was faintly noticeable.

'It would be easier to conceal the mating habits of rabbits in a hutch than keep something under wraps for five minutes in this fucking place.' Disgusted, Craddock slung an empty beer can at the waste basket.

Smith said nothing. He knew the importance of keeping certain details of a crime out of public knowledge, but this was one detail they couldn't keep quiet for long.

Craddock had served from the days when despite publicity of his cases, his name retained a shadowy anonymity on the printed page. The advent of increasingly ebullient, aggressive and critical T.V. reporting drew a resentment from him amounting at times to phobia. The 'meddling medium' he called it, and any officer who appeared upon the screen was in his opinion an exhibitionist who found little favour in his eyes.

Hammertoe lumbered into the office. He used his bulk like a battle tank. Massive, forward-thrusting shoulders directly supported a great lowering black-browed head. Jowled flesh hung over his collar from the back of a close-cropped neck to the front of what had once been a square-jawed chin. Thick thighs swung implacable feet in lurching, elliptical strides.

'Angus, you are buggering up every committee and working party in the building. Who the hell gave you authority to take over the conference room and set up your murder squad in there?'

'There is nowhere else with enough space. It is the death of the Commissioner I am investigating,' Craddock replied evenly. 'If that collection of intellectual wankers cannot masturbate their egos within the privacy of their own offices when I need space for an operational enquiry, then surely they can use the briefing-rooms.'

The weight in Hammertoe's voice was threatening. 'The Commissioner may be dead, Angus, but it is not for you to bury him. There was a time when I might have agreed you cannot run a police force by committee, but I am Acting Commissioner, Angus, and the force will continue to run as Sir Maxwell intended it to be run.'

Hammertoe leaned hugely upon Craddock's desk. 'You see Angus, I am not going to upset the Home Office at this stage of the game. There are too many Civil Servants swimming about in think-tanks these days and I must anticipate the future.'

Hammertoe moved towards the door. 'So move them out, Angus – today.'

Craddock's reply was politely cold. 'As you say, sir. And by the way, could I have your statement on the discovery of the body at your earliest convenience. And ah,' – the accent came in strongly – 'wull ye be sure tae include a full account of your movements on the Sunday.'

He sat back in the trench of his chair to await the counter-blast. None came. He fired again, 'Efter all, we canna upset the Home Office by not showing them we've got a clean hoose ourselves, can we.'

Hammertoe laughed at him, 'Angus, I wish to God you would change your act. The only thing worse than a professional

Scotsman is a professional Irishman. You will have my statement tonight.'

Smith had sat listening with amused interest. 'Both of you gentlemen have considered the problem of statements from senior officers?' he enquired. 'After all, we cannot very well impartially eliminate ourselves.' He looked to Craddock more for support than anything else.

Hammertoe chose to misinterpret the look. 'Oh, Mr Craddock is well beyond suspicion. You spent the week-end with McLean at Brighton, didn't you, Angus? You went straight down there after the "E" Division dinner on Friday night. Came back on the eight-ten from Brighton this morning.'

Craddock was watching Hammertoe above praying hands, each forefinger gliding gently up and down the sides of his long thin nose.

'You were in the company of McLean all day Sunday. You and your wife went to bed at eleven forty-five that night.'

McLean had recently retired from the post of A.C.C., to be succeeded by Hicks. McLean and Craddock were fellow Scots and had been colleagues in the C.I.D. since the rank of Detective Sergeant.

Hammertoe looked down at Craddock with cold amusement. 'You didn't think I would put you on this one without checking first?' The mock incredulity vibrated in the room. 'Did you, Angus?'

Craddock's silence answered that he did.

Smith began to feel uncomfortable. 'I'll get hold of the photographer and cover the P.M.' The statement hung in the air. 'Is that O.K. with you, Guv?' Smith was careful to address the question between the two men rather than at any particular one. It was Craddock who finally looked up balefully and said, 'Get on with it.'

While he was glad to get out of the building for a time, Smith was not happy with his position. Two years in the rank of Detective Chief Superintendent and accustomed to running his own enquiries from corpse to conviction, directing the build up, assessing the evidence and, where no evidence existed, using his instinct to create solid steps of enquiry in a bog of mystery. To size up and interrogate the suspects, to decide when to arrest and when to charge. But this lot . . .

As he left the Yard, the newspaper billboards in front of the underground station screamed at him: 'MURDER IN YARD', 'POLICE COMMISSIONER KILLED IN YARD OFFICE', 'POLICE HEAD – DECAPITATION MYSTERY'

The rain had stopped and a freshening wind drove cloudy galleons across a sky of widening blue and suddenly glinting sun. He looked at his watch. There was time for a walk round St James's Park. Despite the wind, sodden leaves stuck tenaciously to the wet path. A flock of late migrating geese rose in alarm from the lake as a distant Concorde fluttered the surface with imperious thunder and soared upon its majestic way to New York.

As the sound receded, Smith reviewed the day's events. He agreed with Hicks' radio statement about the ease of entry to the Yard. Any police officer from anywhere in the Metropolitan area could get in, as could anyone with the confidence to flash a piece of black cardboard with gold lettering. Alternatively anyone with the ability to pick the locks on the various un-attended service entrances could get in, provided there was a look-out on the perimeter patrol.

Then the body had to be transported to the eighth floor. Assuming the same right, or the same confidence, the basket of a mail trolley being wheeled about the building was a common sight, as was any of two dozen wooden trolleys used to wheel bulky objects around the various departments.

He had told O'Brien to lay on an early action checking all external doors and for a laboratory liaison officer to check all trolleys for traces of blood, however minute. Everyone working within the building on Sunday was to be closely interviewed as to sighting any trolley on the move whether they knew who was with it or not. He knew the Commissioner's office would be locked solid in the absence of attendant staff, but then the Commissioner would be carrying his office keys when he was snatched. So the fact he had seen no sign of forcible entry was of little significance. The offices were cleaned between 8 p.m. and midnight, so no help there.

Smith dwelt upon Simonson's display over the tentative cuts. He made up his mind to dismiss any suicide possibility. Even if some fool had wanted to cover up a suicide, they could have chopped off his head on any vacant lot without risk and with the same result. Nevertheless a benefit performance had been staged. But for whose benefit?

'Possible suspects?' Smith released the breath from his mouth in a lip-spluttering explosion, causing the dingy pigeons scrabbling unconcernedly in the path at his feet to flutter indignantly aside. From Hammertoe, down to any stupid thick-headed P.C. who had been disciplined or turned down on a promotion board. No, discard stupid or thick-headed for this one, he thought. Could it be done single-handed? He reviewed the difficulties. It could, but it wouldn't be easy.

Somebody outside the job? Not connected with the police? Only with inside help and knowledge. Somebody now outside but formerly inside? More likely. Paranoiac promotion-hungry officers, whose original potential had dried up in the energy-consuming rat race for top jobs. Those who had seen the door to promotion slammed in their faces. Those who had been leaned on to retire early. Those who had been told to resign or else –. Those who had been nicked and done time. Smith decided to stop speculating. The possibilities were endless.

He realized he had returned to his starting-point and it was ten minutes to three. Back through the underground station, a quick dash across the traffic in Victoria Street. He pressed on through the diminishing crowds round the market stalls in Strutton Ground, down to Horseferry Road and Westminster Mortuary.

Wingate was waiting inside as Smith arrived, his tripod set up. No casual hand-held snapshots for Scotland Yard photographers. Their pride in the clarity and quality of every detail within focus was renowned.

A young bearded and bespectacled detective sergeant named Neaterkin was gaping open-mouthed at the headless but still uniformed body of his Commissioner.

'Hello Owen,' Wingate greeted him, 'enjoy your lunch?' Smith nodded. 'All right for some,' said Wingate moodily.

'You the exhibits officer, son?' Smith ignored Wingate's crack.

'Yes sir, Mr O'Brien told me to report to you here. He didn't tell me –' He looked down at the body. 'It is the Commissioner, isn't it?'

Smith was looking round the mortuary, 'You've lost the head already, have you?

'Oh no, sir,' Neaterkin looked offended. 'I've been to post-mortems before. Lots of them.' He was quite aggrieved.

'Not your head, the Commissioner's head.' Smith looked enquiringly at Wingate.

'It's in the chiller. O'Brien came over with the body and stuck it in there in case someone opened up a peep show on it.'

'O'Brien should know better, Simonson will do his nut if anything is stuck in the chiller before his examination.' Smith was easily annoyed by unprofessional action, however well-meant.

Wingate was unconcerned. 'I doubt if it will do any harm. You know that bit about the ice-cold brain behind Scotland Yard in the Sunday supplements.'

Smith pulled out several corpse-filled drawers before finding the one containing the head. He lifted it out gently, one hand under the helmet mount, another pressing down on the skull. The sparse grey hair felt cold and brittle under his fingers. The head wobbled precariously as he placed it on the draining-board beside the sink. It settled, leaning enquiringly to one side.

'Right,' said Smith, 'Simonson's had a look at him dressed at the scene. Let's get the clothes off him and see if there is anything else.' Before removing each garment, Smith surveyed every part. No holes, no slits, not even a visible bloodstain on the dark blue material of the uniform.

' 'Ere, that's my job.' The mortuary attendant wandered in, protesting and gesticulating with a cup of tea, slopping the contents on the floor.

'Piss off, this one's spoken for.' Smith nodded to Wingate, who ushered the still-protesting attendant out of the door. 'I'll report this to the Coroner.'

The tunic removed, Smith saw something red through the fine weave of the Commissioner's white shirt. Rigor was still present in the arms and the shirt was removed with some difficulty. Marked by a red fibre-tipped pen, the Commissioner's hairless

41

chest displayed a crudely drawn British flag with an axe buried in its centre. Underneath was written

A BRITAIN FIRST PIG
EXECUTED AS AN ENEMY OF THE PEOPLE
S.O.P.

Chapter V

The initials S.O.P. meant nothing to Smith but, in common
with everyone else, he knew about the Britain First Movement
and he knew, or thought he knew about its leader.

Lieutenant-General Liam Xavier Mulqueen, former G.O.C.
Land Forces Northern Ireland, was a product of the province
itself, where the British Army had since Wellington, found so
many of its generals. But Mulqueen was different. The son of a
Roman Catholic doctor, who found in the British Army a career
free from the bigotry of his birthplace, a bigotry almost genetic-
ally produced by three hundred years of internecine hatred
and murder. A career that grew and, with it, his love of Britain.
Not of England or Scotland or Wales, or even Ulster, but of
Britain: of Britain and the British.

In Berlin, in the aftermath of the war, while still a young
lieutenant, he had seen the rebirth of the new Germanic states,
East and West. He had observed the way in which the peoples on
both sides of the curtain were moulded to conform with the
different patterns laid down by their conquerors. And he came to
the conclusion that the only way to rebuild a sick nation and its
people was to deaden the will by war, destroy the malignancy in
the mind and slowly, very slowly, allow a new pattern of growth
to emerge under careful cultivation.

He had been in command in Northern Ireland for two
months when a secret landing of Czech arms was made on a
lonely beach on Lough Swilly, and safely transported by the
I.R.A. to the vaults of a ruined abbey north of Derry. There
was enough and more than enough to resolve, at least militarily,

the differences between Official and Provisional wings of the I.R.A. The promise of an enterprise so appealing to the minds of both, it could not be resisted. The great ambush ... That, and the thought of the guns brought out 'the boys', sagging spirits revived, and rebel songs on their lips at the prospect of the guns. The long blue steel barrels, the sensual slide of a lightly oiled action, the orgasmic recoil of exploding cartridges ... the euphoria of glory, immortal legend, and dead enemies.

The attack on the British column went in as planned. The Kalashnikov assault rifles rattled and the R.P.G. rockets screamed across the highway, but from concealed positions above and behind them British soldiers poured in a deadly crossfire. The great ambush had itself been ambushed and at its bloody end more than a hundred of 'the boys', some of them boys indeed, lay dead. And more than sixty lay quietly moaning in wounded grief.

And when armed Protestant extremists on hearing news of the battle swept into Catholic areas intent on wiping out what they called the last bastions of the I.R.A., they too were shot down with great impartiality by the British Army.

In the keening and confusing months that followed, a populace numb from long years of bomb and gun, and heavy with the shock of the culminating battles, went quietly to the polls to elect representative members to the reconstituted Northern Ireland Assembly. The barriers came down, the road blocks disappeared. No bombs exploded and children played football in the streets.

Mulqueen had been removed from Ulster long before this. He had carried out his plans without the slightest degree of consultation with his political masters. He knew in any case they would have recoiled in horror from his intentions. It was said he knew of the arms landing and future I.R.A. intentions, through well-placed informants within the organization. He had allowed it all to proceed, with the outcome deliberately planned.

There was talk of court martial, but the media, loudly in his favour, screamed with outrage, as did a large number of M.P.s on both sides of the house.

Mulqueen was placed on the inactive rolls. The knighthood due to him on appointment to his rank and command should have appeared in the next Honours list. The absence of his name was all the more apparent by the blank space in the alphabetical order of newly titled knights, as if that name had been hurriedly removed. There were protests, arguments and discussions and the loudest were in favour of Mulqueen but the coveted 'K' never came. He retired fully from the army, refusing to comment upon or discuss the issue, but eight months later he re-appeared before the public as the leader of a political movement he chose to call Britain First.

And almost simultaneously supporters appeared in all the large cities. Offices in bright decals of red white and blue opened in main streets from Bristol to Aberdeen – and even in Belfast. At first windows were broken and firebombs thrown at the buildings, but as the popularity of the movement grew the attacks subsided.

The general knew the media pitched their product on the basis of a mass assessment of the national intelligence being that of a child of 13.9 years of age.

Everybody understood the general.

In particular Lionel 'Laddie' Landon, Conservative Party M.P. and merchant banker, understood him. To the extent of resigning the party whip and sitting as the original Britain First M.P. He was followed by Sam Quigley and Ellis Skelton, two moderate Socialist M.P.s who feared a refusal to nominate them as Labour Party candidates at the next general election.

The general, thought Smith, was not a man to be idle in retirement.

The revolving doors were spinning with exiting civil staff when Smith returned to the Yard. He waited for the lift, turning over in his mind Simonson's post-mortem findings.

The late Commissioner had been a very healthy man for his age. Before his throat was cut.

Cause of death: massive haemorrhage from deep incised wounds across the lateral and frontal aspects of the throat. After death the head had been removed from the trunk by enlarging the existing wounds with a heavier sharp instrument. No attempt had been made to finely disarticulate the spinal column. Simply brute force with at least three blows from the heavier instrument required to achieve separation.

Bruising around the ankles consistent with the body being suspended by a rope shortly after death. The rope marks were clearly defined and could be related to the original rope if it were found.

Suspension of the body had resulted in a loss of blood from the trunk additional to that incurred as a consequence of the fatal incisions. This considerably reduced post-mortem lividity but there was sufficient to indicate the body had been contained in a compressed state lying on its back, legs pressed into the abdomen. Two indentations two inches wide and eighteen inches apart ran laterally across the back. From these indentations, and from other parts of the torso and thighs, small splinters of wood had been removed. Several pieces of wood-wool shavings had been found adhering to various parts of the body and inside the shirt.

From all this Simonson had stated, 'It is possible to advance the hypothesis, amounting to strong probability, that the body has been contained in a compressed state inside a wooden box for at least two hours, and the box probably one used for the conveyance of china or some other fragile material and would have dimensions not exceeding 3 feet 6 inches in length, 2 feet 8 inches in width and 3 feet in height.'

The writing on the chest had been inscribed after death as the ink appeared to overlie minute blood traces from a probable downward spill of blood when the body was removed from its suspended position. The epidermis and underlying tissue had been removed from the rib cage to preserve the writing.

The two cuts found below the fatal incisions were not sufficient in number or depth to be considered likely as tentative cuts usually found in cases of suicide.

Smith could hear Craddock's voice, penetrating in its anger into the corridor, as he walked towards A.C.C. Hicks' office. Smith waited outside with an interested ear cocked. The door rattled before anything further was said and he managed a couple of disinterested strides before Craddock emerged behind him. 'Smith!'

He turned into Craddock's scowling face, 'My office,' Craddock barged past. 'You would never believe it,' a resigned weariness had replaced Craddock's anger, 'that –' He pointed a finger at his office wall in the direction of the A.C.C.'s suite. 'That –' The discipline of years was being stretched to avoid using, in anger, obscene contempt of a senior, to a junior officer.

Contempt he nevertheless would use without a thought in a more amiable frame of mind.

'That man tells me now,' he looked at his watch, 'at six-thirty in the evening he found a note on his desk when he arrived this morning, saying he was to report to the Commissioner forthwith. He assumed his secretary had taken the message, typed the note and left it on his desk. She had a ten a.m. dental appointment and was gone when he arrived.'

Craddock waved a despairing hand. 'She knows nothing about the message and the commissioner's secretary knows nothing about it either.' He massaged his forehead in frustration. 'Now he can't find it. Thinks he left it on his desk or threw it in his waste-paper basket.' Anger crept back into his voice, and resolution went. 'Or wiped his stupid arse with it.'

'Why didn't he mention it earlier?' Smith enquired.

'He was caught up in what he calls the turmoil of events. In other words, poncing about in front of microphones and T.V. cameras. And he has the absolute gall or stupidity to say he does not consider the note to be of great evidential value. A type-written note, not of great evidential value. My God!'

Craddock held his arms wide and looked heavenwards, palms outstretched as though waiting for the nails to be driven through.

The fact Smith did not have direct responsibility for the investigation lessened any agony to mere annoyance. In spite of himself, he was beginning to be glad not to have charge of this case. There was, and would continue to be, too much on-top interference.

Craddock's door burst open and a flushed and triumphant Hicks entered. 'I've found it, Angus. Look here.' His eagerness was almost obsequious. He held the crumpled note in his hand. Smith leapt out of his chair as he saw Hicks unfold the paper and spread it out on the desk. He was too late.

Hicks looked at him, coldly curious. 'It was in my waistcoat pocket.' He was not wearing a waistcoat. Craddock noted the fact with eyes raised to Hicks' face in silent enquiry.

'I took it off before going to the T.V. studio. The heat of the lights you know. I suppose I slipped it into the pocket before going upstairs.' Hicks was offering an explanation, not an apology.

'Well,' he said, rubbing satisfied hands together, 'all's well that ends well as they say. Get the bottle out, Angus, let's have a drink. Oh, Oh, half a mo' though.' He laid a long forefinger up the side of his nose. 'Better not,' he said, after due deliberation. Craddock was still only speaking with questioning eyes.

'Eight o'clock this evening. At the House. The Home Secretary wishes to confer with the Acting Commissioner and ourselves, including,' he turned a raised eyebrow to Smith, 'whoever will be in charge of field enquiries. Which I presume refers to you, Mr Smith.'

Hicks drew himself up and squared his shoulders, 'It might therefore be, shall we say, inappropriate if we attend with liquor on our lips.'

Craddock poured out an inch of scotch into three glasses and carefully added a further half inch of water. Handing a glass to Hicks, he said, 'We can always suck peppermints.'

Smith went down to the second floor to check with O'Brien, who, on being evicted from the conference room, had re-established the post in two smaller offices on the C 1. corridor. Smith was pleased to see a smooth flow of uniformed officers being processed through the system. Typists clackered noisily in the background as incoming handwritten statements were transposed into typescript.

Neaterkin, the exhibits officer, had established himself in a corner amidst a welter of plastic and brown paper bags, into which he was placing the individual of items of clothing removed from the commissioner's body. A row of bottles held a glutinous array of stomach contents, blood samples, urine, fingernail scrapings and all the other visceral specimens destined for the Police laboratory, whose staff had been warned to work round the clock.

Smith gave Neaterkin the note, now contained in a plastic envelope. 'After you have entered it in the exhibits book, get it up to photographic. Then to C 3 for fingerprints. Tell Mr Rissington he'll probably find A.C.C.'s fingerprints all over it. But if he finds any others, I'll put in a bottle of scotch. And when you get the photostats . . .' He paused and curbed his impatience as Neaterkin wrote down his instructions. He looked up at him, pen poised.

'When you get the photostats, copies to the laboratory to

check the typewriter index. They will scream for the original. Tell them after it's been done for fingerprints but to get on with it, we want to know make and model as soon as possible.'

'Yes sir, I've got it. Will you check and initial my notes.'

The curb slipped. 'If you've got it wrong, son, all I will intial is your request to return to uniform.'

Smith worked his way, past a line of uniform officers awaiting interview, to the adjoining office where O'Brien had set up his empire of statement readers, indices and action books. The phones were manned by three women officers covering eight additional lines. The message file was already thickening.

'How's it going?' O'Brien, in shirt-sleeves, held up a respectful hand while finishing an entry in the action book.

'O.K. Guv. We've got about sixteen sightings of the Commissioner so far, all the way from Hyde Park to Haymarket.' He ran his fingers down a schedule. 'The latest so far, at the top end of Haymarket. He was seen standing on the raised step of a shop doorway looking into the crowd just before the punch-up started.' His fingers ran across the page. 'That was at three-twenty. We have a lot more to get through, so time and place must be regarded as provisional.'

O'Brien reached out and grabbed a passing probationary detective constable. 'See if the tea trolley is still in the corridor, son. Get me a cup of tea and a salmon sandwich, if no salmon, then ham. But not cheese or egg.' He looked at Smith. 'Anything for you, Guv?'

Smith shook his head, 'Haven't time.' The probationary detective held out an entreating hand for money. 'Piss off.' O'Brien spoke with outraged dignity.

'By the way,' O'Brien called after Smith, 'have you seen Henry Dewlip?'

'Not since we left him at the scene. Has he turned up anything?'

O'Brien reached into a desk drawer and handed Smith a small plastic envelope. 'He wanted you to see it before he took it across to the lab.' Smith held the envelope up to the light. It contained a small fragment of white granular substance.

'Cuttlefish,' said Smith.

'Not much doubt about it.' O'Brien agreed. 'Henry found it under the key-board in the back hall Inspector's office. It was wedged between the carpet and the skirting-board. No telling how long it's been there. The cleaner's vacuum would never have picked it up in the position it was in.'

Smith was still holding the plastic envelope to the light. 'Cuttlefish,' he repeated with no surprise in his voice. 'That explains the locks. I suppose there was no sign of forcing?'

'Clean as a whistle.'

The probationary detective came back with O'Brien's tea and sandwich. 'You owe me seventy-eight pence, sir.' Smith admired his courage.

'Some of these kids just don't want to get on in the job.' O'Brien paid with reluctance.

'George,' said Smith, 'as soon as you've finished feeding your face, get on to Commander Brightside. Tell him Mr Craddock wants everything he's got on an organization calling itself S.O.P. I don't know what the letters stand for, but Craddock wants everything he's got by ten tonight.'

'It's nearly a quarter to eight now, Guv. He'll be long gone.'

'With the Commissioner murdered in his office! He's not as daft as that, even if he is Special Branch. You'll find more senior officers, uniform and C.I.D., in the building at midnight tonight than you would at midday.'

The prospect gave Smith and O'Brien some pleasure.

Chapter VI

Smith found Craddock waiting with some impatience in the foyer. The grey old-fashioned homburg hat he always wore displayed dark finger-marks round the peak and brim, all the more apparent because of repeated cleaning. His tartan scarf, another trademark, was crossed under the lapels of a loose-fitting Crombie overcoat.

As they turned from Dacre Street into Victoria Street, the chilling wind hit Smith between the shoulders. He wished he had taken time to get his own coat.

Hammertoe and Hicks had gone ahead by car. Both were waiting in an ornately panelled room. An attendant ushered in Craddock and Smith. The four stood around a large oak table. Crested leather-backed chairs and a Ministry of Works clock on the wall completed the furnishings.

There was an uneasy grimness on three faces at the prospect of an encounter with a senior cabinet minister. Only Hicks appeared at ease, showing pleasurable anticipation.

The reverberations of Big Ben tolling eight still danced in the air as the door opened and a small pear-shaped man owl-eyed the people in the room over half-moon spectacles. 'Ah Hammertoe, Hicks, good evening. You will be Craddock, I don't think we have met.'

Desmond Rachette, Deputy Under-Secretary of State in charge of the Home Office police department, held out a limp hand to Smith and looked towards Hammertoe for introduction. 'Sir, this is Detective Chief Superintendent Smith, he is assisting

Mr Craddock.' 'Ah yes. Smith. The name is not unknown to us.'
There was a lack of warmth in the voice. Smith felt the hand
which was perfunctorily withdrawn.

'This is indeed a sad and dreadful business, gentlemen.'
Rachette took the chair at the top of the table and waved the
others to seats.

Hicks casually slid into a chair on Rachette's left, answering a
glare from the slower Hammertoe with a smile.

'The Secretary of State has asked me to express her sympathy
to you and the entire Force.' Rachette bowed a solemn head to
Hammertoe. 'Regrettably she cannot join us, the business of the
House. The Britain First members are being a bit obnoxious over
E.E.C. contributions. However, as she would be acting on a brief
from my department, it may be more simple and direct if I chair
this meeting. I take it there is no objection.'

The power of Rachette and his civil servants over the
Metropolitan Police, if not absolute, was near enough so to make
his question mere courteous rhetoric.

'That goes without saying.' Hammertoe's reply was accompanied by a look at Hicks that lashed across the table. The latter
closed an opening mouth.

'This discussion is of course completely informal and its
purpose merely to ascertain the existing situation insofar as the
Home Secretary and her duties to Parliament are concerned.'
Rachette, nevertheless, conveyed an air of formality.

'Now first and foremost, the rumour, if rumour it be, that
certain indications exist to suggest the late commissioner met his
death at his own hand, and, shall we say, some cover-up
operation has taken place to conceal the fact?'

Hammertoe cleared his throat noisily. 'Mr Craddock is
perhaps best qualified to answer this question.'

Rachette gave Craddock an inviting smile. Craddock drew a
contemplative chin into his chest and rattled a brief roll of fingernails on the table.

'There were present on the neck of the Commissioner certain
small cuts. They resemble the tentative nicks or incisions made
by an intended suicide. They are present on nearly all throat-
cutting suicides. An absence of such cuts indicates a possibility of
murder. However, their presence does not necessarily indicate
suicide.'

'I am afraid I am not quite with you all the way, Mr Craddock.' Rachette was politely puzzled.

Craddock went on. 'We know the Commissioner was suspended in the air, unlikely to have done it himself. I've never heard of a suicide hanging himself up by the ankles after cutting his throat. If you don't take it from me, you can take it from Professor Simonson,' he leaned forward gathering the fingers of his right hand into a fist, 'this is a case of murder.' He laid his words on Rachette like a gauntlet on the face.

The challenge was rejected in a benign smile. 'Well indeed, Simonson does agree with you without being quite so emphatic. One wishes, at times, our medico-legal friends were always as firm in their convictions, before conviction, as they become after conviction when publishing definitive works.' The final words were addressed to the ceiling and no one replied.

'I digress. May we now examine the ah – mystery.' He put the word on his lips with evident distaste. 'Perhaps I should rephrase and say, the problem, of how entry was effected to Scotland Yard. Despite what I am told are fairly formidable locks.' Rachette looked expectantly down the table. 'Is there, as yet, an answer to that, gentlemen?'

'Cuttlefish.'

Smith did not intend to pause but the pressure of eyes against his face haltered his tongue. Rachette's smile was almost pitying. 'I am sure you did not intend to be enigmatic, Mr Smith, but once again I am in difficulty. The significance of a multi-armed sea mollusc to our debate escapes me.'

Carefully Smith lit a cigarette. 'The bone, the solid core if you like, of the cuttlefish is commonly used by criminals to make impressions of keys. We found traces of cuttlefish in the back hall Inspector's office under the keyboard. Every external key to the Yard is kept on that board.'

Rachette leaned against the back of his chair. 'Ah yes. I see. I understood from my admittedly limited reading of detective fiction, the bar of soap or the wad of Plasticine was used for that purpose. I would have thought the substance you mention was too brittle to be, as it were, impressionable.'

Smith said nothing but reached into his pocket, produced an irregular oval of bony, white material. He took out a key and pressed it into the seemingly solid smooth surface. He removed the key, blew out a residue of powder and slid the cuttlefish bone along the polished table.

It stopped under Rachette's stubby fingers. He surveyed the perfect mould with detached interest but made no effort to pick it up. Then carefully bent a middle finger into the trigger of his thumb and flicked the bone back down the table.

'The point is taken, Mr Smith. However, our purpose here is descriptive language rather than demonstrable action. Nevertheless,' the benignity of the smile was now reflected in the voice, 'the point is taken. There is more to the matter than the honing of budgerigars' beaks.'

'Let us move on, gentlemen.' Rachette cast an oblique eye at the clock. 'One of the many unpleasant aspects of this case was the use made of the Commissioner's body to present what is presumably a political slogan. Do you know anything of the organization? It seems our ah – security services do not.' Rachette had an aversion to the use of dramatic phrasing.

'In a specific sense, neither do we.' The debate had been out of Hicks' mouth too long. 'But my Special Branch are aware of left-wing militants describing themselves as Soldiers of the People. It is a generic term in extremist circles and it would be difficult to pin the label on any particular group. Interpretation of the initials at this stage is mere speculation, but I am having the possibilities fully investigated.'

Smith sighed. It would be pointless to expect Hicks or any of the other top brass to record their actions in the Action book. Craddock would have to speak to him before any further useless duplication occurred.

'Then let us not chase shadows here.' Rachette dismissed the subject. 'There are other difficulties both practical and political. Despite the apparent indications, one might say, all too apparent indications of external influences in this case. And I include the appointment of a most ambiguous nature the Commissioner had with some unknown informant, which he presumably never kept ...'

As Rachette went on, Smith wondered what the meeting was all about. Rachette seemed to know as much about the facts as he did. Smith soon got the point.

'We must, therefore, consider the possibility, regrettable though it may be, the strong possibility of some serving police officer, even of senior rank, being involved in this crime.'

Rachette's enquiring eyes scanned the table, seeking agreement. A succession of heavy heads, pursed lips and downcast eyes showed this to be a question not to be asked. Hammertoe's pen turned between finger and thumb, hitting the table in time to the loud ticking of the clock. He cleared his throat as if the bile of heartburn had reached his gullet.

'As you say, the possibility exists and it is one that has not been overlooked. I took it upon myself to ascertain Craddock's movements over the material times, and he in turn has checked the actions of Mr Smith. Needless to say, both Hicks and myself will agree that our own actions be subject to verification and clearance. Similar action will be taken in respect of every officer, senior or otherwise, who enters the orbit of this enquiry. I have known Craddock for many years. His reputation is, I am sure, known to the Home Secretary. She, and you, may rest assured he will pursue his enquiries vigorously and without favour, irrespective of the direction they may take.' Hammertoe twitched a black eyebrow at Craddock, who got the message.

'Let me make it quite clear, Mr Rachette, I took on this investigation with great reluctance. My reasons were personal. Personal in a domestic sense, not for professional reasons. If it is a question of my integrity my resignation –'

Rachette's voice sliced down the table like a sabre. 'Emotional reactions are not necessary, Craddock. Your personal feelings, and your personal problems are not the issue here. I thought,' the pause was deep, 'I thought I made it clear, there exist practical and political considerations I expect to be treated objectively. However speculative the question may be the possibility of the Commissioner having been murdered by one or other of his own officers exists and for that reason if for no other, the investigation should be taken up by a police force other than the Metropolitan.'

Hammertoe was on his feet. Long arms resting on simian knuckles, pressing white into the table. 'I find the suggestion outrageous.' His body rocked towards Rachette, then, pushing himself upright and clasping his hands behind his back, he addressed the air four feet above the seated conference. 'I regard the suggestion as clear interference with an operational matter. And as an operational matter it is, with the greatest respect,' his voice slurred with sarcasm, 'completely beyond the control and direction of Home Office.'

He glared down at Hicks, an imperative command for support.

Hicks deflected the glare on a barrier of impassive and serious deliberation. Knitted brows and a reflective gnawing upon a knuckle showed he was considering the wider implications. 'I fully realize this is an operational matter, nevertheless, and with great respect,' he gave an exaggerated nod towards Hammertoe who had noisily pulled back his chair and seated himself behind folded arms and crossed legs, 'I appreciate the considerations on which the proposal is formed. The possibility of an inside agency at the Yard being involved has already been raised by the media, although the inferences are still low-keyed. It may do our image a great deal of good if we unselfishly allow the enquiry to be taken over by an outside force at an early stage and before critical comment is made.'

'Images, images,' Hammertoe's Methodist upbringing lay behind his contemptuous snarl. 'Graven images, plastic idols, electronic idolatory and false prophets.' Smith savoured the ·heavy sonority of the words. You're putting on an act, he thought; you must have expected this, you cunning old bastard. Nevertheless, he admired Hammertoe's stand. Whatever personal ambitions his devious mind might harbour, Hammertoe's anger at the implied slur upon the name of a Force he had served for nearly forty years was, if extravagant, also genuine.

'It is being suggested,' outrage took Hammertoe's voice on a higher level, 'that the Metropolitan Police should not investigate the brutal murder of its own commissioner, because to do so might provoke critical comment by the . . .' The search to find an alternative word of acceptable strength caused his mouth to hang open. He failed in his search and spat into Hicks' face, 'Your bloody media.' The shrivelling glare was absorbed by an impassive mask.

'Or even worse,' a sympathetic glance at Craddock, 'because of our alleged lack of integrity. That is how your bloody media would interpret it.' A fist thudded on the table.

'Oh now really, Hammertoe, do let us be constructive please.' The physical enormity of Hammertoe coupled with the controlled violence of his words had unsteadied Rachette. His voice was more pleading than demanding. 'I really thought we had resolved this emotive question of integrity. The Secretary of State fully realizes this is an operational matter.'

He sought refuge and strength by praying in aid to higher authority. 'But it was her carefully considered view that the investigation should be in the hands of an outside force. It would demonstrate, yet again, the desire of the Metropolitan Police not only to be impartial but to be seen to be impartial when the conduct of their internal affairs is called in question. As Hicks has already agreed.' He favoured Hicks with a nod.

'This particular internal affair is not being questioned by anyone.' Hammertoe was unrelenting.

'It is the function of management —' Rachette cut his words nervously as Hammertoe's eyes widened in outrage under a thunderhead of gathering brows. 'No, let me amend that and say it is the function of the civil side to anticipate public disquiet that may, indeed will, be expressed in the circumstances of this case.'

'If, for public disquiet, you substitute the rantings of a few loud-mouthed minor politicos trying to get their names in the papers, then I will accept that proposition.'

'No, Mr Hammertoe. I will not alter my words. Such a statement is not one to be expected by the Secretary of State in discussion of this nature.' Rachette was finding strength at this altar.

'Then, sir,' Hammertoe assumed a dignity to match his bulk, 'you may inform the Secretary of State that if there is to be interference from her office in the operational conduct of this force, she may anticipate my immediate resignation, and I will feel obliged to make a public statement as to the reasons for my resignation.'

The carefully relaxed but alert form of Roger Hicks straightened sharply and bright eyes scanned Rachette's face for its reaction.

Rachette was back in full control and the calm but implacable face and following words reduced Hammertoe's throbbing speech to that of a mere player. 'It is clear gentlemen, this matter is being over-simplified and the wider issue ignored.'

Rachette went on, 'Gentlemen, you have been most helpful. If you would remain, Mr Hammertoe.'

The sudden off-hand dismissal caught Hicks still in his chair.

It took a long quizzical look from Rachette to make him realize he was included in the dismissal. He reluctantly followed Craddock and Smith from the room. They left Hammertoe seated, staring grimly at the panelled wall, club fingers probing gently along his jawline, as though easing a massive toothache.

A drift of smoke from a pile of smouldering leaves stung the air as they entered the car. More than leaves have been burnt tonight, thought Smith.

Chapter VII

They ascended in silence to the fifth floor of the Yard. The heavy breath of dormant life throbbed in the corridor, inconsistent with the latening hour. A cluster of staff officers and branch heads stopped their buzz of speculative conversation and viewed the arrival of the three men silently but expectantly.

Craddock viewed them with some contempt. 'You are like a bunch of bloody schoolkids kept in after school. If ye have got nothing better tae dae awa hame.' The group broke up reluctantly. 'Jist wan thing.' The fragments reassembled. 'None of ye want tae admit murdering the Commissioner before ye go?' There was some relieving laughter. 'Then fuck off, the lot of ye.' The final dismissal was almost friendly.

Craddock turned to Hicks, 'Well sir, will ye be fancying a drink before ye go?' His courtesy was extravagant.

'Yes Angus, I fancy a drink, but I'll go when I decide to go. You run your enquiry, Angus, and I'll run you and the department. Try to remember that.'

The rebuke had no effect. 'We will go down to C 1. and see how your squad is getting on.'

They finished up in Commander Bastwick's office. As a believer in spreading his bread upon the waters, he kept a well-stocked drinks cupboard. The presence of Hicks, Craddock and even Smith was welcome.

Craddock picked up the phone and dialled out. He turned his back upon the room and above the chink of glass and hum of Bastwick's sycophancy Smith heard him say, 'How have you been today, Moira?' There was little tenderness in the question.

'Yes it is terrible. He was a fine man.' The subject was brushed away. 'What did the doctor say?' No emotion on the attentive face. 'I see. Well off to bed with you. I'll sleep downstairs when I get in. Oh, by the way. Any word from Ian?' The 'I see' that followed gave no indication as to the whereabouts of Craddock's junkie son.

Smith handed Craddock a glass of scotch and placed the water-jug before him. He picked up the phone and said, 'I'll get O'Brien up here to see if anything has developed.' Craddock grunted agreement.

Hicks gently swirled the scotch in his glass as if waiting for it to reach a certain consistency before knocking it back in a gulp.

'It might be very useful,' Craddock said to him, 'if your friends in the media could let us have all the film or tape or whatever it is they shot on Sunday.'

'I thought of that at three this afternoon, Angus. Purely as an investigative factor, not as a piece of inspired detection.' The matter-of-factness in Hicks' voice increased the triumph.

'Very astute of ye, sir, very very astute. Clearly a matter that should have been much higher on my list of priorities.'

Smith smiled. O'Brien had listed such action as initial routine.

O'Brien, in shirt sleeves and with an ostentatious cigar in the side of his mouth, entered the room almost before the sound of his single knock reached Craddock's ears. He restrained an impulse to whip into O'Brien both for his failure to don a jacket and the abruptness of his entry. Instead, and ignoring the host Bastwick, he told him to get a drink and report developments. O'Brien was shrewd enough to select a can of beer.

'Nothing significant so far, Guv.' O'Brien jumped back as a fizz of froth shot from the can. 'Drop of old stuff this, Guv. Sorry about the carpet.' Bastwick just rolled his eyes heavenwards. 'Well, sirs, we haven't put the Commissioner beyond the Haymarket. On his own wearing check hacking jacket, grey trousers, tweed cap and umbrella. The uniform on his body, according to his driver who does a bit of valeting on the side, was normally kept in his office. So it looks as though the body was dressed in it after being taken to the office already, er ...' he looked to Smith for help.

'Decapitated.'

'That's the word, sir.'

The sound of the shot froze the room. They all knew it was a shot. The sharp solidity of the discharge penetrated the closed windows two floors above the street.

Craddock swung to the window. Cupping his hands against the reflected interior lights, he saw a uniformed officer running across to a dark folded mass lying on the opposite pavement near the kerb. The whiteness of a limp hand dangled in the gutter. Craddock caught sight of a bowler hat rocking on its crown in the wind.

He knew it was Hammertoe.

He was still alive when Smith reached him. At least, his eyes were still alive. Enlarged in watery tears and glinting in the street lighting, they looked up at Smith asking, in piteous surprise, for an explanation. The light within dimmed and the bloody froth around the mouth subsided. Acting Commissioner Arthur Hammertoe died without an answer.

Hammertoe, once so imposing and impregnable was no less in mass, but sprawled across the damp pavement, limbs unaligned and limp, he was a grotesque hulk, with size but not solidity, the putrescence he would soon become already apparent.

The bullet had entered above the upper lip to the right of the nostrils. Smith knew what the unnatural lack of depth at the back of the head indicated as it lay in a red and white pool. An upper denture, ejected from the mouth, but still connected to it by a string of bloody mucus, lay at the kerb. The string snapped as a fresh haemorrhage dribbled its way down from the shattered skull and out between the open pendulous lips.

Smith straightened up beside the body. A sudden disjointed thought saddened him. It had occurred to him earlier when they had been dropped at the Yard to remind the pensive Hicks to send his car back for Hammertoe. He had decided it was none of his business.

He turned into the face of Craddock and saw the same mute question that had earlier died unanswered in other eyes.

O'Brien was in the thickening crowd of police officers around the body. Smith grabbed him. 'The bullet's gone right through his head. I want it found. Get this lot organized with some search lamps. It will be between here and the Abbey. Look for fresh marks on walls, broken windows and particularly on the ground beneath your nose. Get these gawpers busy.'

Smith looked up the street towards Victoria. From somewhere along there, amongst the offices and shops, the shot had come. Or from ... the headlights of a car coming out of Strutton Ground and diverted left swept across the tree-lined area of Caxton Green.

In the far corner was a small canvas shelter striped in white and orange. He had often used a telephone engineers' shelter as a cover for surveillance.

Smith took hold of Neaterkin, who was about to go looking for a bullet. 'Get back to the factory and draw a gun. Meet me on the footpath across the green.'

Neakerkin looked at him in amazement. 'Get your fucking finger out!' Neaterkin ran.

They approached the shelter from the darkness on the far side of the green. Smith took the pistol from Neaterkin and threw back the canvas clap. The shelter was empty, but a blue haze hung in the air.

The similar stench of urine and cordite remained as the wind blew through the open flap. It raised a thicker, more pungent smell. 'Hash,' said Neaterkin, who had spent a time on the drugs squad.

At one end of the shelter a breast-high parapet had been built from solid four-inch timbers. On top, several sandbags, one heavily indented across the middle. A square hole of about four inches had been cut in the material. On looking through Smith found it framed the circle of police round Hammertoe's body. He estimated the range to be about 120 yards.

Even with an excellent sniping stand and possible use of a night sight, it was, considering the trees and traffic, a very good shot. Was Hammertoe the intended victim? Or would anyone who looked like a copper crossing to the Yard have done? Smith shivered at the thought.

There was no rifle, no cartridge case, but there was a piece of soft blue toilet paper pinned above the square hole.

The same crude union jack flag, this time with small holes punched in it, was drawn on the sheet. Under the flag were the words,

ANOTHER POLICE PIG
LACKEY OF BRITAIN FIRST FASCISTS
EXECUTED AS AN ENEMY OF THE PEOPLE
S.O.P.

'Well it was going to be a long night anyway,' Smith said to Neaterkin in a flat cold voice.

It was after two a.m. by the time everything necessary to be initially done had been done, and Hammertoe's body removed to join that of his chief in the cold, antiseptic, but corruption-laden air of Westminster Mortuary.

They had found the bullet fairly quickly. A clean hole almost in the centre of a shop window twenty yards beyond Hammertoe's body indicated its presence. The vagaries of interrupted trajectory, on its crashing, ripping path through Hammertoe's skull, had deflected it to the right.

The bullet had been found, looking not out of place, in a tray of metal curios. The cupro-nickel jacket had burst into petalled shards, holding the lead core like a stamen.

Smith went to Craddock's office and found him seated behind his desk. He still wore his overcoat and half his face was buried morosely in the folds of his tartan scarf. Smith had not seen him since he appeared over his shoulder looking down at Hammertoe's body.

He remembered Craddock's agonized face as though sharing the pain endured by the victim. That, and the low groan of despair slowly tearing out of Craddock's throat as he turned away.

Craddock did not look up as Smith approached his desk. The hunched shoulders moved slightly as he reached out for the whisky glass in front of him. Smith wondered how long it had been the subject of his contemplation and how many had preceded it.

Craddock drank slowly, but without removing the glass from his lips. For a time he consulted the empty glass like an oracle. Then, apparently seeing nothing, he got to his feet and walked slowly but steadily across the room and placed the greasy homburg on his head, adjusting it fore and aft with deliberate fingers.

'I'm awa hame. Do what you have tae do. Ye don't need me.'

As he left Smith realized he had not looked at him once.

He dialled O'Brien's office. 'Mr Craddock will be leaving for home in a couple of minutes. Get a couple of good men to tail him off, very discreetly. He's not to know.'

'What's it all about Guv?' O'Brien sounded nervous at the temerity of the order.

'There are two down already. Make sure it isn't three. Do you know the number of his car?' 'Oh Guv. Give me credit.' The suggestion that as a matter of self-preservation, O'Brien would not know the number of every senior officer's car at the Yard offended his professional pride. 'OGH 376V a green Princess.'

Smith shook the weariness from his muscles by jogging down the stairs to the second floor. O'Brien, shirt-sleeved and cigar poised, gave him a quick 'Be right with you, Guv' with one hand over the mouthpiece of a phone. He took the hand away and said, 'Go to bed for Chrissake darlin', they will have to shoot another two thousand and forty-nine before they reach my rank.'

He replaced the phone. 'That's been done. Two from the Flying Squad, well tooled up, sat on his tail as he crossed Albert Bridge. They will see him all the way home. Oh, and Commander Brightside was looking for you earlier. He wanted to –' The bell cut him short. 'Bollocks,' he muttered as he brought the phone to his mouth. 'Incident Room, O'Brien.'

He gave an attentive and respectful pause. 'No sir, I didn't say anything obscene when I picked the phone up. Yes sir, he is with me now sir, shall I put him on sir? No sir. Yes sir. I'll tell him right away sir. No sir, no new developments sir. Goodnight sir. That was sir, he wants you in his office right away.'

'Which sir?'

'Mr Hicks sir, is there any other sir?'

'You are getting too cocky, George. You know what happens to people in this job that get too cocky.' Smith was feeling tired again.

'No Guv. What happens to people in this job that get too cocky?'

'Other people start to think you're a big prick.'

'Oh Guv. Guv.' O'Brien was disappointed at the low quality of the riposte.

*   *   *

As Smith entered the office, Hicks was saying to Brightside, 'It is therefore logical to assume I am next on the list.'

Brightside agreed the statement with a firmness more sycophantic than sympathetic.

'Don't sound so bloody pleased about it, Bert!'

Brightside protested his dismay at the prospect.

'Owen,' there was a warmth in Hicks' voice, the warmth of a man seeking and needing friends, 'Bert has absolutely nothing on this S.O.P. faction. We are proceeding on the assumption, and I feel it is the right assumption, that we are dealing with a splinter group of extreme left-wing fanatics with possible Middle or Far East origins, or a combination of both elements operating through or with a resurrected I.R.A. active service unit, in a campaign to destroy the leadership of the force and establish by that means the supremacy of subversive left-wing factions through a breakdown in public order. The motivation is apparent with the murders of the Commissioner and the Deputy.'

Hicks paused to allow assimilation of his words and continued, 'The initials S.O.P. will no doubt be found to stand for "Saviours Of The People". It's the sort of melodramatic title these people assume.' He looked to Smith for agreement.

The inbred caution of years spent avoiding conclusions other than his own struggled against a tendency to agree because he had nothing else to offer. What the bastards called themselves was, to him, unimportant.

'It could well be the case sir.' His voice lacked enthusiasm.

Indeed the weariness was infectious and all three lapsed into a contemplative silence.

The knock on the door was loud and insolent. Smith knew it had to be O'Brien. He opened the door.

'Sorry to disturb you sir, thought you would want to see this.' He handed Smith a message flimsy.

Smith slammed the door in his face, hoping to crush the cigar into his throat, but O'Brien was too quick.

Smith read the message aloud. 'From Associated Press at 2.40 a.m. At 2.30 a.m. this morning we received a telephone call from an anonymous male who said, "I will only say this once. You have five seconds to record this statement." After a five-second interval the same voice went on to say: "From Operational H.Q.

65

Soldiers of the People. The following communiqué is promulgated. Soldiers of the People newly arisen against the forces of fascist tyranny and oppression.

' "In their first operation Soldiers of the People have won a great victory in destroying the leaders of the enemy's most oppressive arm. We shall continue to fight the reactionary aggressors wherever they may be found. Victory to the Soldiers of the People." '

Chapter VIII

Hicks had slept for three hours on the settee in his office. Throughout the building troubled minds had sought similar relief on an assortment of armchairs, couches or desk-tops.

He swung his legs to the floor and sat holding his head cupped in his hands, pondered his stockinged feet, and his future prospects.

He rose, stretched and patted his pot-belly with some dissatisfaction. Must do something about this! he thought. Too many official lunches. Too many dinners. Cut out the booze. Well, cut it down at least.

The radio on his desk bleeped out the eight a.m. time signal. Hicks settled back on his settee for the news bulletin.

'In the wake of yet another murder of a top police officer at Scotland Yard, the Home Secretary has just announced controversial new changes at the head of London's Metropolitan Police.'

Hicks slowly inserted the knuckle of his right index finger into the corner of his mouth and bit lightly upon it.

The news announcer went on, 'In the aftermath of the murder of Sir Maxwell Steype, and the further murder by shooting last night of Mr Arthur Hammertoe, the Deputy Commissioner, the Home Office announced that Mr Desmond Rachette, Deputy Under Secretary of State at the Home Office police department, will take up the post of Commissioner of Police. The post of Deputy Commissioner will be filled by Brigadier Morgan Swarbrick, M.C., one of the army's top specialists in anti-terrorist and counter-insurgency methods.

'This combination of senior civil servant and recent com-

mander of the army's controversial Special Air Service to head
the country's largest police force has already provoked outraged
comment from leading left wingers. Mr Dan Pascoe M.P.,
spokesman for the Tribune group of M.P.s, said . . .'

Above the thunder of words reverberating in his brain, Hicks
became aware of pain in his right index finger. He had bitten
down to the bone. Hicks took the injured hand by the wrist and
held it down between his legs. His head rocked forward and the
long low moan disgorged from his belly had nothing to do with
the pain in his hand.

The radio announcer went remorselessly on, '. . . the Home
Secretary said, "Living as we are in an age of industrial and
political subversion, with armed minority groups striking in-
discriminately at police and public we must defend parliamentary democracy . . ." '

'There's nothing bloody indiscriminate about it,' Hicks
shouted at his radio. 'They are being very discriminating, you
stupid bastard!' He collapsed back on his settee.

He had been sitting there several minutes when the knocking
on the door became louder, and before he could frame a refusal
Craddock came in. He still wore his coat, scarf, and greasy grey
homburg.

'Sitting there as ye are holding your head in your hands, I was
a bit worried to see if it was still attached to your neck. I'm glad
to see it is.'

'You pissed off pretty quickly last night,' said Hicks sullenly.

'Aye Ah did.' Craddock grimaced wryly. 'I felt very tired,
very very tired. I knew old Arthur a long time. A long time.' The
pouches under Craddock's eyes had a bruised blackness under
overhanging brows. His eyes glittered like black ice in shadowy
caverns.

'You heard the news, I suppose,' said Hicks abruptly.
Craddock looked at him in silence, his mouth pursed in quizzical
consideration. Hicks, upright and now coldly composed, stood in
front of the mirror surveying, and gently rubbing, the sagging
underside of his unshaven chin.

'Well?' he asked quietly.

'The new appointments, you mean?'

'Really, Craddock, your Scottish caution can be most exas-
perating at times. What else could I mean.'

68

Craddock's voice took on an edge of sarcastic conciliation. 'Aye well sir, ye see my own career having reached its – now what's the smart word they use now? – its apogee.' He chuckled. 'It used to be peak, then it was zenith, now it's apogee.' Hicks was looking at him with bared teeth. Craddock heard an exasperated 'For Christ's sake' hiss between the spaced incisors.

He went on, 'Ye see, in a career that's been a slow progression over thirty-four years, with several years in each rank, you get time to think more about the job you have to do to enhance your career and not just about making a career out of making a career. If ye follow me, sir?'

The ice shone in the caverns. 'Ye see, I'm more interested in the old dead Commissioner and old dead Arthur, and who killed them, that I am in the new live Commissioner and his sojer boy, and who put them there –'

For the first time Craddock took his hat off. He rubbed a hand through tight bristled grey hair.

'That is unless there is a reason for those that are dead being dead, and those that are alive being where they are now.'

Hicks was looking at him in anticipatory fascination, holding an exposed and bleeding index finger cupped before him.

Craddock looked at it and tutted sympathetically, 'Have ye had an anti-tetanus injection lately?'

Craddock had gone down to the Murder Room. Deep in gloomy thought, Hicks washed and shaved.

As he dragged the old-fashioned safety razor down his cheek, the blade rasped painfully across the bristles. It had been a long time since Hicks had needed to use his emergency office shaving tackle. The blade was blunt and there was no replacement. He scraped gingerly on. The plaster uncurled and hung limply from his self-inflicted finger wound. It was going to be another bad day.

'Damn it. They should at least have consulted me.' He cursed his reflection in the mirror. He cursed the Home Office, the Home Secretary and he cursed Rachette. He double-cursed Rachette.

There were of course precedents for appointing senior civil servants to head the Metropolitan Police. But that was ancient history. It had last happened in the fifties.

The practice of appointing military men to senior police posts also had many precedents, but the precedents were even more archaic.

'Damn them all.' Hicks applied a fresh plaster to his finger. The phone purred rhythmically and persistently in his office until he realized it was only eight-thirty and his secretary not yet arrived.

'A.C.C.' The savagery in his voice brought a momentary pause from the caller, but the reply when it came was unconcerned. 'Morning Hicks, Racey-White here.' Racey-White was Permanent Under-Secretary of State at the Home Office. He went smoothly on, 'I presume that, like the rest of us, you have had an all-night sitting?'

'No,' Hicks was in full control of himself and introduced a lighter note. 'Unlike some, we have been doing a great deal of standing, walking, running, and on the odd occasion, jumping about.'

'Ah yes, you policemen are so grotesquely healthy. But to matters in hand. Firstly, the Secretary of State asked me to apologize for our inability, not our failure, Hicks, our inability, to inform you and your colleagues of the new appointments. But matters of state, Hicks, matters of state. You are well aware there are certain political and private elements who would not approve and are now voicing that disapproval. It was thought we should present a *fait accompli*.'

Hicks came in with dignified restraint, 'Nevertheless sir, I feel, and I am sure my senior colleagues feel, some prior notice should have been –'

'Ah, Hicks.' The interjection was precisely timed. 'The trouble is, you policemen, and of course I am not being personal, let me say your policemen, have such an uncanny gift for ascertaining intentions at the highest level of the Force, we just could not take the chance of a possible leak.'

The voice became harder. 'There have been leaks in the past you know. But let us not go into that. By the way I suggest we go on scrambler – now.'

Hicks depressed the red button. Racey-White's voice took on a metallic edge under the electronic distortion. 'Are we still there?'

Still fresh enough in post to retain a sense of conspiratorial

70

excitement at such clandestine conversations, Hicks replied, 'Loud and clear.'

'Oh, good. Now look here Hicks, we know you anticipated the possibility, and I put it no higher, of a certain improvement in your status had we not been overtaken by recent events. I will only say this to you, and for your ears only, the new appointments are interim and comparatively short-term.'

Hicks resisted an impulse to ask how short the term would be.

Racey-White went on, 'Assuming your, er – loyalties have not faltered and you serve your new, if albeit temporary masters with the same – shall we say flair, you have shown in the past, I see no reason why any former uncertainty that may have existed about your future should not be removed, at some not too distant date.'

Hicks replied stiffly, 'You may rest assured I will serve as I have always served. Without thought for my personal advancement and for what I consider to be the interests of the service.' He was pleased at having avoided any trace of unctuousness in his voice.

The reply, if dryly uttered, avoided any trace of irony. 'Quite so, Hicks. No more than we expected from you. And by the way, in view of the new set-up, our political mistress no longer objects to the investigation continuing in the hands of the Metropolitan Police.'

The line went dead. As Hicks slowly replaced the hand set and sat back, he realized his finger had ceased throbbing.

Hicks called a briefing conference for 10.30 a.m. In addition to Craddock and Smith, Fairchild, the other D.A.C. Crime, Brightside of Special Branch and Dr Dennis Loder, Director of the Police Forensic Science Laboratory were in attendance.

'Right,' said Hicks briskly from the head of the table, 'the position to date?' He looked towards Craddock. He in turn nodded at Smith, 'You take it, Owen.'

Hicks looked disapproving but said, 'Very well then, but let us get on.'

Smith said, 'I take it there is no necessity to review the facts surrounding the finding of the Commissioner's body, the shooting of Mr Hammertoe or the P.M. reports relating to both.'

This was agreed.

'We have nearly completed interviewing the officers engaged on the demonstration last Sunday. We cannot place the Commissioner beyond his presence in the vicinity of the fighting that developed in Haymarket. That in any case would have been the ideal time and place to swag him away. Many people injured in the fighting were being carried by their supporters into side-streets. We are of course interviewing participants on both sides. Any one of several instances of people being thus carried away could be applicable to the Commissioner.'

'What about Mulqueen, the general?' asked Hicks. 'Has he been interviewed?'

'We are told he left the march at Oxford Circus for late lunch at the Savoy. In view of the trouble, police stopped him as he was leaving for the final address at Trafalgar Square. He insisted on going there but agreed to delay his arrival until the factions were separated and the riot quelled. He will be seen in due course when and if we have something definite to put to him. At this stage Mr Craddock has directed he be left in the air.'

'I fully agree, Angus,' said Hicks, 'and when we do see him, it may be better done in my office.'

'Oh aye,' said Craddock, 'I am sure he'll be impressed.'

'What about the T.V. tapes?' Fairchild intervened diplomatically.

'They are being examined frame by frame. The action was concentrated mainly in the centre of Haymarket where the fighting was heaviest and, of course, in juicy shots of the odd police officer lashing out or grabbing someone by the hair. Nothing in the run-through at normal speed appears to show the Commissioner.'

'Thank you, please go on.'

Smith glanced at his notes. 'We have found a trolley, one of those low flat wooden platform things, that are wheeled about for filing-cabinets and the like. There are some blood spots on the platform. If Professor Simonson is right in his hypothesis about the wooden box, such a trolley would be ideal to cart it about the building without drawing too much attention to whoever was pushing it.'

'We know the spots to be human blood, do we?' asked Hicks.

'Oh aye, it would be given the benzidine test,' said Craddock smugly.

'Actually, Angus,' Dr Loder was smiling, 'we use the Kastle-Meyer test these days to establish the presence of blood, but we still use the precipitin test to establish it as human blood.' He turned to Hicks. 'It is human blood. We haven't grouped it as yet, always assuming it is uncontaminated and we can group it.'

'In addition,' Smith came back in firmly to relieve Craddock's ignorance of past developments, 'the trolley was one always parked inside the service door by the Dacre Street car park. It is worth noting that it was found in its original position after use. I think we can assume it was not only used to convey the body from street to office but trundled back again with the empty box. Not only would it carry the empty box, it would give an air of authority to the person or persons wheeling it about. Who looks twice at any of the messengers wheeling trolleys about the building?'

'But late on a Sunday night or the early hours of Monday morning surely the presence of someone wheeling a trolley would arouse some challenge?' Hicks allowed his indignation to fall in Craddock's direction. 'After all, this is Scotland Yard. There are supposed to be one or two detectives about. Perhaps it is only investigators who work at nights!'

Craddock refused the challenge and said nothing.

Fairchild took it up, 'As you said to the Press, sir, there is only a reserve strength on duty and they are mainly office-bound on the phones. The Commissioner's floor would be deserted.'

'It is becoming increasingly clear our internal security is in a lamentable state.' Hicks was still accusing Craddock.

'Ah couldna agree with ye more,' the latter said softly. 'Perhaps ye wull take it up wae your counterpart in "A" Department who has, Ah believe, responsibility for internal security.'

Hicks avoided the issue, 'Can we get on? How did they gain entry to the Commissioner's office? It is double-locked. More of your cuttlefish, I suppose.' He looked intently at Smith.

'No sir, I think they would use the keys they no doubt found in the Commissioner's pocket.'

'And what about the note on my desk. How did that get there?'

'You may be aware, sir, the Commissioner's key is a master for every lockable office in the building. It is reasonable to assume –'

73

'Yes, yes, all right. We shall have to get all the locks changed, will we not? Half the subversives in the country will be crawling over the building opening doors at will.' Hicks turned to Fairchild, acting as note-taker. 'A memo to surveyors department on that and a further one to A.C.A. suggesting separate and distinct identification badges to be issued to all staff, colour-coded according to department. We should have done this years ago.' He favoured Fairchild with a smile. 'Perhaps you can turn your mind to the fine detail.'

He nodded and noted the pad in front of him.

Hicks turned to Brightside, 'Now this murdering bunch, the Soldiers of the People. Just what is Special Branch doing about them?'

Brightside eased the knot of his blue and white polka-dot bow tie in a gesture of restrained indignation.

'At the risk of stating the obvious, sir, we are doing everything we can. My officers are checking on every known subversive group. Our sources have been alerted to supply the slightest scrap of information. We have requested Home Office to increase the number of, ah, special facilities, of ah, –'

'Oh come on, Bert,' said Hicks. 'You are amongst friends. You want to tap more phones and open more letters?'

'I would be obliged, sir,' said Brightside stiffly, 'if the minutes simply showed our special surveillance facilities are being increased.'

'So be it.' As Hicks gained control of the conference his confidence displayed itself in amused patronage.

'Don't let it worry you, Bert. We are all on your side. You S.B. chaps really must try to trust us ordinary mortals. However, I take it you have nothing specific to place before us?'

Brightside considered the question for some time before answering, 'We are thinking of an organization like the old Baader–Meinhof gang in Germany. There are similarities.'

Hicks did not seem impressed. He had made his mind up last night about the nature of the terrorist group. He turned to the other side of the table. 'Well now, can the power of the mightiest brains in the field of forensic science come up with something before I confess to the media "Scotland Yard is baffled"?'

Dr Loder pulled heavily on his pipe and produced a loud salivic burble.

74

'We have and will have a great number of things as our examinations progress. However, I am sure you will use your customary discretion before releasing anything publicly.' He restuffed the pipe, and went on with his nose deep in a large, ancient rubberoid tobacco pouch.

'We have quite a few foreign fibres from the Commissioner's uniform, purplish wool, probably from a jersey or cardigan of some sort. The specimens of eyebrow hair show traces of a white latex-based adhesive commonly used in sticking-plaster. He probably had the stuff slapped across his eyes as a blindfold – Dash it.' His thumb, calloused from long use, flicked repeatedly across the frizzen of a large brass lighter, producing enormous sparks but no flame.

Smith slid across a box of matches and was rewarded with an enchanting smile. 'So very kind of you.'

They sat patiently until the pipe was ignited.

'Now what else. Ah yes. There were also minute traces of the same adhesive on the flesh of the cheeks. So he was gagged as well. The fingernail scrapings produced some further fibres. Brownish, not wool, probably corduroy. Though most unusual to get corduroy. He must have had a fair grip of the garment. Assuming it was a garment, of course. That was in the right hand, ring finger. There was a trace of skin in other nails of both hands. Probably his own skin, though. Too much for aggressive contact. More as if he had dug the nails of his clenched fists into the palms of his hands, and several times too, I would say. Perhaps an instinctive reaction to strain or fear or . . .'

Loder let his voice fade into the stem of his pipe.

'Anyway, we can compare it with his tissue samples and see if it is the same,' he waved his pipe in the air, 'and I'll ask Simonson to have a closer look at the palms. Should be some minor bruising or indentations.'

'I would have thought from what you say such marks would be all too apparent,' said Hicks.

'I am, of course, speaking in relative terms. Large or small, both quantities are microscopic.'

Loder contemplated the volcanic cone of his pipe and re-placed an eruption of burning tobacco with a grimy finger.

'Another evidential factor was adduced.' His eyes were still downcast upon the smouldering pipe. 'The routine swabs taken

75

from the anal region gave a positive reaction indicating the presence of human semen.'

In the silence that followed, the significance of Loder's statement took some time to thud from Hicks' brain to his gut. Craddock and Smith exchanged raised eyebrows.

Hicks controlled his voice but not his words. 'Are you suggesting Sir Maxwell was a bloody pouf?'

'I am making a statement of fact. I am not indulging in emotive speculation.' Loder's voice carried icy reproof. 'If I may continue, it will be seen there are indications which enable one to reach a contrary conclusion.'

He glanced apologetically at Craddock and Smith.

'I hesitate to lecture, but it seems necessary. Three swabs were taken, one from deep in the anal passage, another from midway and a third from the external surface. This is, of course, usual post-mortem practice in all homicides whether sexual assault or perversion is suspected or not.

'The first two swabs were negative. Only the third produced traces of semen. It is reasonable to assume penetration was resisted, but an actual assault and subsequent emission occurred. I have spoken to Simonson on this and he agrees with that conclusion. In other words, the man was victim of masculine rape.'

'Disgusting.' The abhorrence in Hicks' voice was forthright.

'I quite agree.' In their collective and different reactions to Loder's findings, no one had noticed the presence of two figures in the doorway.

Rachette, the newly appointed Commissioner, who spoke, was accompanied by a younger man, yet not a young man; of middle height and figure, who at first sight appeared almost skinny, but for a lithe alertness and upright stance making Smith think of an unstrung bow that, when bent, could unleash the power of a hunting arrow. The thought was germinated by intensely black hair, brushed straight and scalp-close from a central peak above a high cliff-like forehead, towering over a nose peculiarly flattened, boneless and malleable.

Something or someone had at one time struck the man in the face with considerable strength.

Rachette moved to the head of the table, where Hicks, in scrambling to his feet, succeeded in overturning his chair.

Brigadier Morgan Swarbrick followed, his eyes moving from face to face, penetrating, assessing and unblinking.

Hicks pulled up the chair and gestured the new Commissioner into his place.

'No thank you, and do please be seated gentlemen.'

Rachette positioned himself behind Hicks' shoulder. Swarbrick leaned casually upon the edge of a desk, where from the side and rear he could survey the conference.

'I apologize for the interruption of your proceedings, gentlemen.' But there was no regret in Rachette's voice or face.

'May I presume you are all aware of my appointment and that of my deputy, Brigadier Swarbrick, who I now introduce.' He cast a hand towards the latter, who remained expressionless in answer to the acknowledging nods and Hicks' 'Delighted to have you with us, sir.'

Removing half-moon spectacles from a slim gold-coloured case, Rachette leaned across to peruse Fairchild's notes.

'Now Dr Loder,' he interposed another cold smile, 'we have not met for some time, but we have of course spoken and corresponded when I was at Home Office. Particularly over the cost of your new electron microscope, and that dreadfully expensive holograph apparatus. I trust the money was well spent?'

Loder nodded, his pipe going up and down leaving an almost perfect smoke ring in the air.

Rachette, with some deliberation, turned side-on to the conference, bowed his head and clasped hands behind his back. The position allowed him to peep owl-like over his shoulder at those seated.

'It is clear from what I heard as I came in, that quite apart from the horror of his death, my predecessor was subjected to a most degrading and revolting experience. My feelings are that we owe it, not only to his family, but to the service in which he honourably served so long, that this disgusting animal assault upon a helpless victim be totally forgotten.'

He turned to face the table and placed his hands confidingly upon Hicks' shoulder.

There was a prolonged silence. Loder cast nervous, expectant glances at the others.

Smith speared Craddock with his eyes, asking, demanding he

speak. Craddock grimaced and gave a disinterested shrug. He distrusted scientists as he distrusted all things he could not control and understand. And in any case Rachette was right.

'Was he a secretor, the person who committed the assault? Because if he committed the assault, there can be little doubt he committed the murder.' Smith looked only at Loder.

'He was. Oh yes, he was.' Another grateful smile was directed at Smith.

'We have worked on it all night and I can say with some certainty we have a grouping –'

It may have been the increased pressure on his shoulder that made Hicks cut in, but he was in any case determined to get into the act.

'I am quite sure the Commissioner is well aware of the esoteric nature of the conversation you are having with Dr Loder. Nevertheless, Smith, our discussions will continue through the chair. Perhaps Dr Loder, who is qualified and competent to speak on such matters, will deal with it as briefly as he can.'

With Smith put in his place, Hicks returned to his role of chairman, serious yet expansive.

'I am sure we are all grateful to the Commissioner in looking so far ahead and with such compassion. We, in our single-minded anxiety to pursue his predecessor's murderers, have overlooked the necessity to respect his memory. However, let us have the matter on the table,' he paused wishing he had chosen other words, 'and we can dispose of it.'

He looked firmly at Loder.

'Well, I shall try to be brief,' said Loder, ploughing his pipe into the pouch like a mechanical excavator. 'Male semen is, as you are no doubt aware, ejaculated during periods of sexual excitement.' He peered anxiously around as if afraid some present might be unaware.

'This semen consists of spermatozoa carried in seminal plasma. Occasionally, in infertile males, the spermatozoa is almost non-existent. That in itself can be of evidential value if a suspect is similarly deficient.'

He waved a hand to disperse his own smokescreen. 'Sometimes, but not very often, the spermatozoa is malformed, and that also, by its rarity, can be of evidential value if found in a suspect with a similar condition.'

His all-night labours caught up with Loder and he yawned hugely. 'Now,' he said, suppressing a further yawn, 'I suppose the crux of the matter is, that by a biological phenomenon, no, perhaps that is the wrong word, as the condition is more common than rare. Anyway, about eighty per cent of the male population secrete the ABO blood group substance in their semen together with the red blood-cell enzymes which in themselves can be additionally grouped. Various protein groupings can also be made. These factors taken together cannot specify or identify a particular individual, as say a fingerprint can, but they can, if you have malformed spermatozoa coupled with a rare blood group in the AB range, an uncommon haemoglobin count and a P.G.M. (2) factor in the red cell enzymes, be said to come from a minuscule percentage of the male population.'

Loder re-lit his pipe and waved out the spent match with a flourish. His nervousness had disappeared. 'And I can say with certainty we have such a combination of factors in this case.'

'But as you say, this will not by itself specify beyond all doubt, a particular individual, who of course we first have to find.' Hicks was being objective.

'No, but if you do find such an individual and he is the owner of a purplish woollen garment and another garment, in brown corduroy, I would say a jury may be satisfied he was the man who at least perpetrated the particular assault.'

Loder turned sideways in his chair and looked up at Rachette. 'And if you find bloodstains on the clothing of that person corresponding with the deceased's grouping, or in his possession implements that may have been used in the throat-cutting or for severing the head, I will be able to say if such implements were used. It should be understood, in my opinion, if the presence of any of the three evidential aspects were established together with the seminal groupings, they would be sufficient to prove a charge of murder against the person on whom they were found.'

Rachette pulled upon a thin gold chain across his midriff and brought forth a gold half-hunter. He snapped open the cover and looked at the face for longer than was necessary to tell the time.

'I would say further,' Loder was solemnly defiant, 'that much as I respect the motives, I cannot agree to suppress any of my findings in the event of criminal proceedings being brought against any person or persons.'

'No such proposition was postulated, Loder.' Rachette's tone implied a total misunderstanding of his earlier words. 'It was the basic premise that was objected to, not the legal consequences of your findings.' He sighed and went on, 'I sincerely hope past difficulties I have experienced in police circles in being fully understood will be eradicated.'

Smith wondered what the bloody hell that meant.

Swarbrick spoke for the first time, 'How would it be if they admitted, in general terms, to simply killing the unfortunate Commissioner. No need for you to then cast the pearls of police science before the swine of the morbid populace.'

They were, with the exception of Rachette, surprised at the high-pitched Welsh accent. They had expected the flat crisp tones of the modern British officer.

Smith waited for Craddock to give the obvious reply, and saw nothing would come from that quarter. He stepped in. 'In the first place, mainly because we cannot rely upon anyone admitting anything, sir.'

'Then there must be something wrong with your interrogation techniques. What have you got in the second place?'

Smith ignored the contempt implicit in Swarbrick's voice. This was his field. The soldier-boy was out of his depth.

'In the second place sir, whether or not we have a statement of admission, which can always be retracted, we have a duty in law to adduce all the evidence available at the trial.'

Rachette snapped shut the cover of his watch. It was a clear indication that more than his watch was closed.

'Mr Hicks, every development in this case will be reported to me immediately: Furthermore, no precipitate action will be taken against any person without prior reference and approval from me.'

The others stood as he moved towards the door followed by Swarbrick, who turned and asked of Loder, 'By the way, Doc. How do you get the semen from your suspects?' He looked at Smith and Craddock. 'I presume you have methods other than recourse to masturbation?'

It went over Loder's head. 'If the person is a secretor, the same

results can be obtained from a specimen of his saliva.' His reply
was earnest.

'But it cannot be extracted from the urine,' said Smith.

'That is quite true,' Loder confirmed approvingly.

Chapter IX

It was three days before anything like a solid lead developed. Three days and two nights of surveillance, searches and false leads. Of suspects being detained and refused access to lawyers. Squeals of outrage from the liberal press and even the Tory papers none too enthusiastic.

There were parliamentary questions pro and con police action with the back-bench lunatic fringe indulging in a frenzy of well-publicized speculation, conjecture and innuendo, that was almost competitive in its wildness and fervour. With Hicks, and even on occasion Rachette, appearing on T.V. several times a day, soothing, justifying, placating, supporting, denying.

But media interest, although strong, was secondary to the space and time given to the forthcoming General Election, now seven weeks away, and the burgeoning power of Britain First. The General was on the side of Law and Order.

'The brutal murders of two great and eminent public servants demonstrate yet again the evil grasp of an alien cult upon the throat of this great nation. It demonstrates how our youth, indoctrinated in the battery cages of certain places of so-called higher education, may, in some extreme cases, be induced to become foul and degraded murderers.

'Can there be the slightest doubt these Scum of the People, and I refuse to degrade the honourable profession of arms by styling them in their own fashion, so I repeat can there be the slightest doubt these scum are the product of alien influences? Sir Maxwell Steype and his colleague, Mr Hammertoe, died defending freedom. I have no doubt they died bravely.

'Freedom, with the responsibility it demands, is that which people like them willingly die to protect. Licence, in an orgy of liberality, is that which the scum kill to achieve.

'The police and the people of this country may rest assured that within a few short weeks no impediment will be placed in the path of those demanding justice against evil and murderous criminals and traitors.'

O'Brien came into Smith's office with coffee and hope. 'It might be something, it might not.' With a cup of coffee in each hand, the words were muffled behind a Chelsea bun stuck in his mouth.

'What is it?' Smith spoke more to his coffee cup than to O'Brien.

'Harry Pewbone, the D.I. at Hampstead, just phoned in. Early this morning they found a male body in some bushes by the Ponds. It's been there several days.'

O'Brien was having difficulty with crumbs in his teeth, and using the nail on his little finger on an embedded currant. 'Gawd, how long can the human body live on coffee and canteen cakes?'

'You were saying something about a body at Hampstead Ponds?'

'Plastic bag over the head, wrists secured by slip-knots to some chestnut palings. The front of his flies were undone. It looks like one of those partial-suffocation joy trips, a perversion kick gone wrong. He couldn't get his hands out of the slip-knots in time.'

'What makes it of interest to us?'

'He was a civil servant named Alistair Wardoe, single, lived in one room above a shop in the High Street. Pewbone turned the room over as a matter of routine and came up with a diary in an old raincoat, it was the only raincoat and probably in normal use.'

O'Brien licked sticky fingers. He liked a lingering flavour. 'The last entry in the diary was on Sunday. It reads "Meet C.P. 11 p.m. re soldier."'

Smith's took immediate interest. 'C.P. possibly for Commissioner of Police?'

'You know how civil servants minute papers, Guv. Refer to C.P. for report.'

'What kind of civil servant was he? I mean which branch?'

'He was just a middle-grade clerk in some ordnance record section of the defence ministry.' O'Brien was necessarily vague, 'Pewbone hasn't gone into that side of it yet.'

Smith looked at the ever-increasing file of statements he had yet to read. From them he was itemizing further actions that would probably lead nowhere but at least tied up untidy loose ends.

The sky outside was a clear thin blue. Hampstead seemed a nice place to go.

As O'Brien thrust the car along Tottenham Court Road, he filled in the additional particulars earlier ascertained from Pewbone, only interrupting his graphic flow to curse the many cab drivers who had the temerity to cut in on him or otherwise obstruct his passage. O'Brien hated cab drivers.

'There is nothing definite yet on when Wardoe died, but he was last seen alive on Sunday. He was a regular Sunday mid-day drinker, Vermouth and lemonade, in a pub near his flat. Generally on his own, sometimes with a young friend. You know –?'

O'Brien made kissing noises through pursed lips.

'And last Sunday?'

'He came in on his own but was seen to leave with another fellow about twelve-thirty. By this time the bar was fairly crowded but it wasn't one of his usual boy-friends. So far that's the last time he was seen alive.'

As they navigated the complexities of Camden Town's one-way system, O'Brien casually introduced a different element. 'By the way, Guv, did you know Ian Craddock was in the back hall Inspector's office last Wednesday night?'

Smith was mildly interested. Craddock's son Ian used to be a frequent visitor at the Yard when down from Cambridge where he was reading Economics. Craddock was proud of the tall, shy and sensitive youth and used to parade him round the various departments and branches, to the boy's obvious embarrassment. Craddock was keen on his son joining the service as a graduate entrant with all the benefits of accelerated promotion.

It was clear to everyone, except Craddock, this shy reticent youth, for all his apparent intelligence, would never make it as a police officer.

When Ian failed his Part II Tripos, and three months later was sent down after being busted by the local drug squad in the act of mainlining heroin in the cubicle of a public toilet, Craddock, to the surprise of some, stood up solidly for his son.

He got him a good lawyer who in turn got him a conditional discharge at Court. He got him into one of the best drug-treatment centres in London.

But the boy drifted from home like a log on an outgoing tide. Craddock had him picked up a couple of times and brought back. It was no use. The narcosis of shame and failure within him reacted against Craddock's new-found sympathy and under-standing, pulling him out and down into the sad somnolent paths of others like himself.

Occasionaly, when desperation drove him, he would call at the Yard in the discreet late evening and get money from his father.

Craddock in the perversity of pride made no secret of his son's presence, although he no longer came beyond the foyer or the office of the back hall Inspector. There would be a few muttered words between them, a brief handshake, more as a means of exchanging a few notes than as a gesture of filial accord. The son would push hurriedly out of the glass doors leaving Craddock, stony-faced, watching him disappear into the mouth of St James's Park underground station.

'What was he after, another touch?' asked Smith.

'I suppose so. I got it from Jack Colby who was on back hall duty that night. I was checking on those who had access to the office and the key-board. Colby noticed quite a change in him. He was quite clean, reasonably well dressed, seemed more self-assured. He just asked if the old man was in. Colby rang upstairs but found Mr Craddock had gone. Colby was wondering if he should slip him a couple of quid himself when Mr Hammertoe came down on his way out and saw them standing in the foyer. He came over to the lad, all friendly like, and took him into the back hall office. Colby left them to it. They came out about ten minutes later, shook hands, Hammertoe got into his car, and the kid as usual went across to the underground.'

'Hmnn,' said Smith. 'We never did get a statement from Hammertoe. Have you mentioned the incident to Mr Craddock?'

'Mr Craddock I leave to you, Guv.'

'Then don't. Put Colby's statement in the confidential file for the time being, no index card. And tell Colby, I don't want Mr Craddock embarrassed by him mentioning it either.'

O'Brien looked at him sideways, and possibly as a result shot across the lights on Haverstock Hill as they changed to red. He cut neatly across the front of a crossing taxi and answered a protesting horn with, 'And you, you four-eyed, hook-nosed, kipper-faced twit.'

The flat was furnished as tastefully as a rubbish bin outside a fish shop during a dustmen's strike. A card table, at which meals were once taken on a moth-eaten baize top, bore the matted residue of many a careless repast.

Two unmatched wooden chairs, painted livid yellow, contrasted with the blackness of an old armchair disgorging coils of intestinal horsehair from its ruptured sides.

The weightier newspapers lay piled in irregular columns about the room. Oiled flesh rippled from the covers of muscle magazines in caricature of human form.

Heightening the general squalor, a new and expensive hi-fi stretched its smug flat Swedish face across the top of an ancient tallboy. Twin speakers hung on precarious hooks on both sides of the wall. Stereo discs of the cheaper classical issues slotted into a neat rack. The whole was as an altar in a pigsty.

There was a bed, and on it sat a young man with dyed platinum hair, weeping long silent tears that fell into hands cupped upon his knees. He had long once-manicured finger nails, painted green, the varnish cracked and chipped.

'He came up looking for Wardoe. I told him he was dead.' Detective Inspector Pewbone was a large square man whose bulk overwhelmed the small room.

'Does he know how he died?' Smith looked up at a large hook screwed through the plaster into a ceiling joist.

'No no, I wouldn't tell him that.' Pewbone was defensive.

'What is your name, son?'

The youth contemplated his tear-stained palms. He sniffed twice and raised a wet mascara-stained face to Smith.

'Peter,' he said and sadly dropped his head. 'Peter Maydell.'

Smith patted him sympathetically. Maydell's back throbbed

beneath his fingers and the heat through the silk shirt was almost feverish.

Maydell responded to the gesture. 'Please tell me. Please, what happened to Alistair?'

Smith looked up at the hook above his head. Maydell fell to his knees and held up supplicating hands at the hook.

'Alistair, Alistair. I told you not to. I pleaded with you not to. Did I not give you everything? Could I not give you enough?'

All eyes were on the hook as though something still hung there.

'Alistair, Alistair, I told you not to.' Maydell dropped his hands and the long sobs were now loud with despair.

Smith gestured to O'Brien, who lifted him by the armpits on to the bed. 'Come on now, me old darlin'. We've got to be a brave little sailor-boy.' O'Brien grimaced in disgust as Maydell wiped his face with the grimy bed-spread.

'Did he ever use any other method?' Smith asked, gesturing at the hook.

'Oh, no. He would have told me. He used that –' A long delicate finger pointed at a dressing-robe cord draped on the back of the door. 'He would tell me every time he used it. The ecstasy of the orgasm of death. Those were his words, not mine.'

'He never tried it, say, by holding a pillow over his face, or something like that? Did he do anything similar out in the open for instance?'

Smith was reluctant to specify the act, fearing as every detective does the consequences of planting known facts in the mind of a witness.

'He would never do such a thing.' Maydell was shocked. 'Alistair was a very private person. He never frequented ... places, you know.' Smith nodded.

'He only used the cord. He used to say it was the threat of the presence and pressure of the cord and the ability to relieve the pressure at the brink of unconsciousness that achieved and prolonged the orgasm.'

In the aftermath of despair, Maydell became detached and clinical. He went on to tell them how on Sunday he had arranged to meet Wardoe at the pub, only to be told Wardoe had left with another man. 'I am sure it was Soldier.'

'Soldier?'

'That's how he spoke of him. Not as "a soldier" or "the soldier" but Soldier. As if it was his name. I have never seen him.'

He did not know if he was, in fact, a soldier. Alistair had only recently met him. A month ago, not more. No, he did not know where they met or how they met.

'But he was an absolute brute of a man, an animal,' Maydell shuddered in loathing. 'But Alistair adored brutes.' He looked at the hook and began to weep again, quietly.

They waited for the spasm to pass, Smith and O'Brien astride the yellow chairs, Pewbone standing with arms patiently folded across his chest, sullenly resentful of the interference with his case.

'A flagellant?' asked Smith as the grimy counterpane was once again wiped across a tear-stained face.

Maydell accepted the question matter-of-factly. 'No, but he liked to take it – well, brutally. I daresay you find women who like it that way.' He tossed his platinum hair defiantly under O'Brien's chin, hanging loosely open-mouthed, over the back of his chair.

O'Brien sat upright and closed his mouth tightly, but apart from looking hurt, said nothing.   Smith looked at Pewbone. 'What did they find at the P.M.?'

'They could have used it for a funnel on the Mauretania.'

Smith looked anxiously across at Maydell. Surprisingly, it appeared the remark had no meaning for him.

He took Maydell to his feet with a gentle hand under his elbow. 'I want you to go to Hampstead Police Station with Mr O'Brien.' Maydell looked alarmed. 'We just want to get a statement from you, about Wardoe and Soldier.'

He took the youth firmly by the shoulders, 'You will try to help us all you can, won't you?'

Maydell jerked his head in agreement, a glint of tears coming back to his eyes.

Smith said to O'Brien, 'Leave the car, the walk will do him good.' He eyed the overhang on O'Brien's belt. 'It will do you both good. I'll pick you up at the nick later.'

'Do you know where the station is, me old darlin'?' O'Brien made a good job of appearing his usual cheerful self. Maydell nodded in reluctant assent.

'Then lead on, me old darlin', I'll follow you at a discreet distance. We don't want you embarrassed by people thinking you've been nicked.'

'Oh it's all right. I'm quite used to it.' Maydell tried to be cheerful.

O'Brien eyed the platinum hair, the beads, the tight jeans and the green fingernails with a smile that was more a snarl, and said, 'Yeah, well, lead the way anyhow.'

After the interior of the flat had been photographed and dusted for fingerprints, it was torn apart by Dewlip, Neaterkin and a search team from the laboratory.

Inside the record sleeve of Beethoven's Seventh symphony, they found a typewritten list, a carbon copy.

Smith placed the list on Craddock's desk. It read,

```
AK-47 ass. rfls. − 302
PK. 7.62 mm. mach. gns. − 15
R.P.G. 7. − rkt p.jts. − 12
Ammo. 7.62 mm. blts. − 15,000 rds.
    do    7.62 mm. lse.    8,000 rds.
P'tiles    40 mm. HEAT − 150
    do     40 mm. f.mentation − 285


M.V. Glencairn dep. B'fast 25.8
150 Coy. R.C.T. S'raer to A'Dover
41st Ord dep. 28.8 St. sgt. Gredek.
```

Craddock read it with widening interest.

'Aye, come the revolution this lot could be a starter for ten. What do you make of the abbreviations?'

'Apart from the obvious ones, we have rocket projectiles, with HEAT heads, that stands for High Explosive Anti-Tank. Then there are fragmentation heads. There is ammunition of 7.62 millimetre calibre in belts for machine guns and loose for rifles. The rest of it must refer to the ship carrying the stuff from Belfast to Stranraer in Scotland.'

'Ah know where Stranraer is.' Craddock did not like having things explained to him.

Smith ignored it and went on, 'R.C.T. refers to the Royal

Corps of Transport, who no doubt carried the stuff to the 41st Ordnance Depot at Andover. It may be that Staff Sergeant Gredek is connected with either the R.C.T. or the Ordnance Depot.'

Craddock fished in his pocket for keys which he threw on the desk in front of Smith.

'Get the bottle out. This is a job for thinking whisky.'

As he sipped from his glass and sat back in his chair, Craddock spoke to air above his head.

'Now, we are connecting Wardoe with the deceased Commissioner on the basis of a diary entry for last Sunday at eleven p.m. which corresponds with the day and time the Commissioner was meeting someone, somewhere, about a matter of national importance. Wardoe was a civil servant and civil servants, at least in Home Office, do send papers across here marked up to C.P. or C. of P.'

Craddock sank the whisky in his glass and waved it at Smith for a refill. He left the charged glass on his desk, sat forward, gazed at the amber fluid and spoke to it gently.

'But Wardoe was a very low-grade civil servant and worked at the war house. He was also a poufter of great renown. He was having it off with somebody he called Soldier and, working where he was, an association with a soldier is not unusual. The chances of C.P. being simply a reference to the initials of another poufter with whom he wished to compare performance or recommend Soldier to, must be as high and a damned sight higher than a reference to the dead Commissioner.'

Craddock picked up the list in its clear plastic envelope and re-studied the contents.

'Now is this a carbon copy of some official army list of seized weapons? I don't think so. The abbreviations, the layout, the style. Not the work of a skilled typist. We know the arms are of Russian design and manufactured in several Eastern-bloc countries. They were being shipped out of Belfast. The last big seizure of such weapons was over a year ago, when the General finished off the I.R.A.'

There was satisfaction in Craddock's sigh after he drained the glass. Smith refilled it, but not so generously as before. Craddock did not seem to notice, and went on reflecting.

'And now we've got puir wee Wardoe, dead in some sodden

bushes. You think he was murdered?' He held up a hand to still Smith's insistence upon a positive opinion such was the case.

'You know as weel as I do, about twenty times a year, up and down the country, we cut down the likes of puir wee Wardoe from banister rails, shower fitments and tree branches. We find them in parks and fields with hands loosely tied and bags over their heads, or clothespegs over their noses and handkerchiefs stuffed down their throats. If there is one thing about the psychology of sexual perversity I cannot understand, it is how the likes of puir wee Wardoe get anything out of it.'

Smith did not consider the matter worthy of further discussion. He did not know himself. It was something that happened and when it did you had a few photographs taken, left it to a sergeant and a coroner's verdict of misadventure.

Craddock, in any case, was not seeking Smith's opinion.

'But the puir wee man is dead, and it would not have been difficult to get him down to where he was found, tie him to the fence, stick a plastic bag over his head and let nature take its course. He may even have enjoyed it up to a point.'

He considered this possibility for a moment, seeking an answer in the depth of his glass.

'Let's look at Soldier. What can we make of him? Is he an actual soldier or is he one of those Soldiers of the People who write graffiti on a dead man's chest? Or is it just a nickname, like Bomber, Gunner or Sailor? Well, we will find out in due course, because, Owen –'

He looked at Smith and the unnatural symmetry and whiteness of porcelain teeth seemed to fill his face in the grin that did not express amiability or amusement.

'You are right. This little man and his little list is the beginning we have been looking for. Wardoe was murdered all right, as Arthur Hammertoe was murdered, although in his case they used a 7.62 mm. bullet from a Kalashnikov AK-47 rifle.'

Smith was only surprised they had been able to match the bullet to a definite weapon type and said so. 'After all, N.A.T.O. use the same calibre.'

'Oh, they are clever fellows, Loder and his laddies,' replied Craddock with, for him, generous if somewhat condescending praise. 'They did a lot of work with the R.U.C. when the troubles were on and know quite a bit about Kalashnikovs,

Armalites and the rest. After some fancy work in metallurgy, with holographs and chromatographic analysis, they came up with the answer. Mind you, because of the poor condition, they are not saying they can tie the bullet to a specific weapon, but the metal content, the positioning of the lands and grooves on the rifling, are all identical with bullets used in the Kalashnikov.'

Craddock rubbed his hands together. 'We are on our way, Owen, we are on our way. And you are on your way first thing tomorrow morning. To the 41st Ordnance Depot at Andover to see what Staff Sergeant Gredek is made of.'

'What about the Army? Do we bring their S.I.B. into the act?' asked Smith, doubtfully.

'Well now, Owen, laddie.' Craddock's tone took on the grandiloquence of a man who should not be asked for an answer to an awkward if explicit question. He became avuncular.

'Just ask yourself a few questions, Owen. Why didn't Wardoe go to his own people at the Defence Ministry? Why did he go to the Commissioner? And, above all, how did he manage to get the Commissioner to agree to meet him? He must have got in touch with him somehow and he must have convinced him it really was something of such importance he had to deal with it personally.'

Smith could almost taste the whisky on Craddock's breath as he leaned into him confidingly. 'And, Owen, there was nothing in the Commissioner's files about the meeting, not even an entry in his diary. Owen, the Commissioner does not go round meeting informants, like some detective-sergeant. Wardoe must have convinced him there were people around this place who could not be trusted.'

Craddock's eyes turned upwards as if to indicate the area of distrust lay somewhere above even him.

'So I'll leave it to you, Owen, do you think we want the S.I.B. in at this stage of the game?'

'I only raised the question,' said Smith steadily, 'in view of certain words of advice you gave me about taking chances.'

Craddock stared at him in mock surprise. 'You don't actually take advice from other people, do ye?'

Smith could not help smiling back at him but said with some formality, 'I take it sir, you will be reporting these developments to Mr Rachette?'

'You can leave that to me, laddie, away ye go.'

92

As Smith went down to the second floor he wished there had been a third party present in Craddock's office.

There are many indices, manual and computerized, at New Scotland Yard; one of them holds details of all military deserters and others absent without leave. Smith consulted this index before leaving the Yard for his flat in Kennington.

Listed as absent without leave, since the day before Sir Maxwell Steype disappeared in the turmoil of Haymarket, was Staff Sergeant Richard Gredek, Royal Army Ordnance Corps.

Chapter X

A series of conveniently placed military signs guided Smith to the 41st Ordnance Depot. To his surprise it was a fairly small establishment, set in the middle of a recruits' training centre outside Andover, on the Barton Stacey Road.

From outside the centre, Smith saw the brown and yellow board indicating the depot. It consisted of two single-storey flat-roofed buildings of substantial brick and concrete construction, and lay within a perimeter of close-mesh security fencing topped by the short barbs of coiled Dannert wire.

A public access road bisected both sides of the recruit centre and Smith was able to drive up to the gate of the perimeter fence. A bell push set in a supporting pillar was marked 'Ring for attention'.

Attached to a clip-board was an old report he had once received from the Military Police. It was headed 'Royal Military Police, London District.' He held the clip-board in the fold of his arm with the letter-heading ostentatiously facing anyone who approached him.

Smith rang for attention.

After a few moments, a door was opened in the nearest building and a round fat face creased in a frown of annoyance peered across at the gate. Smith gave back a hard-eyes stare and raised a threatening, beckoning finger. A round fat body bore the round fat face cautiously towards the gate. It wore denim overalls graced with corporals' stripes.

'S.I.B.,' barked Smith at the approaching figure. He knew the effect the Army's investigation branch had on military personnel, particularly those who worked in stores. The fat figure broke into a waddling run as a result, eyes zeroing in on the print on Smith's clip-board. He gave the corporal a quick flash at the top of his credit card in his breast pocket and said, 'Sar'nt Major Hume, S.I.B. Open up.'

The corporal fumbled for keys and opened the gate. 'Who is in charge?' snapped Smith.

'Well, I am for the time being, Sar'nt Major,' said the corporal nervously.

'Just call me sir,' Smith persued the papers on his clip-board, 'now you will be –' He turned a page and ran a finger up and down the print hoping for an answer.

'Corporal Ackerman, sir.'

'Ah yes, Ackerman.' His finger stopped and he pretended to read for a moment. 'You are quite well written up, Corporal,' he said with some friendliness in his voice.

'Thank you sir, I didn't get me stripes for slouching about sir.'

Smith eyed the portly figure dubiously but said, 'I can see that. Now let's go inside.'

As they approached the main building, Smith noted the heavy steel bars on all windows and the criss-cross of alarm wires inside the glass. The door through which they entered was of heavy wood faced with sheet steel. Electric contacts at three points indicated it also was connected to the alarm system.

Ackerman showed him into a small glass-panelled office. There was a desk, a chair, a succession of bulldog-clipped army forms hanging from hooks around the wooden frames of the glass panes. Inevitably, there was a large brown kettle on a small gas stove. Three large earthenware mugs stood unwashed on the draining board of a badly chipped sink.

Smith had been caught in the last draft before conscription ended. It took him back.

'Do you fancy a brew-up, sir?' Ackerman gestured towards the kettle.

'A good idea, Corporal,' replied Smith, becoming quite amiable. He waited to see if Ackerman would enquire as to the reason for his visit, but Ackerman had been too long in the Army to volunteer anything.

'Staff Sergeant Gredek. What made him take it on his toes?' Ackerman turned off the tap and looked curiously at Smith.

'But I told the S.I.B. man that came down on Monday all I know about it.' Smith found no suspicion in his voice, more relief that his enquiry did not directly concern the corporal.

'I know that,' said Smith, brusquely, 'but when he got back to H.Q. he went down with a perforated ulcer before he could write up his report. The poor chap is in a bad way. He might not make it.'

'You know sir, I thought he didn't look all that well.' Ackerman nodded wisely at his own prescience.

Smith leaned forward with some nervousness as the door from the main building into the office was flung open. Two denim-clad privates entered. He relaxed as one said, 'Oh goodoh, corp, you making another brew-up?' They saw Smith's hard eye and taking no chances on what the civilian clothes might conceal, came slowly to attention.

'I have told you before not to enter this office without first knocking,' said Ackerman, trying to harshen his high pitched voice. 'I want all these L7A1 m.g.s stripped down, greased up and re-boxed before you finish. Now get out and get on with it!' Smith knew when he was being blinded with science and looked suitably impressed.

'Now,' he said, as Ackerman brought the mugs to the desk, 'about Staff Sergeant Gredek ...'

It was dark and the early evening hour released from the city its nightly plague of mechanical glow-worms creeping outwards to the suburbs along every radial and lateral road. Fumes and frustration writhed in grey plumes in the dry frosty air. Behind layered glass, nebulous shapes steered themselves on to the womb-warmth of living-rooms and the hypnosis of coloured electronic dots.

Caught in the transmigration across and through Fulham Broadway, Smith decided to seek a waterhole and refresh himself before going back to the Yard.

He turned up a side-street towards a quiet pub he knew. With a pint and sandwich he got himself into a corner table and took out his notes on the Ackerman interview.

'I worked with Staff Gredek for about eighteen months,' Ackerman told him. 'The Staff was in charge of the depot. He was a small-arms expert, an armourer, he could strip down, repair and reassemble any small arm in the British Army. And most foreign weapons as well,' Ackerman had added gratuitously.

'Has he been doing anything with foreign weapons recently?' Smith asked innocently.

'We had a load of Russian stuff in from Belfast last summer. At least, it was Russian design but according to Staff it had Czech factory marks. Kalashnikovs, m.g.s and automatic rifles. Cor' Christ them Arabs would have paid a packet ...'

Ackerman coloured into confused gibberish as he remembered who he was talking to. 'Not that ... I wouldn't ... I mean ... you just think ...'

'I know,' Smith said with understanding, 'we all get silly ideas at times.'

With some relief Ackerman went on, 'Anyway, Staff Gredek had them stripped down, cleaned and oiled as though he had been handling Kalashnikovs all his service. The R.P.Gs as well. These warheads can be tricky, you know. We tested them over at Larkhill. Staff Gredek put a HEAT head into the sprocket wheel of the target Centurion every time. You er, know what a HEAT head is in your line of work, sir?'

Smith decided as he was supposed to be in the Army he should display the knowledge he had acquired from research into Wardoe's list. 'High Explosive Anti-Tank,' he replied with aplomb, 'but why shoot at the sprocket wheel? I would have thought the turret ring would have been a better target.'

'Ah,' Ackerman spoke with the superiority of an expert, 'too difficult, too much heavy armour around that area for a hand-held weapon. Knock out the sprocket wheel and the tank stops, see. Can't drive the tracks.'

Smith decided he had had enough on the tactics of armoured warfare. 'You still got the Kalashnikov weapons about? I'd be interested in having a close look at them.'

'No, they went out about a month ago. Got a transfer order through; they went out to some experimental place ...'

Ackerman reached up and unhooked a mass of clipped forms. 'Yeah, here you are: Small Arms Research and Experimental Unit, Addlestone, Surrey.' He grinned at Smith and said, 'You will have to see if somebody deserts from there to get sight of them.'

Smith casually reached out and looked at the form. It was signed 'A. Wardoe, pp. J. Inspan, Lt. Col.'

Smith returned the sheaf of forms to Ackerman and said, 'You never know, do you.'

'Was Gredek married?' Smith offered his cigarettes. Ackerman pretended a reluctance that only increased the malice in his eyes.

'Well, sir. I don't know if I should say what I think about a senior N.C.O.'

'Gredek is an absentee, possibly a deserter, so don't hand me a load of crap. Whatever happens after this he won't even make shithouse orderly in the Glasshouse.'

Ackerman plunged in like a hippopotamus at a wallow. 'Ah, well sir, it was just . . . No sir, he wasn't married. Not that way sir, if you follow me. Not for me to say, sir, but it was pretty obvious at times. Never tried anything on with me though, but him and Private Leopold! And there was that little old civvy he used to meet at week-ends. I saw them once in the Blue Anchor down the road. Gredek squeezing his knee under the table and the old fellow wasn't half enjoyin' it.'

Ackerman, at Smith's request, described the 'little old civvy'. There was no doubt it was Alistair Wardoe.

'Not that Staff Gredek looked like one of them . . . you know, brown-hatters . . . very smart man, very particular, and tough, hard as nails. A right hard bastard.' There was a tinge of fearful respect in the viciousness of Ackerman's voice.

'And that other crowd, he used to meet them about once a week in the White Horse, the pub near the Station; funny bunch, about five of them. Sometimes had a bird with them too. Not bad-looking. They used to get together around the table chatting eighteen to the dozen. Don't know what about. But they never laughed. Struck me funny, that did. All sitting around drinking and yarning away in a pub, but nobody laughing.'

Smith got the best descriptions Ackerman could manage of Gredek's drinking companions. 'Private Leopold?'

'Oh, he bought himself out six months ago.'

'There was one thing about that bunch in the pub with Gredek.' Ackerman put on his deep-thinking reminiscent face. 'Staff Gredek left them early one night and as he waved to them from the door one of them waved back with his fist. Like them

Commies. Gredek came back in smiling all over his face and kicked the fellow right on the shin and walked out again. Must have nearly broken his leg. The landlord came round because he didn't half holler. Then the fellow said he banged his leg on the table. I reckon they were trying to take the piss out of Staff Gredek. Nobody takes the piss out of Staff Gredek.'

Smith came away with the impression that his complimentary, if imaginary, note on Corporal Ackerman's ability was reasonably well founded.

As he sank the dregs of his pint and ordered another, Smith considered a further problem. He had driven round and round the small town of Addlestone. He had used his S.I.B. front at the post office, the local authority office and at various shops and cafés. Although he omitted the police station, he was certain nowhere within or around Addlestone was there any Small Arms Research and Experimental Unit.

There was little doubt in Smith's mind that Gredek was Wardoe's Soldier. A soldier who had left one Army to join another, not only as ordnance quartermaster, but also as front-line stormtrooper.

And Wardoe, where did he fit in? He was clearly in with Gredek, but had he bottled out and gone running to the Commissioner? If Gredek and the S.O.P. got wind of it, it would be good reason to kill Wardoe and Steype. But why all the drama with Steype's head? After all, if a bullet was good enough for Hammertoe ... And why was Hammertoe killed in any case?

As he went to the door, Smith's eyes riveted on a large pictorial notice pinned thereon. A proud fist held aloft the union flag and below the flag it was announced that at 7.0 p.m. that night the Britain First Movement would be holding a public meeting at Fulham Town Hall. All were invited to attend.

Smith decided it was time he had a look for himself at the organization Soldiers of the People used as an excuse to kill top policemen. The political side of the enquiry had been left to Brightside and Special Branch, who had produced a great deal of history that only led backwards.

He found a phone and rang Craddock's extension at the Yard. He had tried previously after his fruitless enquiries in and around

Addlestone; now as then there was no reply. He transferred to the murder room and got hold of O'Brien. The latter had not seen Craddock since early afternoon. Smith gave him a brief on the Andover expedition, for Craddock's ears only, and told O'Brien of his present intentions.

The hall was nearly full when Smith arrived, with late-comers being directed to an overflow meeting on the nearby green where the proceedings would be relayed. Smith had to get hold of the uniformed Chief Superintendent in charge of policing, who knew him, and took him inside to a convenient recess by emergency doors at the back of the hall.

The swirl of red white and blue drapings along the platform and balconies lent garish colour to the drab clothes of the audience, overcoated and scarved against the chill of the unheated hall.

It was the stewards Smith particularly noticed. All young or youngish men patrolling the aisles, watchful, alert, exchanging curt nods with each other as they passed, eyes scanning the audience. Calm, purposeful and assured.

They dealt with the public with a studied courtesy and politeness that was firm, impassive and brooked no argument. 'Not there sir, this way if you please,' and, 'No madam, these seats are reserved, if you will just follow me.' 'Do you mind, gentlemen, these seats are for the Press. I have some for you at the side.'

He saw the discernment with which obvious trouble-makers were sorted out, split up and isolated mainly in aisle seats that could be easily reached. The so-called Press seats were eventually filled by middle-aged couples and others of presentable and conservative appearance.

Spaced inconspicuously around the side walls, Smith saw a few familiar Special Branch faces. They all appeared to have bad colds, and from time to time one or other would hold a handkerchief to his mouth to cover muttered comment into the miniaturized mike of a concealed tape recorder.

As the platform group assembled, the low incoherent mumble of many voices subsided. Ellis Skelton, widely smiling, was followed by the debonair figure of 'Laddie' Landon in impeccable dark grey suiting, except for his shirt. Smith was mildly amused. Red, white and blue stripes hadn't been fashionable since 1977.

Three other men and two women, none of them known to Smith, joined the platform party, who had remained standing. Skelton held up a quietening hand to subdue a scattering of spontaneous applause as the General strode on to join them in the centre. Some recognizable chords were struck on the piano and everyone stood. Smith had rarely heard the National Anthem sung with such fervour.

When the singing died away, the majority of the audience returned to their seats, but seeing a large number still standing, as was the platform party, they too returned to their feet in an embarrassed, noisy shuffle.

The General came to the front of the platform, stood for a moment, then spoke. He did not raise his voice or make any gesture with hand or arm, he simply stated with firm clarity, 'Britains – Britain First.'

The response was thunderously led by the stewards and party stalwarts throughout the hall. 'BRI-TAIN FIRST, BRI-TAIN FIRST, BRI-TAIN FIRST.' The General returned to his seat and the chairman introduced Lionel 'Laddie' Landon to speak about the economic situation. Smith stifled a yawn.

According to Landon, only the strength and discipline of the B.F.M. could pull the country out of the economic morass. He went on with persuasive simplicity into a future of efficiently increased production leading Britain back to its rightful place, pre-eminent amongst the nations of the world.

'Britons out-fought the Germans and out-fought the Japanese! Is there one person here tonight who thinks that under the leadership of Britons in this great movement of Britain First we cannot outwork them?'

The challenge was taken up by several disunited voices well interspersed throughout the hall. 'Fascist pig, fascist pig.' The stewards moved in smoothly, there was no obtrusive violence and Smith noted the expertise with which a 'come-along' hold was applied – the hold where the arm of the offender is trapped between the elbow and wrist with the hand grasped and pulled forward against the limits of the inward curvature of wrist bones and tendons, with agonizing effect. It raises the person upon whom it is applied to his toes in an effort to relieve the pressure

101

and by this means he can be held one-handed and marched in any direction the person applying the hold wishes to go. In each case the direction was out.

The General was introduced as the next speaker, but not by his military rank. Although the media made constant reference to him as the General, and he indeed responded to the title in such circumstances, no reference to his former rank was openly mentioned in any of the movement's propaganda or announcements. He was simply 'Liam Mulqueen, Leader of our great movement.'

As he stood on the platform, Smith found him much taller than he appeared on T.V. The blazing blue eyes sparkled with an inner light, or, to Smith's cynical mind, a cosmetic unguent. He stood with legs astride and left hand firmly clasping a right wrist across the front of his lower body. He made no acknowledgment to the roar of applause other than to allow a light smile to play upon his face, and to swing his trim body from side to side to each part of the hall.

A thought idled across Smith's mind that since the asceticism of Montgomery and the athleticism of Alexander there were no fat generals about – in any army. Still one or two fat N.C.O.s about though, said Smith to himself, thinking fondly of Ackerman.

Mulqueen raised a commanding close-fingered palm for silence. 'Britons, in a few short weeks you will exercise the supreme right and responsibility of free citizens in a democratic society. You will elect a government. It may be a government of cautious class-conscious Conservatives, or of squabbling, squandering and equally class-conscious Socialists. It may even, if you are endowed or accursed with an optimism amounting to fatalism, to be a government of livid and liverish Liberals.

'I say to you Britons, and I say to the devolved Britons of Scotland, Wales and my homeland, it could be, it should be and it will be, a government of men and women dedicated to the enormous task of healing our stricken and crippled nation so that she may stand, yet again, on the mighty thews of her great people, and face the nations of the world in proud vigour and without shame. It could be, it should be and it will be, the Government of Britain First.'

Smith did not know if he was applauding the high rhetoric or because everyone else was applauding and it would draw attention to himself if he remained silent. He gratified his conscience by concluding it was the latter process.

'Tonight in the House of Commons,' Mulqueen pointed in the direction of Westminster, 'miserable, mindless, mewling men of all parties are sitting and debating whether this nation can afford to stay in the Common Market. They have laid out their stall of shoddy goods no one wants to buy, and now find they cannot afford to pay the rent for a site in the market-place.

'Why? Because they have embezzled the profits to fill their own political pockets.

'I said earlier they were debating, because that is what they say they are doing. Is the true meaning of that word not debased by the abject whining, whimpering and wheedling, alternating with pompous bluster, bombast and bunkum, emanating from that place?'

Despite the emotive pitch of the words used by the General, the delivery was quiet but forcefully sincere. Like a briefing before a dawn attack on a four-division front. It was total political warfare, unimpeded by a Geneva Convention of usage and abusage adopted by the established parties. Smith gained the impression that the General was after unconditional surrender, and towards that end no prisoners would be taken.

He went on to deal with defence spending. 'Defence cuts? They have stabbed the Forces of the Crown through the heart. We lie helpless at the feet, not only of any Eastern aggressor! As recent events have shown, we lie helpless at the feet of petty criminals and subversive murderers within our own shores.'

Mulqueen wound up his address by resurrecting the greatness of the nation's past. Once again the gunboats maintained the peace of the world and mighty liners carried the flag of British commerce to every corner of the world. The great bridges were rebuilt and the railways thundered on the power of steam. A never-setting sun shone upon the land at high noon.

If the nation was on a nostalgia trip, the General was going to be in the driver's seat.

He finished by introducing the constituency candidate of the Britain First Movement, and as he held out a welcoming hand to bring him forward someone at the front of the hall cried out,

'Bloody murdering fascist. Killer of innocent Irishmen, Butcher of Belfast, you fas –'

The words were cut off in a gasp of pain as a steward applied the wrist lock. Smith got a glimpse of a twisted youthful face as they wheeled the protestor to a side door. He was fairly certain the face belonged to Ian Craddock.

Smith burst out of the emergency door and ran round to the other side of the building. He found two stewards dusting off their hands with satisfaction. 'That fellow you threw out. Where did he go?'

'He went like a bat out of hell down the road,' said one. 'And with a boot up his arse to help him on his way,' said the other.

Smith trotted down to the main road. Of Ian Craddock, if it was Ian Craddock, there was no sign.

Chapter XI

Smith knocked on the door of Craddock's office and pushed it open without waiting for an invitation to enter. Craddock had the bottle out and his drinking-companion was the Deputy Commissioner, Morgan Swarbrick.

'Come back later, Smith.' There was anger in Craddock's voice. Smith knew it was not because of his intrusion but because his report was not wanted in the presence of Swarbrick. 'No, no, come on in, boyo.' There was a hint of friendliness in Swarbrick's soft voice, or was it just an excuse to challenge Craddock's abrupt dismissal?

'Mr Craddock has been telling me all the nasty grudge-bearing policemen have been eliminated from the enquiry. So what have you been doing today along the paths of righteousness?'

Smith looked at Craddock's tight face and without hesitation related all he had learned about Staff Sergeant Richard Gredek. Swarbrick listened impassively. He was a good listener.

'So, it looks as though your Soldiers of the People are equipped with the fire-power of an infantry assault company?'

'That seems to be the size of it,' said Smith. Craddock glowered in the background.

'But the British Army, despite what you may think, is not entirely composed of fools, boyo. When Ackerman mentions your visit, somebody is going to wonder why Scotland Yard should be interested in Gredek.'

'I am sure you will not press me on the point, sir,' replied Smith, 'but Ackerman has no reason to believe Scotland Yard has an interest in Gredek.'

Swarbrick laughed. 'Oh, dear me. Have you been devious, Mr Smith?' The mockery was, nevertheless, tinged with some respect. 'So what did you go in as? Military Police? S.I.B.? Try posing as Army Welfare next time, you can go in with both feet as Army Welfare.'

'Can Army Welfare get hold of Gredek's I.D. photograph and his blood group?'

The arrow head bowed towards Smith, 'I am sure it can, Mr Smith. I will contact them in the morning.'

Swarbrick swung round in thoughtful silence, his right wrist flicking emptily against his thigh. The swagger-stick was missing. 'We have a problem arising out of all this, that is going to make anything you policemen —' the deep forehead jerked in annoyance, 'anything *we* policemen have ever tackled before seem slightly insignificant.'

Craddock reached for his bottle and grudgingly poured some scotch for Smith and refilled his own and Swarbrick's glass. He and Smith waited, with some scepticism, to learn the magnitude of Swarbrick's problem.

But Swarbrick decided to go back over old ground. He turned to Smith. 'Did Ackerman mention, or did you think to ask him, how the arms were moved from the depot?'

'I thought to ask him.' Smith was not upset by the phrasing of Swarbrick's question; he should have mentioned it earlier. 'Some Royal Corps of Transport vehicles came in one morning. Gredek seemed to be expecting them and, of course, the transfer order signed by Wardoe was in that morning's post. Gredek supervised the loading and away they went.' Smith paused to gather words to excuse his previous omission.

'Two things I should have mentioned, and I apologize for not doing so earlier; firstly, Ackerman noticed the vehicles were all old Bedfords of a type he thought were phased out and, secondly, the R.T.C. men were very smart and in newish gear, smocks and denims. He thought they must be a newly formed company of recruits, but most of them were a few years older than the usual eighteen or nineteen year old recruit.'

'So they bought up some ex-W.D. Bedfords and surplus uniforms. Well boyo, you have a live line of enquiry there.' Swarbrick had to look up slightly into Smith's face, but it did not remove the menace from his eyes.

Hicks barged into the office and pulled up abruptly at the sight of Swarbrick. 'I am sorry sir, I didn't know –' Swarbrick cut him short with a wave of his hand and paced the room flicking the calf of his leg with an imaginary swagger-stick.

Craddock received a glare from Hicks for entertaining the Deputy in his office without including him. Craddock thrust his head in the air in disgust.

'The Britain Firsters are marching again on Sunday.' Swarbrick made the announcement directly at Hicks.

'Yes sir, I've just seen the operation order,' replied Hicks in some puzzlement. 'My department will be providing the usual contingent for plain clothes cover, but the policing will be the responsibility of A.8.'

'I am now fully conversant with the departmental responsibilities of the force. Thank you, Mr Hicks.' The distraction in Swarbrick's voice took the edge from his remark. He turned to face them, black arrow head lowered.

'Britain First is marching again on Sunday,' he repeated. He gave each of them the arrow point in turn. 'Do any of you know what a well-sited Kalashnikov PK machine-gun can do to a closely packed body of marchers?' The question was so phrased as to indicate he did not want an answer even if one was available. 'Well?' he demanded of grim unresponsive faces. 'I will tell you. It has a rate of fire at around one thousand rounds per minute. It has a muzzle velocity of around two thousand, eight hundred feet per second. If they are nicely lined up in file as Britain First marchers are always are, one bullet could produce about five casualties. All fatal.'

'But what is this all about?' Hicks' puzzlement limped around the room as he cast his eyes from face to face for an answer.

'It is about urban guerrilla warfare, Mr Hicks. Your Soldiers of the People have progressed from cut-throat razors and butchers' cleavers to machine-guns, rocket projectors and assault rifles. They have declared war on Britain First. And to let them know what is coming and to let them know just how deeply they can penetrate, they chop off your late Commissioner's head and carry the remains through Scotland Yard into his own office. And to ram the lesson home they put a bullet in Hammertoe outside this very building.'

107

'But they were in no way connected with the Britain First Movement,' said Hicks.

Swarbrick considered the point as if he needed convincing, 'That may be so. Policemen, like soldiers, may have political opinions but not political affiliations. And of course we must keep our opinions to ourselves. But we would be less than honest if we did not see ourselves desiring anything other than a well ordered society, it is what police work is all about, is that not so?'

He received no answer. 'In that delightfully archaic phrase, the object of a police force is to achieve the preservation of public tranquillity.' The Welsh voice dwelt lovingly yet mockingly on the syllables. 'And while we have a politically apathetic society consuming tranquillizers by the ton, we also have a minority who are solely on political pep pills, some of whom see the police as trying to shut down their source of supply so they bump off a couple of them just to let everyone know the police cannot protect themselves, let alone ordinary people.'

'Why didn't they go straight for Mulqueen or Landon?' demanded Craddock.

Swarbrick smiled at him almost pityingly. 'Newton's Third Law, my dear Craddock, every action has an equal and opposite reaction. Have you seen the opinion polls?'

Craddock vented dry spit at the floor to give his opinion of opinion polls. Swarbrick ignored it and continued.

'Since the murder of Sir Maxwell and Mr Hammertoe, Britain First have increased their share of the vote from 23.4 percent to 26.8 percent. Had they murdered Mulqueen it might well have jumped to 30 per cent in sympathetic reaction.'

'So why kill anyone?' asked Smith.

'Smith, you have the ability to ask the right question. The answer you will have to supply for yourself. In arriving at it, consider the half-filled bucket of water you can whirl around without spilling a drop. Because of the speed, centrifugal force gives you, so to speak, a bloodless revolution. But if your bucket is heavy with centuries of tradition and parliamentary democracy, it can only be revolved slowly and a lot of water or blood is going to run out before it comes over the top.'

Smith considered it without answering. He had to admit he had never been much good at physics.

'And on Sunday, gentlemen, the bucket may be raised upwards above forty-five degrees.'

Swarbrick had offered a hypothesis demanding a practical solution. The silence almost hummed as the neutrons and protons of cerebral energy fought for stability as the awful prospect in the mind threatened to reach critical mass and explode.

Craddock scratched his head and said, 'We will have to prohibit the march. The Commissioner can make an order prohibiting any march for the purpose of preventing disorder, can't he?'

Hicks did not think much of the idea, 'Only if he can obtain consent from the Home Secretary and agreement is rarely, if ever, given these days. Indeed, it is rarely sought. In case you have forgotten, Angus, your uniform colleagues have a tradition of upholding and protecting the democratic right to demonstrate.'

'Aye weel, if they are going to exercise that tradition on Sunday, you will have to replace the mounted police with an armoured division.'

'We are not going to prohibit the march!' Swarbrick was grimly decisive, then, suddenly aware of his new role, qualified his words by adding, 'At least not on the basis of what Smith has found out today. That would mean public disclosure and destroy anything we might gain.'

'Man, you are taking an awful chance.' It was not a protest from Craddock, merely a statement of fact.

Swarbrick shrugged and sniffed through his battered nose like a boxer.

'We could prohibit this one but with Parliament about to be dissolved for the election we would be powerless to prevent any further pre-election meetings of Britain First. We would only be delaying the possibility of an attack, with our chances of recovering the arms considerably reduced.'

He sniffed again and even wiped the tip of his mis-shapen nose several times with his thumb. So far as Swarbrick was concerned it was seconds out of the ring.

'I take it, sir,' Hicks sparred cautiously, 'the decision will rest with the Commissioner?'

Swarbrick smiled pleasantly and handed his glass to

109

Craddock. 'It always does, Mr Hicks. Is that not so?'

He drained the recharged glass after raising it in salute. 'Your choice of malt is to be commended, Mr Craddock.' The appreciation was firmly expressed.

'In the meantime, gentlemen, only those in this room are aware of the matters discussed and we may assume our discussions are totally secure,' the arrow pointed at each head in turn, 'may we not?'

The threat in his parting words hung vibrant in the air as Swarbrick left the room.

'Now just what the hell has been going on?' Hicks demanded to know.

The beginning of the week brought a few positive factors to the attention of Craddock and Smith.

They were in a report from Dr Loder on examination of the material from Wardoe's room. Some wool fibres found adhering to the head of a nail on one of the chairs were identical in every respect with wool fibres found on the dead Commissioner's uniform. In addition, the blood group AB obtained from Swarbrick's sources as the blood group of Staff Sergeant Gredek, was, in that respect only, similar to the blood group derived from the secretion deposited on the body.

Ninhydrin tests for fingerprints on the typed note left in Hicks' office were negative. The typeface used could be attributed to four different models but if the original machine could be found it should be possible to attribute it to the note.

When it was ascertained that Wardoe was not employed at the main defence ministry building but in an Ordnance complex in Holborn, Smith accompanied a puzzled but uncomplaining D.I. Pewbone there as his sergeant to enquire of Wardoe's colleagues, civil and military, as to any known reasons why he should meet such a tragic and 'accidental' end.

They were particularly interested in Mr Wardoe's personal effects he might have left in his desk. A drawer was opened. A brush matted with long-dead hair and granules of dandruff lay inside, with a soap case in peeling chrome and ancient rust, a record token, a broken fountain pen, and two copies of *Muscle, The Magazine for Men*. 'I would never have thought Wardoe was interested in physical culture.'

Did he have an official diary? A wry smile, 'No, he did not come within the scale of issue, his duties were purely clerical.' Did he have any friends? 'Oh dear no, rather a solitary man, he came and he went, so to speak, alone.' A knowing smile, 'He was, er, ah, as you probably know, rather eccentric.'

May we use your office typewriter just to copy out a list of his effects? An anything-to-get-rid-of-you look. 'Please do, you will find paper in the drawer.'

Did he make visits to military establishments? Shocked surprise, 'Goodness gracious no,' then suspiciously, 'Why do you ask?' We have to try and find someone who may know his next of kin.

According to Dr Loder, it was highly probable the carbon-copy list of arms and the list of property were produced on the same machine but as the first was a carbon copy a definitive standard of proof could not be assured. The paper on which both lists were typed was identical.

Chapter XII

The reason given by Britain First in its notice of intention to demonstrate was, 'To make a visible protest against the Government's economy measures in cancelling orders for the Multi-Rôle Combat Aircraft by one-third, thereby reducing the nation's already lamentable defence forces still further and causing widespread unemployment in the aero and allied industries.'

An intended route of demonstration was delivered to police showing an assembly point at Hyde Park north. The procession would exit from Tyburn Gate to Park Lane, Grosvenor Place and down Victoria Street past Scotland Yard into Parliament Square, up Bridge Street to Victoria Embankment by the River Thames. Along the embankment to Horseguards Avenue, where a petition of protest would be handed in at the Ministry of Defence.

Details of the march were barely in the hands of police before the Popular Front of International Marxists and Socialists served notice of an intention to demonstrate on the same day, from Tower Hill to Trafalgar Square by way of Cannon Street, Queen Victoria Street, Victoria Embankment and Northumberland Avenue.

The P.F.I.M.S. wished to peaceably protest 'against war-mongering fascists who are endangering world peace.'

There was no actual point of contact along the route of either demonstration, but barely two hundred yards of Embankment Gardens separated Northumberland Avenue from Horseguards Avenue.

And on the southern flank, the broad brown Thames would roll quietly to the sea.

There was much coming and going between the Yard and Home Office with Rachette, Swarbrick, Hicks and Ormerod, the public order operations chief, in frequent conference and consultation with Home Office officialdom. In the end it was decided to make an empty threat and a passionate plea. At least as passionate as the ambiguity of civil service self preservation would allow.

Identical letters were sent to both parties.

'With regard to your proposed demonstration, the purpose and intention of which has been notified to Police. I am directed by the Commissioner of Police to draw your attention to the Public Order Act, 1936, Sec. 3, ss. (1) & (3).

As you may be aware this section of the above statute confers upon the Commissioner the power to impose upon the organizers of a procession such as you intend, conditions necessary to maintain public order.

It further empowers the Commissioner, with the consent of the Secretary of State, to make an order prohibiting such a procession for a period of three months, should he have reason to believe there may be a breach of public order.

Whilst the Commissioner would be reluctant to exercise his powers under the Act, you are reminded of their existence and requested in the public interest to cancel your proposed demonstration.

You will be aware in these troubled times, the demands upon police manpower are such, that to persist in your intentions, may result in a considerable section of the community being deprived of police services and placed at risk.

I am also obliged to point out, there are certain risks and dangers inherent in a demonstration such as is proposed. Police may not be in a position to adequately anticipate or prevent such risks and dangers in a manner consistent with public safety.

You are therefore asked to consider these factors and once again requested to cancel your proposed demonstration.'

The B.F.M. replied in reasonable terms, saying they realized only too deeply the pressures and strains under which police had to work amidst the lawless and anarchical conditions the Government had allowed to fester and grow amongst the great mass of law-abiding Britons. They would be most happy to accede to the request, and forgo their democratic rights in the public interest.

However, they understood certain other parties intended to demonstrate and regrettably they would only relinquish that right should the other parties agree to do likewise.

Should the other parties refuse to do so, they would consider the overriding need to protect the Nation required their message be brought before the people.

They noted the risks and dangers pointed out in the police letter, but 'our members will never be deterred from their duty to the nation however grave the risks and dangers may be.'

To show how moderate and reasonable they were, the B.F.M. promptly released the police letter and their reply to the media.

The reply from the P.F.I.M.S. was predictable in the circumstances. There was none, at least to the police letter.

But the media got hold of one of the extremists from the students' union and, with him nicely posed on Tower Hill, asked him what the left intended doing. 'The solidarity of the workers' movements will not bow down to the lackeys and running dogs of the capitalist regime. We will march despite the threats of police to curtail the peoples' rights to democratic protest.' He found inspiration in the hulk of H.M.S. *Belfast* lying embalmed on its riverside bier just across the Thames. Pointing to it he cried, 'We carry the spirit of the worker martyrs who died on the Odessa steps and on the streets of the city for which that ship was named. Death to the fascists! Worker Democracy must live!'

It was not quite enough for another Eisenstein revival at the National Film Theatre.

Sunday leave for four thousand six hundred and forty-eight police officers was cancelled.

Chapter XIII

There was still some warmth in the late autumnal sun and Smith stood shirt-sleeved at the window of his office looking down on, and almost enjoying, the quiet of a Sunday morning in Victoria Street. A few out-of-season tourists were camera-clicking their way towards Westminster Abbey and Parliament Square. A solitary taxi beetled past and dry gutter-gathered leaves swirled and settled in the wake of its passing.

An ominous number of police began to assemble in the street and take up positions along the route of the B.F.M. march. The tourists, seeing the unusual concentration, brought their cameras up into the high port. Focal length and exposure timings flicked into correct setting with the casual expertise of gun hands in a Western movie.

'Jesus Christ, they won't be carrying bodies into the building today.' O'Brien came into the office with some Sunday papers. 'I had hell's own job getting in myself. There must be more coppers in the building than there are in the streets.'

He settled down by the portable police radio and opened the centre page of his paper.

'Where are the *Times* and the *Observer*?' Smith surveyed the pile brought in by O'Brien. 'Guv, those are papers for people who think they rule the world.' He swung the centre page of his paper round to Smith, 'This is for people who don't care who rules the world so long as she's got big tits.'

Smith returned to the window and surveyed the opposite roofs. Uniformed police, and plain clothes men, identifiable in yellow armbands, the colour of the day, hung uncertainly over parapets and balconies. In the distance, the growing resonance of massed voices came muted through the windows.

He craned into the corner looking towards Victoria. He saw nothing, but the shouting was louder and becoming meaningful. The cadence and rhythm had the discipline of a drum. He had heard it before but not in such volume and triumph.

'BRITAIN – BRI-TAIN FIRST'

The syllables were shortly but definably interrupted. There was a silence of five paces between shouts, but it was a silence filled with the stamp of steel tipped shoes.

A marching beat designed to accentuate the words, 'BRITAIN – BRI-TAIN FIRST' Crump – Crump – Crump – Crump – Crump – 'BRITAIN – BRI-TAIN FIRST' Crump – Crump – Crump – Crump – Crump – 'BRITAIN – BRI-TAIN FIRST.'

The combination of voice and sound had a rousing excitement.

As the leading ranks, five abreast, appeared in view Smith saw each man wore identical dark blue double-breasted blazers with brass buttons brightly shining. Light beige trousers lifted in sharp creases above highly polished heavy-soled black shoes. A plain blue tie on a white shirt completed the outfit.

Taken as individuals, it was the sort of outfit worn by any young man seeking to impress his week-end girl-friend with his smart attire. Smith grinned to himself as he imagined the argument there would be among his uniformed colleagues as to whether or not the get-up constituted a law-breaking political uniform under Section 1 of the Public Order Act. He dismissed it from his mind. It wasn't his worry.

'BRITAIN' short, sharp and loud with challenge. 'BRI-TAIN FIRST' deeper and with menace. Each marcher, and by now they filled the extent of his view across the window, carried a red white and blue British flag, about eighteen inches square, of the sort sold on State occasions.

During the five-pace beat, the flag was held out to the front on stiff extended right arms. On commencement of the shout it was brought smartly back to be held diagonally across the chest.

Smith saw with some surprise at least fifteen black faces, three stalwart bearded and turbanned Sikhs, and more than a score of Asians amongst the marchers.

116

The precision and smartness of the parade – the word demonstration, Smith thought, was too, well, democratic – betokened hours of training and rehearsal. Parade was the better word.

There were women interspersed among the marchers, wearing single-breasted blazers and skirts in the same colours as the men. As in any choral work, their higher-pitched voices lent range and clarity to the volume of sound.

Smith estimated about five hundred 'uniformed' marchers passed before they were followed by the body of the demonstration. Varied in dress, they walked rather than marched, compressing into sudden knots as the less disciplined pace varied, or rushing forward with giggling squeals from the girls as a space developed in front. Their shouting did not have the unison of the lead marchers, and such of them as had flags waved with gay abandon.

Despite the normality of the people engaged, a fervour reflected from the crowd like a long flash of sunlight on bright steel.

Smith left the window and walked to the corner where O'Brien sat listening out on the operational channel.

'All quiet so far, Guv,' he said in answer to a quizzical eyebrow from Smith. As though in confirmation a voice on the radio said, 'Alpha Lima Point Two – tail of march passing Grosvenor Gardens – no incidents.'

A different voice came in, 'Alpha Romeo Point One – estimated two-thirds of march passed Buckingham Gate. No incidents.'

The central controller asked, 'Alpha Delta One – how are things your end?' 'Alpha Delta One to Control – head of march now in Parliament Square. No incidents.'

Above the voice of Alpha Delta One could be heard the stacatto of 'BRITAIN – BRI-TAIN FIRST'. As they listened O'Brien said with some envy, 'That lot will need to sink a few pints before the end of the day to get their voices back.'

The radio clicked on, 'Alpha Delta One to Control – head of march now approaching Whitehall end of Parliament Square – no incidents.'

'What cover have we got in the Square?' Smith knew the answer but felt in need of reassurance.

117

'Well there must be about two hundred and fifty uniform men –' 'No, from the Department?' Smith was seized by an angry nervousness.

'We've got sixteen men on foot on the pavement. Two with binocs and a radio up in Big Ben, two more on the tower of St Margaret's Church in front of the Abbey and six on the roof of the Treasury building. All armed except the two on the church, it being Sunday and all.'

'Alpha Delta One to Control – head of march now crossing into Bridge Street – no inci –' The last syllable was masked in what Smith thought to be a roar of static. A heavier reverberation followed. Smith and O'Brien stared at the radio, willing it to speak.

The voice when it came was an octave higher. 'An explosion – somebody's fired a shell at the Treasury building.'

The controller cut in. 'Use your call sign and report the incident please.' There was another roar ending in an explosive thud. The observer came back, 'There's another one in the same place. They are shooting right over my head!'

The controller was calm and precise. 'I repeat, use your call sign and report the incident please.'

They could hear the heavy indrawn breathing as nerves calmed and wits were gathered in. 'Alpha Delta One to Control – two missiles, apparent source tower of St Margaret's Church, fired across Parliament Square through second-floor window of Treasury building and exploded inside. No casualties amongst marchers. Casualties, if any, at seat of explosion not known at this stage. Procession calm and intact. Main body has not yet reached the square. Procession now halted on directions of police. Alpha Delta One – out.'

Smith took a quick look out of the window. The marchers were standing patiently. A few began to sing 'Why are we waiting.' If the sound of the explosions had reached them, it had not made much impression.

'Well at least nobody should be hurt,' said O'Brien, 'Civil servants don't work on Sundays.'

Smith gave him a withering look. 'The Home Secretary, several M.P.s from all parties, Rachette, Swarbrick and God knows how many senior civil servants and M.I. people decided to view the march from the Treasury building. I don't know which room they were using but it's ten pounds to a pinch of shit it was on the second floor.'

O'Brien deflated on a long 'Jeeesus Christ,' then said, 'I don't think I'll take the bet Guv, and believe me, I've got plenty to stake.' He went on to ask, 'What about Mr Hicks?'

'You don't think you could keep him out of an act with a cast like that? Craddock and Brightside are there as well.' Smith picked up a personal radio and tossed it at O'Brien, 'Come on, let's get down there.'

They ran down Victoria Street past the amorphous body of the march, a buzz of rumour and speculation now flittering up and down, words spattering in the air. 'The reds have opened up with a machine gun.' 'Six bombs have gone up at Whitehall.' 'There are about two hundred dead up in the Square.' And inevitably a bold voice saying, 'Now everybody keep calm,' as a self-appointed leader of men tried to assert himself.

In twos and threes, some of the marchers broke away and began walking back towards Victoria Station.

At the front of the march, the blazered cohort stood steadily enough, most of them in the military 'At ease' position. At the behest of police they began to march, in silence, across Whitehall and over Westminster Bridge. A police cordon across the lower end of Victoria Street cut off the remainder of the column who were being directed back from whence they had come.

At Northumberland Avenue, the main body of police had the P.F.I.M.S. solidly blocked from access to the marchers.

As Smith and O'Brien turned into Parliament Square, a thin plume of smoke drifted from a second-floor window on the Treasury building. A black stain shadowed the weathered limestone surround.

Whitehall was a checker-board of vehicular colour. Red fire tenders, white ambulances and blue police cars. It was an appropriate combination, thought Smith, the colours of disaster.

The sounds of disaster were also present, the belligerent scream of two-tone horns, a clangour of bells, the shouts, 'Get a stretcher over here' – 'Any oxygen bottles on that tender?'

The activity and inactivity, men running, gesturing, directing. Others standing, waiting, wondering. And all over, pervasive, the contagion of uncertainty and fear.

O'Brien was repeating himself into the personal radio. He

turned to Smith, 'No good Guv, I can't raise the men we had on the church tower. Maybe they have nicked somebody or are chasing them,' he said hopefully. 'Go and find out,' Smith could see a gathering of helmeted heads appearing above the castellated parapet of the tower. They all appeared to be looking down at something behind the parapet.

Smith made his way to the second floor. On the stairs stretchered bodies were going down, some white-faced in shock, other shrouded and still. He kept clear of the room where the projectiles had exploded. A coming and going of harassed doctors, saline and plasma, of ambulancemen and firemen, indicated that his presence would be merely obstructive. A familiar voice led him down the corridor to the next room. 'We had men on the church tower to provide against such a contigency. There has been gross neglect somewhere and I will want to see these men as soon as . . .' the voice trailed away into, 'Oh my God, what a shambles, what a bloody shambles.'

Hicks stood over Craddock, his face buried in clenched fists, rocking back and forth from the waist. Craddock sat in a chair, head bowed, looking old and small inside his overcoat, the ends of his tartan scarf hanging disconsolately to the floor.

Rachette, white-faced and pensive, was staring from the window into a faraway distance.

Swarbrick was the only one who noticed Smith standing in the doorway. 'Ah now, perhaps Mr Smith can tell us why the Metropolitan Police failed to pluck a rocket projectile out of the air?' There was no levity in his voice.

'Was it one —'

'Yes Smith, it undoubtedly was one, an R.P.G. 7V with fragmentation warheads. And in the hands of a very good man. A soldier, Smith, a very good soldier.'

There it was again, 'Soldier', 'Soldier', Wardoe's Soldier, Swarbrick's Soldier, Soldiers of the People, nothing but bloody soldiers.

Craddock was glad to see Smith, as if he was no longer alone. He stood up and asked, 'What about the men on the church Owen, what have they got to say about this?'

'I don't know, we couldn't raise them on the P.R. O'Brien has gone across to find out.'

'I suppose you realize, Smith,' Hicks was in icy control of

himself, 'the Home Secretary and the Private Office senior staff have virtually been wiped out. She is dead, Smith, a Minister of the Crown and three other Members of Parliament, slaughtered in our presence – not to mention Mr Brightside.'

Smith experienced, not for the first time, the callous euphoria that protects the mind from the impact of outrageous death. A macabre pun slid silently across his lips, 'Don't forget the bright side.'

'What is there to smile about for God's sake?'

'I am sorry sir, it was a ... grimace, not a smile.' Smith felt they knew he was lying. He fought down a vomit of panic. The bite of reality gnawed at his guts. He sought refuge in sycophancy.

'May I say sir, it is a relief to find the Commissioner and yourselves unharmed.'

'All due to the fact the room nextdoor was so small, boyo.' Swarbrick seemed to reflect on his words. 'We moved in here before the parade arrived.'

Smith noted his use of the word 'parade' as fitting his own earlier assessment and was childishly pleased. 'And Mr Brightside?' he asked.

'He remained to point out the various personalities of the B.F.M. From what I saw of him, the first round probably impacted in front of him. I am afraid there will be nothing physically left to identify him.'

'You said, sir, it was an expert using the weapon. If so it implies the people in the building were the intended target and not, as we anticipated, the B.F.M. marchers. Or was he not so expert and, intending to hit the marchers got in a –' Smith tripped over the words ' – lucky shot?'

'Not a chance. We are about fifty feet up on a corresponding height with the tower. I saw the trajectory, nice and flat even though we must be on the edge of extreme range for an R.P.G. And the projectile has a secondary rocket that gives it a great deal of accuracy. No, boyo, we were the target all right.'

'Excuse me, gentlemen.' The timorous sobbing tones bore little resemblance to O'Brien's jaunty voice, but it was O'Brien, white-faced and with tendrilled hair sweat-plastered on his forehead. His frame shaking.

'The two boys on the church tower, Ross and Graham, they

are both dead. Both been shot, they are lying up there.' His voice trembled as if in disbelief at what his eyes had seen. 'Graham was still alive when they found him. He said a police inspector in uniform came up into the tower with two constables, they were carrying a case like the ones used for A9 portable transmitters. He thought they were going to set up another reporting station but before anything was said the inspector pulled a gun and shot him.'

O'Brien paused as if seeking to recall further detail and added, 'Three times, shot him three times.'

Without warning he came forward on his toes and with gathering momentum fell on his face.

Chapter XIV

The national papers got the communiqué in good time for all Monday's editions.

'In an action against the fascist and reactionary group calling itself the Britain First Movement, Soldiers of the People struck down nine political collaborators and three of their repressive police lackeys.

However our primary target was the fascist column and as this was not attacked the soldier comrade in charge of the operation will be tried by a Court of Comrades.

Finding and sentence will be duly promulgated.

Freedom to the People.'

The leader writers, reaching into the past and resurrecting lifeless clichés, studded their articles with 'ghastly carnage', 'senseless slaughter', 'unholy holocaust' and 'death of democracy'. They 'stood aghast', 'recoiled in horror' and 'demanded to know.'

Some of course, rebuilt the gallows and required the restitution of the Prevention of Terrorism Act. Others appealed for calm and would not be panicked into an over-reaction.

The Britain First Movement were promptly into print with a half-page pronouncement in heavy type.

'Britain First shares with the nation a sense of shame, sorrow and anger, at the murderous attack directed against the roots of parliamentary government. We mourn with the relatives and friends of the dead and extend our deepest sympathy to the many grievously wounded.

However, we must ask the nation to remember it was the consequences of weak and unwise governmental policies that permitted the rise of those murderous beasts who drenched the Mother of Parliaments in the blood of her children. We of the Britain First Movement are proud of the courage and resolution shown by our members as they stood fast and firm under a hail of fire from the murderous Red terrorists. It was the courage of Britons who stand and will die for Britain First.

Liam Mulqueen`

The cabinet had met in emergency discussions on the Sunday night, amid a gathering crowd of morbid sightseers, and after a reshuffle, a new Home Secretary was appointed.

When Parliament assembled on the Monday all other business was put aside while Sunday's killings were debated. To the surprise of all, and to the anger of many backbenchers on both sides, the government made an offer of coalition to the opposition. This would have the effect of postponing the forthcoming general election.

The screams of anger came loudest from the Britain First members but were only slightly less hysterical than those of the more dogmatic members of both sides. For twenty minutes cries of 'Never', 'Shame' and 'No Surrender' rose in crescendo.

Nevertheless the opposition front bench sniffed more than tentatively at the coalition pie. The aroma stirred the juices of political appetites as power-hungry men and women in both main parties realized in the event of an election they, at best, might only eat by supping at the table of Britain First with a very short spoon, or at worst watching powerless as Britain First scoffed the lot.

Although a free vote was demanded and obtained, the whips on both sides went out, pleading, demanding, excoriating, but the shellbacks, optimists and never-say-die men resisted and the motion was defeated 283 to 278 with 43 abstentions. The vote of Britain First members was decisive in bringing about their first major parliamentary victory. The House gloomily adjourned at 5.30 a.m. on Tuesday morning.

Later that day the pound fell 3.8 cents against the dollar and the latest opinion polls gave Britain First 31.9 per cent of the vote.

With the remainder of Sunday, and all of Monday and Tuesday morning, taken up with the grim business of body identification, multiple post-mortems, scene-searching and frenzied statement-taking and making, it was late on Tuesday afternoon by the time they got round to forward planning at Scotland Yard.

The Commissioner, Rachette, and A.C.C. Hicks were in favour of the immediate release of Gredek's photograph to the media. It had been repeatedly but fruitlessly published without specifying the crime for six consecutive days in confidential police circulations, under the heading 'Arrest on sight'.

Craddock protested against the proposal, with Smith offering what support he could, on the grounds that to do so would simply warn Gredek they were on to him and make the task of finding him even more difficult, with the prospect of him fleeing the country altogether.

Deputy Commissioner Swarbrick secured a compromise agreement to delay media involvement for six clear days.

With the additional presence of Bruce Bolsover, National Co-ordinator of Regional Crime Squads, and a languid gentleman from the Security Service introduced as Mr Black, a name to which he frequently failed to respond, discussions were opened for the implementation of joint planning devised by Swarbrick, Craddock and Willie Woulover, Brightside's successor as special branch operations chief.

The plan was named 'Operation Zip Fastener' and called for police raids beginning at midnight Thursday on the homes, offices, communes or whatever places used, frequented or occupied by people with affiliations anywhere to the left of moderate socialism.

One in every three police officers engaged in the operation would be armed. C.S. gas, or 'smoke' as it was euphemistically named in official references, would be available, and every officer carried a photograph of the – to them – mysterious Gredek.

Rachette closed the 'Zip Fastener' meeting by saying despite the gravity of the matters under investigation, he trusted all would recognize the need for courtesy, tact and consideration to be shown to the persons subject of the searches and every care should be taken to put them to as little inconvenience as possible. Turning to the stenographer he added, 'Please ensure my comments are fully recorded in the minutes.'

Bruce Bolsover departed for Birmingham to lay the plan before a conference of Chief Constables whose forces were involved in the operation. Mr Black recoiled from Craddock's invitation to join him for a drink as though an attempt was being made to compromise him, and left hurriedly in whispered conversation with Willie Woulover, and with several nervous glances over his shoulder.

At 10 p.m. that night, Craddock and Smith were in the murder room reviewing the input of the day's work. It was heavy in quantity but, in quality of substance, not inspiring. Detective Inspector George O'Brien awaited their pleasure, tentatively fingering a faceful of surgical tape that held his nose, broken in his fainting fall, in place.

He was called over by one of the girls on the phones to take a call from the news agency. It was another communiqué from the Soldiers of the People.

'A Court of Comrades has considered the case of the soldier comrade responsible for the misdirection of the attack upon the assembled fascist forces of Britain First.
The soldier comrade has confessed to being a revisionary traitor in the pay of the fascist police.
As such he has been executed.
His remains will be found in Highgate Cemetery.
Freedom to the People.'

Despite immediate steps by police to seal the area around the cemetery, Craddock's car had to wend its way through an increasing jam of press cars, outside broadcast T.V. and radio vans. Swains Lane was a brilliant chiaroscuro as T.V. lighting cut into the darkness.

Led by Craddock, who brusquely pushed aside out-thrust microphones and stonily ignored the shouted questions, Smith and O'Brien entered the cemetery. Uniformed police kept the reporters at bay.

On the way out they had discussed the likely area within the cemetery where the body would be found. Their unanimous conclusion was not wrong. The body of a man lay, face down with arms outstretched, in the grass near the grave of Karl Marx.

Smith could not help grasping Craddock's arm in suppressed excitement; the body was clad in a thick polo-necked sweater of purple wool above a pair of heavy corduroy trousers. A crudely torn piece of white cardboard from what had once been a carton of some kind was pinned on his back. It bore words in thick red letters, 'EXECUTED AS A SPY. S.O.P.'

They stood looking down at the body for a time, not wanting it touched or moved until Wingate, who had just arrived, had taken his pictures. The face buried in the frosted grass was not visible. The lank untidy hair was blood-matted at the back of the neck and strangely, unnaturally, an envelope, sealed but un-addressed, had been inserted between the middle fingers of the outstretched right hand.

Wingate went methodically about his business, his lens covering every angle around the body and immediate area of ground. Finished, he turned to Craddock and said, 'We can turn him over now and get some shots from the front.'

'Don't move him!' Smith's voice cut into the night. He turned to Craddock, 'I think we had better get everybody back a bit. It might be booby-trapped.'

Craddock stood impassive and with set face a few feet from the body. Without lifting his eyes from the corpse he said to the uniformed inspector from the local station, 'Get on wi' it. Move them back.' His stance indicated he would remain.

Smith saw in Craddock's deep-set eyes, as they stared into the prostrate back, a glistening brightness. Was it anticipation? Or fear? He put it down to the high-intensity lighting and the coldness of the night, but the wavering gleam under the deep shadow of the wide hat-brim troubled his mind. It was unusual for Craddock to play the role of spectator at the scene of a crime and this was the second time it had happened.

Smith began with the envelope. Grasping it with a pair of tweezers he moved it gently. There was no resistance, no wire attached to the part hidden by the fingers. He held the envelope out to Neaterkin, who made a circuitous approach and let it fall into a clear plastic bag.

Lifting one finger at a time, Smith probed the ground under each hand, working his way up to the armpits. There was still some body warmth in that area. He has been killed within the last two hours or so, he thought to himself.

He carefully unpinned the notice of execution from the purple wool sweater and again Neaterkin tiptoed reluctantly forward with another bag.

There was nothing under the legs but the torso was the problem. Its weight could be holding down a spring-loaded contact that would complete a circuit to the electric detonator of an explosive charge buried under the body. The possibility brought beads of sweat to his brow as he eased his hand under the body, and worked it along both sides from crutch to back. He felt nothing other than the stickiness of congealing blood lying in the cavity between chin and breast.

He got to his feet and holding his bloody fingers away from his clothing looked around for something to clean them. Neaterkin provided a piece of cotton waste from his various supplies.

Wiping his fingers, he took a few steps to Craddock's side. He still stood on the same spot, head hunched into the folds of his tartan scarf, every line on his face a black canyon carved deep by the glare of the lights. The bright eyes drilled into the back of the body and through into the very ground beneath.

Smith said to him, 'I think it's clear. I'll take a chance and turn it anyway.' He moved towards the body, hesitated and looked again to Craddock. 'I think you should get back a bit just in case, Guv.' The head moved slowly in a gesture of refusal.

Smith shrugged and bent over the corpse. He pulled the right arm down to its side and placed the left leg over the right. Grasping the right side between shoulder and hip he pulled the body upwards. As he reached the point of balance he knew ... He suddenly realized whose face he was going to see and recoiled from the corpse in a panic of alarm and anguish.

He hoped it would fall back upon its face but the centre of gravity had been passed and it fell on its back like a sodden sack to reveal the face of Ian Craddock.

Smith was dimly aware of the cold dampness of the ground on his knees. He looked at Craddock, still standing, unmoving, but a little more erect, as if he had gathered more strength to carry a burden that had always been there, and was still there.

'You knew!' Smith bayed at him from his knees, 'You bloody well knew.' He got to his feet and approaching Craddock, hissed into his graven face in a mixture of anger and remorse, 'Why didn't you say, you knew it was your son, why didn't you say?'

Slowly Craddock reached up and took his hat from his head. He stood for long moments as other faces turned one to the other in wonder. Then, turning, he walked from the light into the etched darkness. Smith saw the silhouette stop and the hat drop from his hand. Craddock threw back his head and raised both fists to the heavens. He stood thus silently, but the anguish and despair could not have been more keenly felt by the witnesses had he howled at the moon.

And over it all the giant carved face of Karl Marx frowned down from its plinth, rejecting the sacrifice as unworthy.

The envelope had been opened at the laboratory and the letter inside photographed. Smith read the copy with increasing gloom. It was not something he wanted to show to Craddock.

'To my father,

Despite the enormity of my crime, my comrades, in consideration of my past service have granted me the privilege of writing to you.

I do not seek your forgiveness for fighting the people's battle against the repressive forces you serve.

My only regret is the betrayal of my comrades. This I can only attribute to the sight of your face amongst the gin and whisky drinking parasite politicians on Sunday.

I was taken in my memory to my childhood with you when we stood in the highlands watching the stags on the mountainside. You still remembered your working class origins in those days. You spoke of your elder brother who died in 1938 fighting for the Spanish workers in Andalucia.

It is a pity you did not choose to fight and die with him. It was my anger of your betrayal of your class that diverted me from the objective assigned by my soldier comrades.

This is my only regret.

Freedom to the people.

Your son of No Name.'

It seemed to Smith that bitter recrimination stood out on every line.

He grudgingly admitted there was no self-pity in the letter, and although the boy was blaming his father for his death, one could see from reading it, he had made no plea for mercy. He could see the comrade soldiers agreeing to allow young Craddock a last letter but he could only see them leaving it with his body if the content suited them. And this it clearly did.

Perhaps he had been forced to write it? Smith did not think much of the possibility. The boy had been shot twice in the back of the neck; there were no other marks of violence on the body.

As Simonson had pointed out at the post-mortem, the killer knew what he was doing. He had not stood behind and fired into the base of the skull with, especially in the dark, just the chance of not administering an immediately fatal coup de grâce.

'You may be surprised to know, my dear Smith,' Simonson had said, 'just how resilient the human brain can be. You can shoot bullets into it, even stick crowbars through it, without necessarily causing death. At least not in the short term, but your killer ... well I am not saying he knew that. In fact, bearing in mind what he did to Steype, I think he had other things in mind, but he was standing in front of the victim who was kneeling with his head held down. The shots were discharged at point-blank range into the back of the neck and downwards through the body, penetrating nearly every major organ en route. Both bullets finished up in the pelvic region.'

Smith's thoughts returned to the letter. Craddock's son was, in effect, saying he was responsible for the missiles fired through the Treasury window. That he, Ian Craddock, had aimed and fired the weapon.

Smith considered the little he knew about the youth. He was certainly not the trained soldier of whom Swarbrick had spoken. This shy, reticent intellectual who had cracked down the middle in an immature conflict of the mind between philosophical perfection and physical reality, between Life with a capital 'L' and what life really was about.

The post-mortem had revealed no signs of recent drug-taking, the forearm and buttock scars of his past addiction had long healed over. The crack in Ian Craddock had been repaired by a weld making the original material much stronger, but it still did not make him an instant expert with an R.P.G. rocket launcher.

Oddly enough, he could see the young Craddock killing Steype. The fearful indecision of the tentative hand jerking the blade across the soft suspended throat. A spasm of anger at the man who stood for all his father's failings as a parent, for a mother whose incurable illness and suffering were secondary to the obsessive duty of the hunter ... man-hunter.

All this and suddenly – slash – slash – slash.

Disgusted with the speculative and inconclusive nature of his thoughts, Smith came down to earth. 'It's a right load of bollocks,' he said.

O'Brien, who was driving the car taking them back to the Yard, looked at him anxiously, 'What is, Guv?'

'The reason for young Craddock's murder, that's what is. They are trying to have us over, and I don't like being had over.' It was six in the morning and Smith was tired and becoming angry. Perhaps even unconsciously inducing the anger to combat the fatigue.

'This Court of Comrades, this killing last night, this stupid letter, it is all a load of bollocks. These bastards never intended to hit the B.F.M. column on Sunday. They hit what they intended to hit. Maybe they realized afterwards they made a big mistake and put up Craddock's kid as a patsy.'

'Or maybe not,' said O'Brien. 'They have destroyed Craddock, and, through him and the kid, punched another hole in the credibility and the integrity of the police.'

'I don't know,' Smith felt his anger evaporating in a sudden wave of sickening lethargy. 'I just don't bloody well know.'

Smith found Craddock lying on the cot he had had put up in his office shortly after the Steype and Hammertoe murders. He was not asleep, just lying, head on clasped hands, gazing through half-closed eyes at the office wall on which hung a wide photograph of solemn-faced senior officers in row upon posed row, of compressed two-dimensional figures, wherein no single individual could be seen beyond a range of three feet.

'I presume you have come to tell me the result of the P.M.?' Smith stood uncertainly in the doorway as Craddock swung himself out of the cot and bent over to lace up his shoes.

'I thought you might be asleep.'

'No, I had slept, though. Does that surprise you, Owen? I was asleep until about five minutes before you came in. Deep asleep. No dreams. Does that surprise you?'

The repetitious mock-seriousness of the question required some form of answer. Smith said lamely, 'I'm glad to hear it.'

'The P.M., what was the result of the P.M.?'

'Shot twice downwards through the body from the back of the neck.' Smith felt he had to qualify the brusqueness of his tone and added, 'It must have been instantaneous. There would have been no pain.'

Craddock smiled, a slow pensive smile.

'To a man about to die, Owen, a millisecond of pain could be a thousand years of agony. In any case, I would rather my son lay there in agony, but alive until I had been able to say . . . just a few words to him.'

He turned to Smith with some excitement in his voice as a thought came to him, 'The envelope, what was in the envelope?'

Smith gave him the photocopy. Craddock rummaged about on his desk for his spectacles until Smith spotted them resting on a chair beside the cot. He gave them to Craddock saying, somewhat apologetically, 'It may be your son didn't actually write it. Or he may have been forced to write it.'

Craddock waved him into silence as he read the letter. The resurgence of animation in him faded and his face stiffened.

He scanned the pages, nodding slightly from time to time as if wishing to acknowledge agreement with the written words. On coming to the end of the three pages comprising the letter, Craddock returned to the first page and re-read it yet again.

With each single page spread out before him on the desk, Craddock looked up at Smith and said, 'Ian wrote it all right, I have not the slightest doubt about it, and nobody forced him to write it either.'

There was a hint of satisfaction in Craddock's voice. Smith was not puzzled by it, indeed he almost shared in the satisfaction. There was something in the letter. He had not seen it, but Craddock had.

'Why don't you go home and get some sleep, Owen.'

Unlike Craddock, Smith's sleep was restless and largely consisted of a still trancelike state of semi-wakefulness, with the distant day noises intruding through his mind in a constant drone. Thin blades of light slipping past apertures in the heavy curtain drew his eyes into far galaxies of cosmic dust.

Despite his failure to sleep it was the insistence of his bladder that brought him, heavy-eyed and sweating, from his bed, rather than a desire to face the rest of the day . . . and night.

The urinary relief was not the relief he now demanded as he sat with the bed-sweat chilling on his skin.

He reached across for the bed phone. 'Cora? Owen Smith . . . Well I've been busy . . . Are you tied up at the moment? . . . Then for Christ sake come over to my place and give me a short time.'

It was two in the afternoon when he returned to the Yard. O'Brien had not come in, and the house-to-house reports from the area around Highgate cemetery were piled on his desk.

The usual unproductive results of the great ability of the public to mind its own business were present, but at least two witnesses in the vicinity of the cemetery had heard the sound of shots twenty minutes prior to the notice of execution being phoned to the news agency.

A preliminary lab report was in on the Ian Craddock exhibits.

'The two bullets recovered from the body are of 9 mm calibre and fired from the same weapon that killed Ross and Graham on the tower of St Margaret's Church. Further tests are in being to ascertain the type of weapon used. Early indications favour the 9 mm Browning automatic pistol, as issued to H.M. Forces. It should be noted, no cartridge cases have been recovered at either scene.

'The exhibit described as a purple sweater is of wool fibres identical in all respects with fibres found on the uniform of the deceased Sir Maxwell Steype. It should be borne in mind the garment is one sold in large numbers at multiple stores and other garments from that source may give similar results.

'The exhibit described as brown corduroy trousers produced fibres identical to those found in the finger-nail scrapings of the same deceased person. The reservations attached to the purple sweater will also apply to the latter garment.

'On the sole of the right shoe, minute fragments of wood shavings were found, similar in nature to particles of wood shavings found on the body and shirt of the deceased Steype.

Again it cannot be said that these exhibits had a single source but taken together the probability of the three exhibits having a singular origin of exchange must be considered extremely high.

'The blood sample from the deceased Ian Craddock is of Group "O"; sub-group classification in the protein, antigen and enzyme ranges will be available in due course, but it can be stated categorically the secretor grouping AB deposited on the deceased Steype did not emanate from the deceased Ian Craddock.'

The result was less than Smith anticipated. He hoped there would be traces of the dead commissioner's blood found on Ian Craddock's clothing or at least on his shoes.

It must have been a strip-off job all round. His thoughts were interrupted by the arrival of a still yawning O'Brien. 'Night duty I don't mind, Guv. But day *and* night duty is severely interfering with my sex life.'

Chapter XV

At ten that morning Swarbrick and Hicks had presided over a briefing conference of all Divisional commanders and C.I.D. chiefs at the Imber Court police sports centre, to the west of London. Operation Zip Fastener was due to begin at midnight.

Although the London end of the zip would not be pulled tight until two in the morning, surveillance on suspect premises would begin at midnight as the operation commenced in the north. It had been decided to hold the briefing at Imber Court instead of the Yard to avoid speculative headlines in the evening papers as watching reporters jumped to conclusions about such a gathering of senior police in the light of recent events.

For all the satisfaction of a pleasant post-briefing luncheon, Hicks was not looking forward to his afternoon appointment with Craddock. As the car bearing Swarbrick and himself sped down the Kingston bypass, he was surprised to find consideration of the death of Craddock's son had brought a more personal and domestic sense of tragedy into the case, for him, than the murders of Sir Maxwell and Hammertoe.

He had not seen Craddock since before the so-called execution. He could only hope the man would see reason; the last thing he wanted in the circumstances was an abrasive argument. He genuinely felt sorry for the old man and shuddered to think what his own reaction might be if his own fifteen-year-old son went the same way.

As if reading his mind, Swarbrick broke into his thoughts, 'Do you want me in with you when you see Craddock?'

Hicks was tempted to accept, but his image shield slipped

smoothly into place. 'No, no. I think it best if I deal with this alone. I am sure he will appreciate the position. After all, it is what he wanted at the outset.'

Swarbrick gave a twisted nod of the head as if in admiration of Hicks' decisiveness. 'See if you can find out what his opinion is of his son's letter.'

'In what respect?' Hicks was puzzled.

'There is something about the content that is unnatural. I don't just mean in the way he reviles his father.'

Swarbrick paused as a speeding truck pulled into their lane, causing the driver to brake sharply in a welter of subdued curses.

As they resettled in their seats, Swarbrick went on, 'This business about highlands and stags, the elder brother killed in Andalucia, I feel it has an implicit meaning other than what is expressed in the words.'

Smith had hardly settled in with O'Brien to discuss further action on the results of the Highgate house-to-house enquiries, when Craddock rang down for him.

He had a number of personal articles laid out on his desk and was in the process of stuffing them into his briefcase. He handed the case to his driver and told him to wait at the front of the building.

Smith did not find his actions altogether unexpected, but felt it incumbent upon him to express some surprise and said, 'You on the move, Guv?'

'Owen, I am anticipating the inevitable, and don't try to bullshit me. You know what must happen as well as I do.'

'I must admit I could see the possibility. When did they tell you?'

Craddock drew himself up and said with some anger, 'They don't have to tell me, nobody has to tell me. With my own son a murdered member of a gang of criminal political cut-throats, they don't have to hit me over the head for me to realize my position is totally impossible.' His bitterness subsided as he dismissed it with a wave of his hand.

'And I won't be engaged in any stupid story-book one-man-band stuff, Owen.' He placed a confiding arm round Smith's shoulders, 'But you will keep in touch with me, Owen.' He gave him a look almost beseeching in its supplication. 'I would like to know how things go on.'

'Of course I'll keep in touch.'

Craddock smiled, his smug, secretive, confiding smile. 'I want to show you something.' He brought Smith the photocopied pages of his son's letter. 'Look at this.'

There was an almost childish eagerness in his voice, 'See, it's a crude personal code. Owen, the boy was never north of St Andrews with me and the only stags we had ever seen together were up the road in Richmond Park.'

'I thought there was something more in the letter than what was written, but I took it to be something personal between you and Ian. It was the reference to your brother killed in Andalucia.'

'That is where the message is concealed.' Craddock's eagerness was just under control. 'I did have an elder brother killed in Spain and he was on the loyalist side. But he was killed in 1937 on the Guadalajara front, not in 1938 in Andalucia. Ian knew that perfectly well. He spent the whole of a summer vacation in the Guadalajara trying to find his grave.'

The bitterness crept into his voice, 'He could not find a present hero in the family. He had to go back to a dead man in an old foreign war to find one.'

Smith thought of Craddock's D.C.M. from Anzio and silently sympathized. Instead he asked, 'So what is the message?'

Craddock acknowledged his digression with a wave of his hand and became businesslike once more. 'I have gone over this again and again all morning. I began with the word "highlands" and went over the whole of Scotland on the map from Stirling to Cape Wrath, to see if some place in the area had relevance to the enquiry. Nothing ... I then realized the only way he could introduce "stags" was by using "highlands" and that "highlands" was just window-dressing to lend an illusion of reminiscence to the letter. So I went through the various species of deer, antelope and so on. I cannot find anything relevant. But stags have horns, and the horns have points, and it is just a pointer to the key phrase and that is "Andalucia in 1938". Some one – some thing – some place, Spanish. No, more specifically, Andalucian.'

Smith looked at him, puzzled at his avoidance of the obvious. 'What about the cypher experts across the river? We should let them have a crack at it.' The reaction, even for Craddock, was startling in its vehemence.

'Those pimps! Are you suggesting I make these ... *people* ...' he gave the word greater loathing and contempt than any obscenity, '... a present of this case? This is a criminal enquiry. All right, there are political extremists involved and they have killed some politicians. But their killings ... their murders, Owen, their murders are public murders, murders committed in the streets, murders to be investigated by policemen, not by an anonymous bunch of class-conscious military men and civil servants.'

The tirade suddenly stopped in an almost inaudible mutter, 'Bloody interfering busybodies.'

Smith was surprised. Craddock's regard for the security services used to be one of respect. A slightly amused and condescending respect, but respect nevertheless. Something had happened to change that. Perhaps they had found out about Ian before his death and downgraded Craddock's security clearance? But then he would not have had access to the S.B. computer. He would never have been allowed to take charge of the investigation. Was that what Rachette had been getting at when he wanted an outside force to take over?

Smith wondered if the old man was seeking not only his son's regeneration but also his vindication. He dismissed the thoughts from his mind. They were now irrelevant.

He decided not to place the fly of the lab report in Craddock's filial ointment. Craddock would be aware of it in any case and chose to ignore its significance. But his reasoning on the letter was no delusion.

'So what do you make of Andalucia, 1938?' he asked.

'I haven't got it yet, but it is a location, an address. It would not be something so obvious as Andalucia Road, but I am sure he was trying to get something like that across. It will be a place-name or something indigenous or peculiar to Andalucia, corresponding with the name of a street or an apartment block. The figure 1938 must be a reference to the number, 19 or 93. Some permutation of 1938.'

Smith accepted the conclusion as more than reasonable. It

should not take very long to check out. He asked Craddock, 'Why do you want this kept quiet?'

Craddock gave him another of his grow-up-son-there-are-a-lot-of-nasty-people-about looks.

'Without even going back to Steype and Arthur Hammertoe, just give a bit of thought to the fact that somebody got the bright idea for all the police, except poor old expendable Brightside, to move out of the room at the Treasury before the rockets arrived.'

'So whose idea was it?'

Craddock shrugged and said, 'I am not sure. I was over in the corner with Brightside when Hicks came out of the political crowd and said we were moving nextdoor. It clearly wasn't his idea, he was more than in his element. I have since asked him who suggested it and it was proposed to him by Rachette, but it may have originated on the political side.'

Craddock pondered upon it for a few moments. 'There was plenty of space in the room for everyone. I've got to admit we could not get everyone at the windows, but it is damned peculiar nevertheless.'

Craddock gave Smith a look of genuine concern. 'So just watch your back, Owen. Watch your bloody back.'

They were interrupted by a light knock on the door and A.C.C. Hicks entered, solemn-faced.

'Hello Angus,' he said quietly, and looking meaningfully at Smith added, 'Could we have words in private?' Smith made for the door but Craddock held him with a restraining hand. 'No need, no need.' Craddock was almost jovial. 'I know why you're here, sir, will you have a drink.' His cheerfulness, courtesy and respect took Hicks by surprise. He did not persist in his direction to Smith.

'Why, thank you, Angus.' The glass was carefully poured and handed over with some ceremony. Hicks held it carefully in both hands as if bearing a chalice containing the last unction.

'I am deeply sorry about your son. I believe I can understand how you feel.'

Craddock gave an eccentric hunched shake of his head, accompanied by a palm-waving gesture, almost Semitic in its expressiveness. 'We have lived with the possibility for some time.'

'You appreciate we will have to make...' Hicks sipped in his whisky for words, 'shall we say ... adjustments.' It was not a question so much as request for Craddock's implicit understanding.

'Oh aye, Ah do, Ah do that.' The old sardonic tone returned. 'Dinna fash yoursel! Ah knew last night in Highgate Ah would have tae make ... adjustments.' The sadness in the crooked grin took the edge from the bitterness in his voice.

'Ah saw the medical officer, this morning. A very understanding man, who also knows about adjustments, and the necessity to make them. He diagnosed extreme exhaustion.'

The grin lost some of its sadness, 'He could be bluidy right for a change.' Craddock toasted the absent doctor.

'He prescribes a prolonged period of rest, an avoidance of stress situations, and if Ah follow his advice Ah might live tae draw ma pension.'

'I think you are very wise, Angus,' said Hicks with great sincerity.

Craddock brought out his coat, hat and scarf from the wardrobe. Hicks and Smith watched in silence. 'Ah'll say cheerio for now then.'

Hicks shook his hand emotionally. 'Keep in touch Angus, let us know if there is anything we can do.'

Craddock nodded and turning to Smith said, 'Will you let me know when the coroner releases ...' He hesitated for a moment, then hardened his tone, 'When he agrees to release the body. I can make arrangements for the funeral.'

Smith nodded and Hicks, snapping his fingers as if remembering something of importance, called after Craddock, 'Hang on Angus, I'll come down on the lift with you.' He then told Smith to wait in the office until he returned.

Smith consoled himself with the last of Craddock's twelve-year-old malt.

Smith decided to do the research into Craddock's Andalucia theory himself.

Hicks had returned after seeing Craddock from the premises, requiring a briefing on the events of the previous night. He seemed particularly interested in Craddock's reaction to his son's letter. 'Did Mr Craddock really have a brother killed in Andalucia?'

'He has certainly spoken in the past of an elder brother who was killed in the Spanish Civil War,' replied Smith with careful truth.

'Rather odd thing to say in a letter though?'

'Not in the light of the lad's political views. He was dying for a cause as his father's brother died for a cause. He was making a gesture, a political gesture.'

'Yes, that could be it.' After a satisfied consideration of the conclusion, a gratefully received dismissal, 'Thank you Smith. That will be all for now.'

As Smith compared the list of towns in Andalucia he had compiled with the street index, he was gratified to find those responsible for naming London streets did not go frequently to Spain for inspiration, although there was a Spaniards Road and a Spanish Place.

Those apart, a Seville Street and a Cadiz Street were the only other probables and he was dubious about the latter as it appeared outside the ill-defined boundaries of the stipulated region.

He was considering the best means of ascertaining the names of unlisted apartment blocks that could well have Andalucian titles. There must be several Almeria Apartments, dozens of Malaga Mansions; as for Granada, there was even a cinema chain, Alhambra ... where the hell did Alhambra come into it? He remembered. He crashed his fist on the table. He remembered, Wardoe, bloody Wardoe.

He kept himself in check as D.I. Pewbone answered the phone from Hampstead Police Station. Smith casually asked him how the inquest had gone on Wardoe, and listened patiently to the difficulties Pewbone had encountered with the coroner's predilection for an open verdict rather than a more positive one of accident or misadventure.

He praised Pewbone's handling of the affair and asked, 'By the way, did you check out that hi-fi equipment against the Stolen Property Index?'

A slightly piqued Pewbone replied it was naturally one of the first things he would do. 'There was no trace, it was straight.'

Smith apologized for implying that Pewbone would be so remiss in his duties. That had not been his intention. 'I just want

to check out the price he paid for it, who were the suppliers?'
Pewbone said he had no idea.

Smith replied evenly, 'I happened to notice when I examined
it in the room, just inside the cover of the record player there is a
little plastic label, supplied by somebody or other. Have a look
and tell me who they are.'

He held anxiously on the line as Pewbone went to his property
store to check. It seemed to take him a long long time.
Eventually Pewbone's surly tones came back.

'Sorry to keep you Guv. One of my sergeants had the key in his
pocket. Got it now, it's the Alhambra Radio and Hi-Fi Centre,
21 Nevis Mews, Camden Town.'

It required some effort of will to keep the exultation out of his
voice and continue a casual conversation with Pewbone on his
chances of promotion on the next selection board.

As he put down the phone he realized Ian Craddock had not
even wasted the word 'highland'. Ben Nevis, highest of the
Scottish mountains. Young Craddock had probably got away
with it in the letter because nobody referred to the peak as simply
Nevis, it was always Ben Nevis. They had missed the connection.

He lost some of his euphoria as it came to him the number 21
in Nevis Mews did not permutate out of 1938. He sat puzzling
over it for several minutes, then cursing himself for a fool as he
ran his eyes across the figures 1938 for about the twentieth time,
saw at a glance the sum of the figures totalled 21.

'Pay pontoon or-five-card tricks only.'

He realized he was laughing in silly giggling bursts like an
excited schoolgirl and reproachfully brought himself under
control. Where did he go from here?

Hicks had told him Cyril Fairchild would be taking over from
Craddock but Fairchild was in Geneva liaising with the Swiss
police on some very hush-hush fraud enquiry. He would not be
back until the following night.

Then there was Operation Zip Fastener due to commence at
midnight. He had no direct role in the operation. That was
largely down to Special Branch with assistance from the local
divisions. But he was on stand-by throughout the operation with
O'Brien and a small team from his squad, to move in if some
positive development came out of it.

He looked at his watch, just under six hours to midnight.

Plenty of time to go and at least have a look at the Alhambra Radio and Hi-Fi Centre. He told O'Brien, in the presence of Neaterkin, that he was going out for a couple of hours to see an informant.

Not wishing to be encumbered by an unparkable car, he walked to Victoria and took the underground to Euston, then a taxi to Camden Town.

He found Nevis Mews just off the northern end of Camden High Street. At the entrance to the mews a tawdry decaying sign over a shop front said, 'Alhambra Radio & Hi-Fi'. Posted over the front of the shop window, whitewashed to opaqueness on the inside, a peeling poster proclaimed a closing-down sale had occurred more than two months previously.

On the front door, faded white lettering stated, 'Trade enquiries. Workshop in mews at rear.' For ten minutes Smith gave the front of the shop a steady examination as a member of a bus queue at a stop on the opposite side of the street. The scabrous façade presented nothing but the white of its dead eye and the sores of its decomposing paint. If life existed within, no tremor broke the pallid surface to denote its presence.

Smith took the first bus to its next stop, crossed the road and circled the block to enter the mews at the end opposite his original point of observation.

Heavy double wooden doors bore the number 21 and the words 'Alhambra Radio & Hi-Fi Trade & Repairs only'. The doors were secured by newish multi-lever padlocks in chrome steel, three of them, top, bottom and centre. The latch and hasps were in the same metal, secured to the wood of the doors through metal plates by countersunk bolts.

For a store dealing in radio and hi-fi, the precautions were not unusual. Smith tried to pull the double doors forward to make a space between them large enough to shine his pencil torch through the crack. They would not budge.

'Can I help you, friend?' The menace was all in the last word, not in the deep interested tone posing the question.

Smith turned. In the darkness the shape of a tall man in a white open raglan raincoat stood facing him, sideways on like a fencer. The right hand was buried deep in the raincoat pocket and the pocket lifted slightly as Smith moved towards the man, who stood about eight feet away.

Smith decided to play it straight, or at least reasonably straight. He slowly lifted his warrant card from the breast pocket of his coat and shining his torch on the gold lettering said, 'Detective Sergeant Smith, Hampstead Police, are you the owner?'

The man did not move, but said, 'I have an interest in the business, or at least what was the business. We went bust, as you saw at the front.' He moved a little closer to Smith but still kept his fencer posture. 'So what can I do for you, Sergeant Smith?'

'I am making enquiries into the death of a man named Wardoe, trying to find his next-of-kin. We found some hi-fi equipment in his room. It's got your firm's label on it as supplier. I was hoping if he had bought it from you on hire purchase he would have shown a guarantor on the contract from whom we could get some information.'

The dim figure seemed to weigh the solidity of Smith's statement. The slightly uplifted raincoat pocket dropped and the stance became more square. But the hand still remained inside the pocket.

'Wardoe? Yes, I think I remember him. He is dead you say? Someone has killed him?'

'No, no we don't think so. It looked a bit suspicious at the time, but we are satisfied it was accidental.' Smith shrugged his shoulders and added, 'He was a little bit that way,' he waved a gay hand. 'Tried something a bit too elaborate and it backfired.' He laughed coarsely but got no response. 'So we are stuck with the hi-fi and all his bits and pieces cluttering up our property store, and we are rather anxious to find his relatives and get rid of it.' Smith paused as a thought struck him.

'And, of course, if there are payments outstanding on the hi-fi you've probably got a good claim to it, Mr ...?'

'Barton, my name is Barton.' The man waved Smith to precede him towards the mouth of the mews. 'I don't know if I can help you, most of our invoices and copy contracts are with the accountants, but I will have a look.' He steered Smith towards the shop front. 'The office is at the back of the shop.'

Smith felt himself firmly but courteously eased into the recessed door at the shop front. Barton said, 'I don't see very well. You have your torch, perhaps you will kindly open the

144

door.' He passed two keys over Smith's shoulder, a cylinder and a mortice.

The door opened. Smith threw a thin wand of light into the interior. 'You will find the light switch over on the right-hand wall.' Behind him Barton closed the door.

For several seconds the neon tube flashed and flickered, giving Smith a view of Barton as a series of images. The fair close-cropped hair was now dark and of thick, wavy, luxurious length. The drooping moustache running into a cropped beard added depth to a shallow rounded chin and the smoke-tinted glasses in heavy black frames accentuated the darkness of a sallow complexion that should be fresh.

But there was just enough of the tiny lobeless ears showing beneath the thick hair from Smith to be sure he was face to face with Staff Sergeant Richard Gredek.

The tube hissed into uninterrupted life. Barton/Gredek ushered Smith into a small office at the back of the empty shop. The floor was littered with empty cartons, display signs, advertising blatter, bumph, and brochures ... and curly little clumps of wood shavings from packing cases. Thick heavy curtains were drawn across the inside of the window.

Smith saw that Gredek's right hand was no longer in his coat pocket and indeed there appeared to be no weight in the pocket. If there had been a gun, and Smith was sure there had been, Gredek must have dumped it somewhere in the shop behind him as he went forward to switch on the light.

Smith felt better at the thought. It meant Gredek had fallen for the story. He could leave Gredek on ice for a bit. He wanted more out of this than Gredek, even though he badly wanted Gredek. You will come in due course, you bastard. He smiled down at the oiled head as it pored over a sales ledger.

On the right-hand side of the office a heavy steel door, secured at two points with the same heavy padlocks, indicated access to the workshop. In the left corner, an unlit staircase disappeared into the darkness of probable living accommodation.

'I am afraid I cannot help you, Sergeant.' Gredek closed the ledger. 'It was a cash transaction, during our closing-down sale. He obviously took advantage of the reduction. It was quite a bargain, thirty per cent discount.'

'I see. Well, it was worth a try.' Smith let the disappointment

145

in his voice hang in the air, then as he turned towards the door, asked, 'By the way, do you live on the premises?'

'No, but I do, Sarn't Major.' Smith winced at the voice.

Bending into the office from half-way up the stairs, the fat figure eased itself down, one hand on the rail, the other swollen by a black metallic chancre in the form of a Browning 9 mm pistol.

'Ackerman,' said Smith in disgust, 'Corporal fucking Ackerman.'

Gredek removed the heavy-framed spectacles, sat back in the old wooden office chair and surveyed Smith with interest. The absence of the tinted glass made his cold blue eyes seem brighter against the artificial darkness of his hair and skin.

He took the pistol from Ackerman. Smith saw a practised thumb reassure itself the safety was off. The cold eyes never left Smith's face.

'You know him?' Gredek's voice held some dubiety.

'He's S.I.B. He was the second one to come to the depot when you decided to have it away.'

'The card you produced earlier. Put it on here.' The pistol waved from Smith to the desk. Smith ignored him. Ackerman moved towards him.

'Stand still man!' Only an N.C.O. trained in the British Army can halt a man in his tracks by the pressure of words. Ackerman stood still.

'Ackerman,' said Gredek, 'you will never be anything more than a corporal storeman, if you serve for fifty years.' He gave Smith the chill of his blue eyes.

'If I had had to shoot you through his back, I would have done so. Now take out the card and put it on the desk.' He made his point with the pistol aimed squarely at Smith's face. Smith placed the card on the desk.

Gredek handed it over his shoulder to Ackerman, and said, 'Read it out.'

Opening the centre fold, Ackerman cleared his throat, and with both hands holding the card in front of him read with some formality.

'This is to certify that Owen Smith holds the rank of Detective Chief Superintendent in the Metropolitan Police and this is his warrant and authority to execute the duties of his office. Signed, Maxwell Steype.'

'Looks like he is civvy law, Staff,' said Ackerman with some apprehension, 'there may be others around the place.'

Gredek weighed the possibility calmly, 'No, I don't think so. He was alone when he happened to cross the road in front of me back in the High Street. It was only when he entered the mews I took an interest in him. If there was anyone else they would not have split up so far back.'

Smith glanced at his watch. The action generated a sudden response from Gredek. The pistol thrust forward. 'The watch ... drop it on the floor.'

Puzzled Smith did as he was told. 'Strip off,' the pistol gestured menacingly.

Smith sat on the edge of a packing-case, one leg swinging idly. He suppressed an inclination to say 'Get stuffed'; he felt it would be tempting fate. But he knew his nervousness was showing, as an attempt at a contemptuous smile failed to distend the frozen muscles of his face.

Gredek moved towards him, the gun firm in his right hand. A long leg lashed out from the hip.

Behind the meniscus cartilage inside the knee there is a ganglion of nerve endings. A blow to that point need not be particularly severe to produce a degree of pain beyond mere agony.

Smith felt the nerve centre explode and distend in an excruciating spasm, contracting genitalia and clutching heart and lungs in a searing vice. All he could utter from his gaping mouth was a long soundless scream.

As the pain subsided into almost pleasurable fire, Smith found he was lying on his side grasping his injured knee. It was an effort to stand on the nerveless leg, but he managed to hobble back to the edge of the packing-case ... He slowly loosened his tie.

'You are not going to be arrogant, are you?' Gredek walked around Smith as he stood awkwardly naked with his hands clasped on top of his head. 'Steype was an arrogant man, he actually spat on me.' Gredek wiped his left hand across his face as if he still felt the residue of saliva. 'He did not die an arrogant man.'

Ackerman was turning out Smith's pockets on to the desk. 'That's the lot, Staff.'

Gredek poked through the contents with the muzzle of the pistol. He pushed to one side the fountain pen, silver-cased pencil, gold lighter and packet of cigarettes. The cigarettes he ground beneath his heel, then, telling Ackerman to fetch a hammer, had him smash the rest on the concrete floor.

'For Christ's sake,' said Smith as he saw the valued articles broken into the ground. 'My name's Smith, not James Bond.'

He felt the muzzle of the gun on the back of his neck, then dropping from ridge to ridge down his vertebrae like a child's stick along railings, it came to rest at the level of his sacrum. The muzzle was withdrawn then punched into the fused bone. Smith grunted at the slow heavy pain.

'Now we have plenty of time, Mr Smith, you will tell us what took you from Wardoe to the depot and to Nevis Mews. It is beginning to look as if there is more than one traitor in our midst.' He completed a circuit round Smith. 'Our chattering corporal here, for instance.'

Ackerman coloured and made whining protest. 'But Staff, if I hadn't recognized his voice, you would never have known he was the same fella that was nosing around the depot.'

'Stop snivelling, Ackerman, and do not assume I have to rely on you for intelligence.' Gredek picked up Smith's warrant card. 'Isn't this nullified by the death of the issuing authority, to wit, Sir Maxwell Steype?'

Smith shook his head, 'No, I can still nick you.'

'Arrogance, Mr Smith? Do you remember what happens to arrogant men?' Gredek's patience only emphasized the threat. He contemplated Smith's shivering nakedness and went on, 'Obviously we overlooked something with Wardoe. I wonder what it was? The intricacies of the civil-service mind are difficult to unravel ... The man should never have been allowed to survive for as long as he did. When dedication to a cause reaches a state of fanaticism it becomes dangerous. It becomes ... not a question of the end justifying the means, but of the means justifying the end. Rather appropriate in Wardoe's case, don't you think.'

Gredek smiled at the thought, 'Despite his fawning masochistic affection for me, his revolutionary ardour turned to hate, and hate to treachery when his schemes were rejected and the realities of urban guerrilla warfare explained. He failed to appreciate it was not our intention to die with him . . . to join him in death as revolutionary heroes, but to kill and run, to destroy without being destroyed. To live in order to achieve, Mr Smith.'

He sat on the edge of his desk facing Smith with contemplative folded arms, the gun resting in the crook of his left elbow. Smith wondered if he could span the intervening seven or eight feet between them before the arms could unfold and the gun be brought to bear. His weak quivering knee gave him the answer as he tentatively pressed the ball of his foot on the floor.

Gredek's reminiscences had ceased for the moment, his eyes seemingly downcast at the floor. Only the slight upward turn of the brows gave an indication of his watchfulness. The bastard is waiting for me to try it, thought Smith.

'Yes, do relax Mr Smith, nakedness gives no cover to muscular tension.' Gredek brought his eyes into Smith's face. 'Now where were we? Ah yes, Wardoe and his treachery. No, I think I give him too much credit. His petty homosexual jealousy would be more accurate a term. When deprived of his intended martyrdom, he went running to Steype. His knowledge of civil-service jargon and a false elevation of his rank to that of Assistant Secretary gave him personal access by telephone. Fortunately in his arrogance – yes Mr Smith, he was another arrogant man – he refused to discuss detail with Steype unless they met personally. So all Steype knew was what Wardoe told him on the phone, that a large quantity of arms were in the possession of a revolutionary group who intended using them on the streets. Again fortunately, we were in a position to forestall that meeting and negate the knowledge in the head of Sir Maxwell Steype.'

Gredek was pleased with his analogy.

Ackerman, who had earlier disappeared upstairs, came down again with three steaming cups on a tray.

'Nice cup of tea, Staff. All right for him to have one?'

At Gredek's nod of approval, Smith accepted the tea gratefully. The shivering was becoming difficult to control. It increased the ache in his lower spine and the threads of fire coursing outwards from his injured knee had no warmth in them. Yet it amused him to think he was being subjected to the hard –

149

soft system of interrogation. He wondered if they would give him a cigarette.

'And so Mr Smith, what did Wardoe leave behind that took you to Andover?'

Smith decided to exploit the situation, 'I can talk better with my clothes on.'

Gredek looked at him, long and hard. 'You had better say something positive by the time you put your shirt on, otherwise it will be full of holes.'

As Smith pulled up the zip on his pants and reached for his shirt he said, 'Wardoe left a list in his room. It itemized the arms transferred from Belfast to the 41st Ordnance Depot.'

'We found the list on him before he had his accident. He was taking it to Steype. There was nothing else in the room. Someone in our group is working for you, Smith, you have only seconds before your kneecap is permanently disjointed, so before I get to your elbows, I'd better have his name, and don't be tempted to try young Craddock on me. I know it wasn't him.'

Smith saw the anger in Gredek's face. The pistol was presented at his right knee.

'Hold it for Christ's sake. He made a copy of the list, it was in a record sleeve.' The muzzle wavered.

'You should have got some music-lovers to search the room. Wardoe had made a carbon copy of the list and put it in the sleeve of Beethoven's Seventh.' Smith in a nothing-to-lose attack of aggressive contempt said, 'Search the room? You stick your noses in a few drawers and call it a search?'

It was perhaps fortunate he was interrupted by the ringing telephone. It made three distinct rings and was silent. Gredek responded by dialling out, listening for a number of ringing tones, then replacing the receiver. At his directions, Ackerman produced a roll of adhesive tape and Smith was bound hand and foot. Another length of tape was placed firmly across his eyes as a blindfold. His legs were kicked from under him and he was allowed to slump against the far wall.

Smith heard the padlocks on the steel door leading to the workshop being undone. Within a few minutes the sound of bolts being drawn from deeper inside the workshop. Voices, an exchange of greetings, 'Good evening, Comrade Soldier.' 'Good evening, Comrades.' An exchange of comment about the weather, some laughter, an approach of footsteps, the footsteps of several people, sudden silence.

'Who is he?' A new voice, accentless, mature.

'Police. Senior C.I.D. A Chief Superintendent, from Scotland Yard.'

'But what is he doing here, Comrade Soldier?'

'I am afraid there was some laxity in the search of Wardoe's room. There was a copy of the list left behind in the sleeve of a record. Comrade Solan, do you have an explanation?' Gredek's voice was stern.

Yet another voice, hesitant, unsure, half-afraid, 'My instructions were to search ... to search for material showing Wardoe's association with our group. To search and leave no indication of a search. It was difficult. That painted friend of Wardoe came knocking at the door for him. Howling his head off ... there was a danger of attracting attention. I am sorry comrades, I did not think to look inside record sleeves. I am sorry ...' the voice trailed into mumbling silence.

'How does he know of this place?' Again the mature voice.

'We had not reached an answer to that before your arrival, Comrade Brent. And on reflection it may not be prudent to await an answer. While I am satisfied he came here alone, and reasonably certain his presence is not known to others, we cannot be sure. I suggest immediate evacuation to rear headquarters.'

The proposal was discussed mainly between Gredek and the mature voice of Comrade Brent. Another voice with a slight London accent, responding to the name of Comrade Grey, said he could have suitable transport at the premises to remove the equipment within forty minutes. He was despatched to this task. Evacuation was decided upon.

From the workshop came the scrape of heavy boxes being dragged towards the outer doors, of metallic clatter and muttered curses. Like soldiers everywhere the Soldiers of the People did not relish hard work. In due course a chinking of cups and the sounds of laboured movement were replaced for a few minutes by muted conversation. Ackerman had introduced another tea break.

The roar of a diesel engine brought Smith's efforts to achieve some movement in the adhesive tape around his wrists to a stop. The revving engine indicated a large vehicle being manoeuvred

151

into the mews. A draught of cold air brought further discomfort to Smith's cramped limbs as the outer doors were opened.

He pondered upon the chances of some passer-by putting in a call to police at the sight of a heavy truck being loaded up late at night; the possibility was remote. A patrolling copper? Not much chance, and he hoped there would not be one. Another dead policeman wasn't going to help recruiting.

It must have taken them nearly an hour to load the truck. Smith tried to estimate the actual time and concluded it must be around nine. O'Brien would not be greatly concerned about him as yet. He would enviously assume Smith had fallen in with good company in some pub, and was making up for a lot of lost time.

The thudding, uneven bark of the diesel engine again split the night as the vehicle eased its way out of the mews. Smith heard its roar receding up Camden High Street. Northwards? It didn't much matter.

Gredek was speaking as they came back into the office. 'No, comrade, I do not think we should abandon our base here totally. The man may have been acting entirely on his own initiative on information from a source within our group, and it is important to find that source. The deviationist Canada has already done considerable damage to our cause. If there is another in our midst it is important to find him.'

'I had great faith in Comrade Canada,' the mature voice of Brent was heavy with regret. 'That he should have given you a false direction from the committee to change the target is still difficult for me to believe.'

'As I told the Court, Comrade, he arrived after we captured the post with, as he said, revised orders from the operational committee based on late intelligence, that the room was full of Government and military security people and Special Branch. Making it a more productive target. We could see several people moving inside the room. It seemed a reasonable proposition. We only learned at the de-briefing that he had given false directions and had allowed his personal hatred to supervene.'

'Yes, I suppose we should have suspected something with his insistence on making such a ghastly exhibition with Steype.'

'This does not resolve the question of our present position, Comrade Brent.'

Smith, unsighted and shivering, would not have warmed to see Gredek's cold eyes indicate his form, lying bound and slumped against the wall.

'It is a military decision and as such your responsibility, Comrade Soldier. I will respect your judgment.' Comrade Brent, thought Smith, was another of the world's great buck-passers.

'Then if you will tell Comrade Ackerman to report to me, I will give him his orders and join you in the car.'

The soft footsteps stopped at Smith's side. He felt Gredek standing over him, as if the air pressure was increased by his presence. Smith braced himself for what he expected. A primeval tension drew his lips back in a snarl of fear, and he hunched his neck protectively into his shoulders. He heard a metallic clicking and knew that a magazine had been removed, inspected and slammed back into the butt of a pistol.

'You interfering fool. You complete fuck-up.' He felt Gredek pull him forward as if testing the binding on his wrists, then force his head forward on his chest. Smith lost control of his bladder.

'You want me, Staff?' The anxious voice of Ackerman. Smith lay cringing in a limp pool of embarrassment.

'Yes, now listen carefully, I want you to hold on here until early morning.'

'How early, Staff?' Ackerman expressed dubious reluctance.

'At least until six a.m. That will give you ample time to get back to the depot without being missed. It is necessary for you to hold on here to ascertain if there is any follow-up by police.'

'But Staff –' said Ackerman in a long whine, 'what about me?'

'We will secure everything on the outside, you do the same on the inside. Even if they come well equipped it will take at least ten minutes to break in. That will give you plenty of time to get out through the emergency door and away.'

'What about him?' Ackerman seemed more settled in his mind with Gredek's explanation.

'I will leave him with you, and I will leave the Browning with you. I've just checked him, he is well secured, and the gun is cocked. Before you leave you must finish him. Understand, there must be no slip-up with him. Put him in the inspection pit next door with at least two feet of sand on top of him. We may want to use this place again.'

'Why not do him now, Staff?' Ackerman seemed eager to have a witness present when the killing had to be done.

'No. He'll be insurance for you if something goes wrong. You can hold them back with him as a hostage, should you need more time. But he has to be finished irrespective of anything else. Is that perfectly clear?'

A still-reluctant Ackerman agreed and Smith heard a sound of locks closing and bolts being slammed home. It took Ackerman several minutes to secure the interior of the building.

'What about taking the blindfold off?' Smith asked as he heard Ackerman's footsteps passing.

He was answered by a kick in the thigh and Ackerman's resentful whine, 'It's all your bleedin' fault you stupid nosey bastard. I suppose you think you were clever with your S.I.B. bullshit.' He aimed another kick at Smith but it was only a half-hearted swing of his foot grazing the top of Smith's leg. Ackerman's mind was occupied with the problems of the passing night.

He caught sight of the consequences of Smith's fear.

'You've pissed yourself.' He found the discovery amusing, and made comic noises of disgust. 'Eeuugh, you dirty bastard. You'll be shitting yourself before the night's out, won't you, eh?' A little dig with his foot to Smith's hip-bone reinforced his demand for an answer.

'Won't you, eh? Be shitting yourself before the night's out, won't you?' Another dig with his foot had more weight.

Smith had swallowed a great deal of pride since he entered the premises of the Alhambra Radio & Hi Fi an aeon ago. He forced down the largest portion yet and regurgitated a bile of humility, 'I suppose so,' he said.

Apparently satisfied, Ackerman retreated. Smith heard his heavy tread on the wooden stairs followed by a rush of water into a kettle. Ackerman was making yet another pot of tea.

Taking advantage of his absence, Smith began exercising his bound legs by stretching them out and in with his back pressed against the wall. Alternating this movement by rolling to and fro on his hips restored the blood supply to his lower limbs in a painful surge of pins and needles. His knee started throbbing again, but the joint felt stronger. By pressing down on the soles of his feet he managed to raise himself progressively upwards against the wall until the sound of Ackerman's descending feet made him slump back to his original position.

The creak of the wooden office chair, accompanied by slurping sounds of hot tea being drunk and the rustle of a newspaper, indicated that Ackerman was settling down for a long night. And clearly, no tea was coming to refresh Smith's parched throat.

More to relieve the cramp in his fingers and wrists than in an attempt to release his bonds, Smith tugged at the plaster tape behind his back and found the overlapping end on the crossover between his wrists was loose by at least an inch.

Stretching every tendon to its utmost, he could grip the loose end between forefinger and thumb and pull it further. Pressing the loosened tape against the cloth of his coat, it gripped with sufficient strength for him to manipulate his arms and completely remove that section of the tape between his wrists. He now had some six inches of tape to grasp and by taking it in a ball, from the fingers of one hand to the other, succeeded in rolling and pulling it from wrist to wrist until the tape was completely removed.

Smith sat with his freed hands behind his back and wondered what he could do next. Ackerman's tea drinking would have finished by now, but the occasional rustle of the paper showed his attention was still on the pages.

Estimating the distance between Ackerman and himself at about twelve feet, Smith knew he could not tear the plaster from his eyes, unbind his feet and jump Ackerman without the latter casually pumping several shots into him before he even gained his feet. He must wait and hope.

More than two hours passed before a chance came. The phone rang three times and stopped. It rang again and Ackerman answered on the fourth ring. As Smith remembered it, the phone was on the far side of the desk against the wall. Ackerman would have to turn his back to him to answer it, unless . . . Never mind the unless.

Smith tore the plaster from his eyes, restraining a shriek as half his brow hairs were pulled out by the roots.

Ackerman had his back to him, listening intently to what he was being told, then asking, 'Does that mean they are likely to carry out searches in the London area?'

Smith was on his feet, he saw the hammer Ackerman had earlier used to smash the articles from his pockets lying on the floor six feet away. He hopped forward and had it in his hand as Ackerman spoke into the phone, 'Yes Comrade, I will carry out Soldier's orders and then evacuate immediately.' He replaced the phone hurriedly, turned and saw Smith.

The surprise in Ackerman's face did not delay his reactions more than a split-second. Smith saw the gun come up and point fully into his chest before he had bent for a second jump. He saw the forefinger whiten at the knuckle . . . nothing happened. Panic distorted Ackerman's podgy face, his left hand drew back the slide to re-cock the weapon as Smith heaved himself forward, his arm swinging backwards.

The hammer thudded into the side of Ackerman's head just above the left orbital ridge, the useless half-cocked pistol dropped from his hand and his body followed it in a swinging curve away from the impetus of the blow.

Unable to keep his balance on bound feet Smith also fell heavily to the floor and found himself gazing into the corporal's half-closed eyes. The deep rasp of his stertorous breathing brought pungent odours into Smith's nostrils as the acidity rose from Ackerman's stomach in turgescent waves. A thickening ooze of blood welled from a star-shaped impacted wound on the forehead.

Kneeling above the comatose body, Smith pressed a gentle finger on the area just above the wound. He could feel movement beneath. Cursing, he unwound the tape from his ankles and staggered to the phone. Ackerman was dying from a fractured skull and he wanted an ambulance.

Then, making his way into the shop, he threw the internal bolts, pinned back the cylinder lock and, with a cold chisel found in the desk drawer, smashed open the mortice lock on the front door. The night air steamed around his sweat-soaked body as he drew it into his heaving chest.

Back to the phone, trembling fingers making him mis-dial, then shivering seconds waiting for O'Brien to answer. Cutting into him as he reached 'For Christ's sake, Guv, where –' Smith told him where, and to get there quick with a full scenes-of-crime team, photographer, fingerprints and forensic.

Smith fell back into the chair and, with his forearms resting on his thighs, looked down at Ackerman's body. His breathing was quicker, shallower, and his face fell into a creamy pallor, smoothing the coarseness of his bulbous nose and pouting lips. Beside him lay the gun. The useless half-cocked gun. Smith leaned forward and picked it up. Whatever had made it jam had saved his life; he was interested to know what it was.

Pulling the slide back to its full extent, he saw for a start there was no cartridge in the breech. A fresh round would have to be jacked into the chamber by actuating the slide, and that had jammed. With some difficulty Smith drew out the magazine and found the answer. The top cartridge had been inserted wrong-way-round with the bullet thrust downwards leaving the end of the case protruding above the jaws of the magazine. In such condition, the slide could never go forward.

He looked at the body with some pity. Ackerman had been served up to him on a plate. But by whom? Gredek?

Ackerman died in hospital within an hour of reaching the casualty ward, and without regaining consciousness. The cause of death was shock accompanying intercranial haemorrhage due to a fractured skull.

After dictating a concise report, Smith was kept in hospital thirty-six hours for observation. He needed no drugs to sleep most of the time.

When not sleeping, Smith lay in the hospital bed in that languorous somnolent twilight where thought and dreams intermingle.

The geese arrowed across the surface of a warm black lake – Brent, Solan, Grey and Canada. Where were they heading? They could just as easily be Sparrow, Raven, Thrush and Robin. Names . . . groups . . . cells. Black, White, Brown and Green, how many names, how many cells?

Brent, unruffled, smooth, the political commissar, whose actions were the consequence of action by others, a sage of the past event.

Solan and Grey? Captains in the people's army, ideological psychopaths, blind to reasonableness by their own reasoning. And Canada, the particular member of that species, was now extinct.

157

The Soldier: Smith saw him as a hawk, sometimes as a vulture but never as a goose.

Only Grey had a tangible emanation, a real source. He had access to a heavy goods vehicle. Forty minutes it had taken him to bring the truck to the mews. Say, fifteen minutes one way by car, and twenty-five back with the wagon.

Could be anywhere within a five-mile radius of Camden Town. Probably the most densely populated part of London, with more transport firms within its boundaries than anywhere else in the country. As a positive lead, too hit-or-miss, but bear it in mind.

Why didn't they use the ex-W.D. trucks? Because they were too risky, or located at too great a distance from the workshop? Or were these vehicles just not under their control?

And why did Gredek have such a touch of the seconds in suddenly deciding to evacuate? Because he was ultra-cautious? On the logical assumption that Smith, being there, must be there because someone sent him?

Or because it was suddenly inconvenient to be surrounded by a flock of geese?

Ackerman, poor bloody Ackerman, why did he feel sorry for the fat corrupt corporal? Because he had killed him ... or because he had been conned into killing him?

The loose tape, the jammed pistol. Suppose he had been meant to take Ackerman alive? The misplaced round, the empty breech on a gun Gredek had stipulated was cocked and ready. He remembered hearing the magazine withdrawn, but the snap of the slide action jacking a cartridge into the breech was never present. Had he in his mindless fear failed to interpret the true meaning of Gredek's actions? In the long seconds it would have taken Ackerman to free the jammed pistol, he could have torn the tape from his legs and subdued him with nothing more than a slap on his podgy face.

And Ackerman would have talked, he would have screamed the house down. But whose house would have fallen?

While Smith lay in hospital questioning his conscience, the results of Chief Inspector Dewlip's lab team began to accumulate from their examination of 21 Nevis Mews. Under the microscopes, scientific instruments and test tubes at the Police

laboratory, ghosts appeared. Rope from the pulley of a roof-mounted hoist was identical in size and pattern to the pressure marks embedded in the ankles of Sir Maxwell Steype.

In the workshop a flagstone sloped towards a drain. From crevices around the drain and in the flagstones, despite previous use of a high-pressure hose, tests revealed traces of human blood. Due to contamination and the passage of time, the blood could not be grouped. There was little need.

At the side of a coke-burning stove, an old butcher's cleaver was found. It had, at one time, been used to chop firewood. It had also been used to chop through the pharynx and the fourth cervical vertebra of the late Commissioner.

Strands of purple wool from Ian Craddock's sweater had threaded themselves on wood splinters as he had brushed against rough walls and doors. The curls of wood shavings on the floor of office and workshop were identical with similar fragments found adhering to his corpse and to the body of Sir Maxwell Steype.

Test firings of the Browning 9 mm automatic pistol produced lands, grooves, barrel markings and striations to leave no doubt this was the weapon used to kill the two officers on the church tower, and Ian Craddock.

Operation Zip Fastener slid to a close before Smith's release from hospital. The immediate results were thirty-seven arrests for possessing stolen property amongst various groups who themselves considered private possession to be a crime. Another twenty-three were arrested for assaults on police conducting searches. Four members of a dormant I.R.A. unit were arrested for possessing explosives. Their lives, and lives of many others were saved by the recovery of the explosives from the bedroom of a large block of flats on the outskirts of Birmingham. The ancient gelignite was exuding nitro-glycerine and about as stable as a naked flame in a gas tank.

In addition, the operation collected 248 complaints against police and seven Parliamentary questions.

There was little discernible gain in the battle against the Soldiers of the People.

A.C.C. Hicks, in minuting the papers on Smith's conduct, considered he should be suspended from duty pending disciplinary action for neglect in failing to inform senior officers of his intentions. There was also the question of Ackerman's death.

As he said to his counterpart in 'A' Department, 'Justifiable homicide it may be, but damn it, did he have to hit the man with a hammer? It was most ... unpolicemanlike.'

Cyril Fairchild, Craddock's successor at the head of the enquiry, required to make a written recommendation, respectfully pointed out he would be in a difficult, if not impossible position, if Smith was removed from the investigation at this late stage. He generously went on to say it was common practice to reconnoitre an intended target before direct action and it was hardly Smith's fault he had been captured. In addition, Smith was acting in the best interests of security by not revealing his intentions.

Swarbrick, as Deputy Commissioner, was the final arbiter in a matter of force discipline. With fine diplomacy he agreed Smith's conduct was hasty and impetuous and should there be a recurrence he would not hesitate to have Smith severely disciplined. However, there were certain mitigating factors and subject to Smith receiving strong words of advice from Mr Fairchild, no further disciplinary action would be taken.

Chapter XVI

Smith had spent four hours updating Cyril Fairchild when Willie Woulover of Special Branch came into the murder room with a sparkle in his eye and the self-assurance of a magnanimous millionaire about to throw a fortune at the feet of the ignorant poor.

'I think the Branch can put this one back on the rails,' he said to Fairchild with assumed modesty.

Fairchild looked at him with interest, 'Go on.'

'Various intercepted telephones of known leftists produced a great deal of activity within half an hour of Zip Fastener starting in the north. The calls never began from an intercepted source, but from a public call-box. They had, of course, to go to an intercepted source and at the beginning simply said, as a for instance, "Skua. Pigs are flying amongst the sea birds." We had only a limited number of interceptions granted but we anticipated the use of call boxes to pass on details of police activity, so as soon as Zip Fastener began we installed scribers under the dials of public phones adjacent to suspect premises.'

'Without Home Office authority?' questioned Fairchild with a severity that might not have been assumed.

'As it is not a device for recording or hearing speech, it does not contravene the Privacy Act,' replied Woulover.

Without offence Fairchild conceded the point.

'Well, sir,' Woulover ploughed on, 'as soon as we saw a suspect make a call, it was just a matter of going into the box afterwards and noting the numbers. Obviously, we could not get the correct sequence of the number dialled, but by feeding the random numbers we obtained by this means into the computer, for comparison with the known phone numbers of left-wing extremists, we have gradually linked the chain from north to south. There were one or two gaps, due to repetition of similar digits, but in the main computerized permutation has filled the gaps with as little as five known digits on a nine-figure combination.'

Smith refrained from saying, as they knew of such left-wing existence before the operation and it was reasonable to assume they were in communication, it did not help much merely to have that fact confirmed. He was glad he held himself in check. Woulover had not yet played his ace.

'Within two hours of Zip Fastener messages were being sent from the leftists saying "The pigs are flying South."'

'We had a casual surveillance on a farmhouse near Dunmow in Essex, a man was seen to leave the house at 1.50 a.m. and use the call-box on the main road. There were two identical digits in the number dialled but the computer permutation corresponds with the phone number at 21 Nevis Mews.'

The call to Ackerman! The thought flashed through Smith's mind.

'What was the result of the search?' he asked.

'It wasn't searched,' said Woulover ruefully. 'It was only a Priority Three target. Surveillance only. The occupant was a known Anarcho-Communist but not considered militant or at least extremist.'

'And just who is this peace-loving occupant?' enquired Fairchild.

'He is a junior lecturer in Economics at the University of North London. Name of Julius Ploume. Apart from being a contributor to various left-wing publications and a willing participant in any leftist action at the university, he was considered more of a theorist than an activist. He has a hobby, by the way ...'

Woulover treated himself to the luxury of savouring his words before speaking.

'He is a bird watcher,' said Smith, spoiling the broth.

'Well not exactly,' Woulover tried to retain the piquancy but the flavour had gone, 'He's a naturalist with a special interest in the migratory habits of wild geese.'

'Looks like your Comrade Brent,' said Fairchild. 'Can he be identified?'

'Only by voice, for what that is worth,' said Smith, 'they wiped the place clean before they left.' He turned to Woulover. 'By the way, did your men see anything of a heavy goods vehicle around the place?'

'Yes they did,' Woulover answered grudgingly, 'at least at daybreak they noticed the back end of a trailer sticking out from behind some stables next to the house. It was still there when they broke off the observation.'

'You mean the place is no longer under surveillance?' Fairchild asked sharply.

'No sir.' Smith had some sympathy for Woulover's pained expression as he went on to say, 'All negative observations were pulled in at the conclusion of Zip Fastener. We simply haven't the men to provide permanent cover. In any case the house lies about four hundred yards up a track from the main road in the middle of some open fields. There is not an inch of cover within half a mile for daylight observation, but I've arranged for two men to go in as close as they can when it gets dark.'

'To do what?' Smith felt the pain in his knee again.

'Passive surveillance, to observe and report. Don't worry about them, Owen, the Branch men don't go around trying to get their names in the papers.'

Smith took the implied reproof without rancour. 'I am sure, Willie, their names would be wrongly spelt in any case.'

When the implications of the farmhouse near Dunmow were explained to Rachette, he ordered Swarbrick to take full charge of the operation. Within an hour he and Smith were on board a Force helicopter heading east along the river.

Above Tilbury they turned due north, and as they approached the target from five hundred feet Swarbrick put aside his map and said to Smith, who sat holding a camera, 'We are going to make a run past at this height just to the west of the house. Get as many shots as you can. We will go straight on to Thaxted, turn and come back at a thousand feet and give you a chance to get some more pictures.'

As Woulover said, the house lay in the middle of a flat expanse of ploughed fields. No hedge or coppice stood closer than six hundred yards. A rutted track, shallow-ditched on either side, ran from the house to the main road. A small van and a dark blue

163

saloon car were parked by dilapidated stables. Of the heavy vehicle there was no sign.

The house itself was not large, merely a rectangle of stone blocks, under a steeply pitched slate roof. It was nothing more than a couple of farmworkers' cottages joined together.

As they droned past on the second run, Smith saw the white blur of an upturned face peering from a bedroom window.

They were seated around the table in Rachette's office with the still-wet prints of Smith's photographic reconnaissance in front of them.

'If I may put it quite bluntly,' said Swarbrick to the Commissioner, 'I don't think it is a matter for the police.'

Rachette pulled his spectacles down until they rested on the very tip of his nose. He took them off altogether, peered through the lenses at arm's length, and replaced them on his face.

He sighed deeply and said, 'You are recommending military aid to the civil power?'

Swarbrick nodded. 'If they are in possession of the weaponry we believe them to have, I can see no alternative. I would not wish to be responsible for sending in lightly armed police officers to take what may well be a fortress.'

Swarbrick reinforced his position, adding, 'As we know, after the Treasury massacre the Attorney General promised the House the persons responsible would be charged with high treason, and of course the death penalty would be implicit upon conviction. So these people have nothing to lose.'

Rachette sighed again, 'Ah yes, our political masters are forever making things difficult. But I see no reason to change previous policy, whereby we secure a strong perimeter around the place and simply wait them out. The military would adapt to a passive role in this manner, would they not?'

Swarbrick shrugged his deceptively narrow shoulders. 'They would have to be amenable to the directions of the civil power, but if these people are allowed to remain in situ and a prolonged siege develops, then their sympathizers are going to develop the situation into a martyrdom concept, with attendant demonstrations and possible attempts to break the perimeter. It could lead to far greater bloodshed than a pre-emptive strike at the house.'

'You don't mean an air attack?' said Rachette incredulously.

'No sir, no, no, no. I would not think of it.' Swarbrick laughed at the suggestion. (He had in fact considered it but dismissed it as politically unacceptable.) 'There is an armoured-car squadron at Colchester. If the freezing weather holds we can get them in the fields around the house beyond R.P.G. range and simply blast them out.'

Rachette shrank into his chair like a turtle into its shell at Swarbrick's explicit words. He searched his mind for reasonable and pacific alternatives, then reluctantly stretched out an arm from the shell and pressed the inter-com button. 'Kindly arrange an immediate appointment for myself and Brigadier Swarbrick with the Home Secretary. We will be over in about fifteen minutes.'

Chapter XVII

There was no moon, only the early winter frost sparkling in the opalescent radiance of starlight. Across the glistening fields the solitary house stood up, a black excrescence in the surrounding plain. From a cluster of chimneys at the centre of its slate roof, a wisp of grey smoke shrouded the stars like the last frozen breath of a mastodon dying on the ice.

Swarbrick, looking almost fraudulently small in police uniform and greatcoat, stood in the narrow road conversing with the Chief Constable of Essex Constabulary and an army major in command of the armoured-car unit. Occasionally he would point his swagger-stick towards the house and sweep the cane in small arcs across the dark horizon.

Smith, huddled into the collar of his sheepskin, remained in the background with Fairchild. They had no place in the tactical operation. Their role would only be played when the occupants of Appleshaw Cottage were brought into custody. At this stage they were at best merely reluctant witnesses.

A few minutes earlier, two platoons of infantry, accompanied by an equal number of uniformed police officers, had filtered into the darkness to outflank both sides of the house and take up positions in the rear. In the still air the sound of their entrenching tools could be heard thudding into the frost-hardened ground as they prepared cover in the flat plain devoid of natural shelter. But apart from the hanging smoke nothing indicated their noisy efforts disturbed the sombre stillness of the darkened cottage.

A hundred yards down the road, a generator panted like a heat-stricken dog for a few minutes until its sound was drowned in a heavier, deep-throated growl as the Saladin armoured cars started engines and moved into positions around the perimeter of the field. It was two minutes from the zero hour set for four a.m.

Swarbrick picked up a loud hailer and walked briskly along the rutted path, his dark blue uniform merging into the darkness as he approached within a hundred yards of the house.

The generator howled into the night. There was a thud of thrown switchgear and two thirty-inch searchlights threw back the darkness with brilliant lances.

Smith saw Swarbrick kneeling in the shallow ditch, the bull horn at his mouth.

'My name is Swarbrick. I am the Deputy Commissioner of the Metropolitan Police.' The amplified voice rolled against the dark walls and across the fields. The formality of his introduction continued.

'We have reason to believe there are certain persons wanted by police for murder and other offences within the house known as Appleshaw Cottage. I am in possession of warrants under the Firearms and Explosive Substances Acts to search this house and outbuildings. I therefore call upon the occupiers and all persons within Appleshaw Cottage to leave the house and assemble outside the front door. I must warn you that Police are aided by military forces who surround the house and who will be called upon if armed resistance is made.'

Swarbrick paused, seeking some response from the darkened windows, but no light or movement disturbed the mute solidity of the cottage. He tried again. 'I repeat, any armed resistance will be met with such weapons as are necessary to overcome any armed resistance you may offer. I appeal to you to evacuate the premises peaceably. You have five minutes to comply with this request.'

Swarbrick placed the loud hailer on the lip of the ditch and, still kneeling, gathered his arms across his bent knee and pulled the lapel-mounted transmitter of his personal radio across to his mouth.

'Metro 2 to Control. I don't think they intend to respond. My intentions are these. At the end of the five minutes I will announce my intention of approaching the house where I will again demand entry. If no positive response is made and if no hostile act is made against me I will call up the personnel carrier

167

with the police assault team on board. No aggressive action should be initiated by police or military forces unless the occupants use automatic or heavier weapons. Metro 2, over.'

Smith shivered in admiration at Swarbrick's calm pronouncement. He found difficulty in adjusting to the ominous reality before his eyes. The stark menace of the solitary house, the slight crouching figure of Swarbrick, the crisply hoar-frosted field now marked by the passage of many feet and intersected by the tracks of heavy wheeled armoured cars, the tunnels of light damming the surrounding darkness; it was Highgate cemetery all over again but on greater and more impersonal scale.

A sudden mechanical whine startled him as a Saladin adjusted its turret a few degrees to the left. The short-barrelled 76 mm gun sniffed at the cottage. Smith turned to the also spellbound Fairchild and grasped his arm.

'If things warm up sir, it might be a little less draughty behind that armoured car.'

Fairchild swung crossed arms across his chest several times as the cold began to bite. 'I believe that is what they call a contradiction in terms, Owen, but who am I to be pedantic. Lead on.'

They walked across the field to the nearest vehicle and took a position behind its reassuring bulk. Smith peered from behind the shoulder-high plates around the rear wheel and saw Swarbrick reaching out for the loudhailer.

Suddenly from the stillness of the cottage, a long white shaft stabbed the ground a yard in front of Swarbrick's outstretched arm and almost immediately Smith heard a fearsome rrrrrrrrr-ripping sound. He saw Swarbrick fall into the shallow depression and lie curled in a tight ball.

Another shaft of tracer hissed out of an upstairs window, probing into the tunnel of a searchlight; its core exploded in a shower of dying sparks. The orange-coloured tail of a rocket projectile arched lazily towards the armoured car behind which Smith and Fairchild stood. They watched helplessly as it plunged into the ground about twenty yards in front. A shower of earth spattered their shoulders as they bent into the shelter of the hull. From the turret, a sharp voice cried, 'Shoot – Shoot – Shoot.'

Pressed behind the hull, Smith felt all twelve tons of the

vehicle jerk against his shoulders as its gun blasted shell and flame at the walls of Appleshaw Cottage. Around the field other guns joined in. Instinctively, Smith dropped to the ground and found himself staring at the massive ribbed wheels as they jerked backwards on the recoil of each shot. Fearing the vehicle might reverse in some tactical manoeuvre and grind him into the earth, Smith rolled over and over away from its bulk. On each upward turn he saw the white lines of tracer bullets overhead. One long burst riveted the steel mantle close by the gun turret and flew upwards and outwards in angry ricochet as their passage was denied. He heard the hissing beat against the air, as if a huge flock of ... geese ... wild geese, were flying through the night.

He raised his head towards the cottage. It still stood but writhed in repeated convulsions of flame and smoke as the shells struck. Suddenly, a tongue of blue-white flame tore out of the shattered roof and in the accompanying roar the building pulled its external walls upon itself in a blanket of smoke and dust as nearly three hundred R.P.G. warheads detonated under the impact of an exploding shell.

The surviving searchlight held the swirling ruin and in its beam cautious infantrymen approached the scene in the sporadic rush and cover of a battle drill; only the rising smoke and small guttering flames from charred timbers opposed them.

Smith got to his feet and saw Fairchild sitting up on his knees and grinning sheepishly at him from behind the armoured car. His expression changed to one of alarm as the engine baroomed noisily and he jumped up and ran to Smith's side as the vehicle lurched forward and moved towards the gutted cottage. Smith saw Fairchild's lips moving and realized he was being spoken to, but his head was full of the ringing tinnitus of auditory nerves still vibrating in rebellion against the earlier oppression of tyrannous noise.

He gesticulated with his hands as his voice boomed within his skull. 'I can't hear a damned thing.'

Fairchild grimaced in sympathy, 'Me too,' he mouthed.

They followed in the wake of the armoured car and as they neared the ruins, Smith saw Swarbrick walking towards them, apparently unharmed. He did not know whether to be pleased or not but he was certainly surprised.

They stood before him as he beat the dirt from his greatcoat with his swagger-stick. 'Well Fairchild, an excellent demonstration of police and military co-operation, was it not?'

Fairchild hesitated. 'I must admit, it is my first experience of police and military co-operation. It was very . . . thorough?' He put the word to Swarbrick as a question.

Swarbrick lowered his brow in reply, 'Effective, might be the better word.' He looked across at the smouldering rubble. 'And words are now what we will have to choose . . . carefully. You and I, Mr Fairchild, are off to Essex Police H.Q. to compile the preliminary report.' He turned to Smith with grim geniality.

'As for you, boyo, this is where you come into your own. You know what you're here for, don't you?'

'Oh yes,' replied Smith, 'To pick up the bloody pieces . . . as usual.'

From past experience of mass morbid psychology, the police knew that crowds would be attracted to the scene as soon as the communiqué on the night's operation reached the early-morning radio audience. Already the local inhabitants, awakened by the gunfire, some curious, some frightened, were congregating at the road blocks set up to keep them and later arrivals away from the scene.

Answering the telepathy that seems to arise from every disaster, receivable only by the omniscience of reporters, a noisy few of these were also at the barriers clamouring for admission and interviews, screaming in outrage at the stolid repetition of the unfleshed communiqué by the Police Press officer.

As radio reports disseminated the release, filled out by graphic words from local people speaking of the distant flashes and thunder of battle, daylight brought to the sky above the cottage a circling fleet of helicopters and light aircraft hired by the media.

Below, Smith cursed the clear still air that permitted this circus to wheel and dip over his head as he supervised police and firemen in the grim task of locating and packing human remains.

Shortly after ten in the morning, a propaganda masterstroke was effected by Marxist students from Essex University.

One of their number, being a licensed light plane pilot, hired a Piper Aztec at the nearby Southend airport, and joining the media squadron circling the ruins made a slow, illegally low, run

170

across the area and dropped a large wreath of red flowers squarely on to the smouldering debris.

A policeman, pickaxing away on top of the rubble jumped back startled as the wreath flew past his face. He fell backwards, wrenched his back, and suffered a mild concussion as his head struck a pile of bricks. He was the only casualty listed by the forces of law and order during the entire operation.

A fireman got to the wreath first and surreptitiously pocketed the card attached to the frame as a souvenir. When relieved, later that morning, he proudly displayed it to the waiting reporters at the Press check point. It read, 'To the memory of the gallant proletarian martyrs who gave their lives in the people's struggle against Fascist oppression.'

By two in the afternoon there was a walk-out at three car plants, a forty-eight hour strike in the Welsh, Yorkshire and Scottish coalfields, and similar action at several shipyards. There were fights and near riots at these and other industrial areas, between those inclined to fight on both sides, who either violently agreed or disagreed with the night's action.

Ignorant of all this, Smith and his men worked on. The stables behind where the cottage had stood were only slightly damaged. Smith thought perhaps it was because the armoured-car crews were from a famous cavalry regiment, prepared to do or die – or anything else; provided it didn't frighten the horses.

There were no horses in the stables, only four 1½ ton ex-army trucks, on and around which were scattered dozens of assault rifles, machine guns, rocket tubes and boxes of ammunition; all the signs of a hurried attempt to load up and get away that was never made.

In the early darkness of late afternoon, a small convoy of police vans crept away to the nearest mortuary with eleven bodies, in twenty-five major portions. Two of them were female, six retained identifiable features, and Smith looked at them all. And he examined the backs of hands, looking for the long thick blond hair he had noted there, and between the knuckles and first flexure on the fingers of Richard Gredek.

He sat down wearily amongst the dead and lit a cigarette. Gredek was not numbered with them.

Smith left Dewlip and Neaterkin to finish the work at the

171

mortuary. It was just after nine in the evening when he reached the north-eastern perimeter of the Metropolitan area beyond Epping. The car radio spoke of demonstrations getting out of control in Whitehall and spreading to Trafalgar Square and along the Embankment. Riot conditions prevailed at Whitechapel, with running fights going on as far as the Mile End Road.

A gathering of International Socialists, Marxist-Leninists, Anarchists and Communists with a sprinkling of old-fashioned moderate socialists, intent on marching to join the Whitehall demonstrators, had run into an equally hurried gathering of Britain Firsters rallying to the call for greater action against the forces of treason and subversion.

To avoid the troubles, Smith swung in around the North Circular Road and approached the Yard from Victoria.

O'Brien rose to greet him as he entered the Murder Room, tired, dirty and smelling of cordite and death.

'Hullo, Guv. When do you get your Dunmow battle star?'

Smith glared at him in disgust and, walking through without a word, slammed the door of his office.

With a shrug of his shoulders, O'Brien went back to his desk. 'Miserable bastard,' he muttered. He addressed the door of Smith's office. 'If you can't take a joke, you shouldn't have joined up.'

He picked up the first of a pile of messages and reports accumulating on his desk and wearily looked at the banks of boxed index cards that had grown along the length of the office wall since the start of the enquiry.

'Oh fuck it.' O'Brien cursed and unlocked his desk drawer. There was still a third of the contents left in his whisky bottle. He took it out with two glasses and, without knocking, went into Smith's office.

He was seated behind his desk, one leg across the corner, an arm draped over the back of his chair and his chin sunk into his chest. His dull eyes stared fixedly at the blank wall.

'Ay yi yi yi,' O'Brien gave his imitation of mock Yiddish despair. 'My life, we thought we had troubles when this was just a simple case of murdering the Commissioner of police already. All we had to do was nick a couple of Assistant Commissioners or something easy like that. Now look at us hobnobbing with politicians and generals.'

He rolled his eyes heavenwards. 'A simple case of murdering the Commissioner of police! Just go out and nick a couple of Assistant Commissioners! Jesus Christ, simplicity itself.' He began to laugh.

Smith found he was laughing himself. A few snorting chuckles at first, then an uncontrolled flood of breathless guffaws as pent-up emotion welled out of his guts. He drained the whisky in a gulp and subsided in a fit of sputtering coughs.

'Anything of any consequence been coming in on the reports and messages?'

'No, nothing much,' O'Brien took out the message form he had stuffed in the pocket of his shirt. 'I was just going to clear the messages through the indices when you came in.' He looked at the form.

'Leopold' . . . he repeated the name, 'Leopold . . . He is one we have on the request list to all forces – all stations to inform us if he comes to notice.' He scratched the back of his neck. 'I can't think where he comes into the frame . . .'

'I can.' The words came from the back of Smith's throat. O'Brien saw the dull film vanish from his eyes. 'He was Gredek's boy friend in the Army.'

'The S.O.P.?'

'No, the real army. He was stationed with Gredek at Andover, He purchased his discharge and disappeared.'

'Oh Christ, yes. Sorry, Guv.'

'Who turned him up?'

O'Brien looked at the form to ascertain the originator of the message. 'The passport squad . . . man in the name of Herbert Arthur Leopold, born Luton, Bedfordshire, 28th July, 1960 has applied for a passport. I'll get his card from the index.'

He was back in twenty seconds. 'It all checks. Same names, date and place of birth. He is identical. The same particulars were given by our Leopold when he enlisted.'

Smith picked up the message form. 'He is asking for the passport to be delivered to an address at 139 Agar Crescent, Notting Hill, London W. 11.'

'Do you reckon Gredek is with him?'

173

Smith shrugged. 'It's a chance. No more than that. But it's a chance.'

'Leave this one to me, Guv.' O'Brien's anxiety showed. 'You've been up all night again. You've got to get some sleep.'

'We'll both get some sleep,' said Smith calmly. 'It would only show out if we crashed it this early and found they were still out on the town. We will go in about five-thirty in the morning. Get hold of two good men off the squad, authorized shots. Tell them to be here at five a.m. but don't tell them what it is about.'

'What about Mr Fairchild?' O'Brien's anxiety increased. 'We should let him know.'

'Smith's reply was firm. 'No, he is still at Essex police H.Q. at Chelmsford with Swarbrick. As far as they and anybody else are concerned, this is just a routine enquiry on a past associate of Gredek. We'll do it on our own. I joined the police force, not the bloody army. I've had a bellyful of soldiers ... whatever army they may be in.'

Before he settled down for a few hours sleep, Smith phoned Angus Craddock to let him know Gredek was still alive ... but he said nothing of the possibilities he anticipated at an address in Notting Hill.

O'Brien and his two picked men, Detective Sergeants Devoir and Loach, were sitting in the Murder Room munching bacon sandwiches and drinking coffee as Smith entered a few minutes before five. He gratefully accepted similar sustenance unwrapped for him by O'Brien. He then checked the loading of their .38 Smith & Wesson pistols and made sure the personal radios were working effectively. He noted with approval that, like himself, they all wore dark windcheaters, jeans and soft soled tennis shoes. He had known idiots turn up for an early-morning raid in formal suits and hard leather shoes with the intention of knocking on the front door and shouting 'Police'.

They stopped the car at the beginning of the street. Agar Crescent, as its name implied, curved away to the left. The house at number 139 was out of sight and should be about the middle of the crescent. Smith sent Devoir to reconnoitre the exterior.

Already the stirrings of a new day could be heard around them. The rumble of the first underground train, the whine of an electric milk float, a speeding newspaper delivery van taking full

174

advantage of the empty streets, the proud solitary footsteps of a worker who, for a short time, shared the city with only a selected few.

Devoir loped noiselessly back to the car. 'It's the usual Notting Hill gaff, sir, a basement, ground floor and two upper floors. All the rooms separately let out, but we are in luck, according to a card on the door, Leopold lives in the basement. There is a gap between the houses about six up from 139. We can climb over the fences and cover the back pretty easily.'

'Make sure you are covering the back of the right house and don't forget you are only there to stop anybody coming out of the back. I'll give you five minutes to get in position.'

Devoir and Loach made their way back along the street. Smith followed at a slower pace with O'Brien. He felt O'Brien shivering alongside him as they waited outside the front of the house for the others to get in position. He knew it wasn't the cold and certainly wasn't fear. It was the involuntary trembling of adrenalin surging into the system with the anticipation of danger. Very useful when you are actually in action but a damned nuisance when you are waiting for it to occur.

The basement door was recessed at the front of the house below street level where six steps led down to an untidy mess of strewn garbage and rubbish bins. The curtains were fully drawn across grimy windows. No light gleamed behind them. Smith led the way down the steps, carefully avoiding the rubbish.

His shaded torch swung over the locks. There were two, an old Yale and what he thought was a flimsy back plate, screwed on to the inside of the door. He noted, with satisfaction, that the wood was old and rotting. With a strip of flexible plastic, he eased the tongue back on the Yale. Holding it in position, he stood to one side as O'Brien, gun in hand, flexed his right leg, then thrust his foot against the second lock. Smith prayed there would not be a security chain.

The door swung back against the force of O'Brien's foot and crashed against the side wall. Smith hurled himself through into the room.

In the dim glow of a guttering paraffin stove somebody jerked upright from the bed on his left. A face, momentarily slack-jawed, gaped up at him as he leaped on to the bed, a hand snaked out to the top of the bedside table, nails scrabbling. But

Smith already had his own hand deep into the thick hair of the head below him and pulled upwards with all his strength.

There was a strangled, squealing pain-filled curse, and the hand came away empty from the table, to grab at Smith's wrist in an instinctive attempt to free the clutching fingers. By now, Smith had his feet braced firmly against the side of the bed. He heaved the squirming body on to the floor and dragged it across the room.

A bedside lamp came on, and he saw O'Brien seated across the other occupant of the bed, a young man, unknown to him, who was staring cross-eyed down into the barrel of O'Brien's pistol, thrust into the cavity between his nose and upper lip. Smith's grip tightened even further and his loins churned in gratification.

Glaring up at him from between his legs, where he held the head suspended by its hair, was the hate-filled face of Staff Sergeant Richard Gredek. He struck down strongly with the heel of his left hand across the bridge of Gredek's nose. The blood poured from his nostrils. Then, almost solicitously, but still holding Gredek by the hair, he took out a clean handkerchief and gently soaked up the streaming blood.

Gredek sat in the detention block of Cannon Row Police Station, situated almost opposite the scene of the Treasury massacre. His nakedness was concealed in a rough blanket. He had been allowed to wash and, at his persistent request, was given the use of a comb to arrange his dark hair. He was quite composed when Smith entered his cell.

He rose and threw an end of the blanket across his shoulder. There was a quirky smile on his lips. The gesture was too exaggerated and contrived; Smith knew what to expect. Gredek held up an imperious hand.

'Save your breath, Mr Smith. I will only say this. You are standing here now because I allowed it. You could have had Ackerman alive, and from Ackerman all the rest of them . . . and I don't just mean those silly . . . geese.' His nostrils flared and dark traces of dried blood lay within them. His injured nose made him speak as if with a bad cold.

'I assumed, Mr Smith, as you purport to be a senior detective, you would be capable of drawing a logical conclusion from given circumstances. Instead you simply lash out with the nearest blunt instrument you can lay your hands on.' He gestured towards his injured nose. 'It seems to be fairly typical of your approach. You kill Ackerman and as a consequence you must accept responsibility for the slaughter of those fools at Appleshaw Cottage.'

'I know where I made my mistakes,' said Smith. 'What's your excuse?'

Gredek drew himself upright. 'I am a soldier, Mr Smith.' He repeated the statement with greater emphasis. 'I ... am a soldier.'

'Yes, but whose side are you on?'

'No more, Mr Smith. I say no more.' Gredek turned his back on him and stood gazing at the small barred window high on the wall.

'Perhaps, like me, you talk better with your clothes on.' Smith spoke as if recalling a fond memory. 'I'll have them brought in.'

Without turning, Gredek let the blanket drop and threw it backwards in silent contempt.

Smith grinned, and trying to make it appear of little consequence said, 'Maybe it's just as well. As I told you in the basement, anything you say may be given in evidence.'

In the absence of Swarbrick and Fairchild, he awaited the arrival of Hicks in the anteroom of his office, to report the arrest of Gredek.

Hicks, who had been relegated more and more into the background by Swarbrick's dominance, was delighted to be the first recipient of the news.

'Excellent work, Owen, commendable piece of initiative.'

Smith received the praise with a half smile and a seemingly grateful nod. He wondered what his reception would have been if it had turned out differently.

Hicks picked up his red phone. 'Good morning, Commissioner. Good news, sir, we picked up Gredek early this morning at Notting Hill.' Smiling into the mouthpiece he waved Smith to a chair. 'No sir, no violence or disturbance, the arrest was effected quietly and without trouble of any kind.'

Smith leaned forward uncomfortably, to speak. He should have mentioned Gredek's nose, but Hicks' attention was directed entirely upon the instrument in his hand. He sat back. In comparison with recent events it was relatively unimportant, besides ...

'It is very kind of you to say so, Commissioner. Yes, sir, I will get on to Chelmsford right away and inform Brigadier Swarbrick of the development. Thank you, sir.' He replaced the receiver and, leaning back in his chair, slapped the palms of his hands twice upon his upper abdomen.

'Well Smith, er ... Owen, as you heard, the Commissioner is very pleased with us. I will get on to the Deputy and let him know of our success.'

Hicks clasped his hands together and contemplated the top of his desk. He allowed himself another pleasurable smile. 'I'm sure he also will be very pleased.'

He rose and stretched out to shake Smith's hand in dismissal, 'I suggest you just wait in your office until he gets back before we take any decisions on what charges to prefer against Gredek.'

He was dozing in the armchair in his office when the door swung open and Swarbrick and Fairchild entered. Smith started guiltily to his feet. Dammit, at Swarbrick's rank they sent for you, they didn't come crashing into your office.

'Resting on your laurels, boyo?' Swarbrick swept past him and took the chair behind his desk. He looked meaningfully at Smith's legs.

'Glad to see you managed to keep your trousers on this time.' He gathered up the papers on Smith's desk and dropped them on the floor, occupying the vacant space with his elbows and propping his chin on the apex of his knuckles; he moulded the malleable shapeless nose with his forefingers.

'I thought you had been warned against playing your one-man band on this particular pitch, boyo?' The question was disinterestedly posed.

'It was just another routine enquiry. One of hundreds we have carried out since the beginning.' Smith tried not to sound defensive.

'I thought routine enquiries were for sergeants and detective constables?'

'I had a hunch about this one. It just sounded good to me.' He regained his composure. 'Gredek is inside, isn't he? Does the how, why, or who, matter at this stage?'

'What's he got to say about it, Owen?' Smith was glad of Fairchild's intervention. He handed them copies of his report on the arrest. They read in silence.

'So he admits nothing.' Swarbrick threw his copy on to the desk.

'He said enough to me at Nevis Mews.'

'But you were alone then, Owen. There is no corroboration. You know what the defence will do to that,' Fairchild said reproachfully.

'Well, there was Ackerman,' Swarbrick sneered, 'but as Gredek says, you lashed out and now we haven't got Ackerman. So where is the evidence, boyo?' He picked up the report and read from it, 'Gredek refused to allow blood or saliva samples to be taken.' The report was again contemptuously thrown on the desk. 'It looks as though the seminal obsessions of the good Dr Loder are not going to be gratified.'

'I think we can give him something to work on.' Smith was quietly complacent. He went on, 'Gredek and Leopold had something of a second honeymoon last night. We've got swabs from Leopold and we've got the bed sheets –'

Swarbrick interrupted him. 'I would be inclined to think that, apart from Gredek, Leopold's body and bed would have been as busy as Oxford Street during the summer sales. Gredek may have been the most recent passer-by, but what about the others?'

'We do have an actual blood sample, sir.' Smith was now patiently polite and making it obvious. 'Gredek put up something of a struggle as I grabbed him and to restrain him, I was obliged to . . . lash out . . . I hit him on the nose and staunched the blood with a nice fresh handkerchief. Dr Loder tells me it should be enough for a full grouping.'

Swarbrick eyed him with respectful suspicion, then laughed, 'You may be a bit more far-sighted than one gives you credit for, boyo.' The chuckle subsided. 'But you still have no evidence to pin the Treasury massacre on him. It was Ackerman who you first saw in possession of the Browning that killed the policemen on the church tower.'

He rose from behind the desk. 'After all, you cannot hang a man for high treason just for killing a Commissioner of Police.'

He pushed a forefinger into Smith's chest, the deep hard eyes boring upwards into his face.

'You leave Gredek to sweat in his cell. Neither you nor anyone else is to see him unless I give authority. That direction will also be passed to the duty officer at Cannon Row ... Clear?'

Smith nodded. Swarbrick was right, without an admission from Gredek he might, with luck, be convicted of complicity in the murder of Sir Maxwell Steype, but without a confession ... of nothing else. Twenty-four hours alone in a cell might make him open his mouth, but Smith doubted it very much.

In the absence of an immediate requirement to work, and as a gesture of appreciation, he took O'Brien, Neaterkin and Dewlip to dinner. As they left the Murder Room he saw the studied but reproachful indifference on the faces of Devoir and Loach at not being included in the party.

He concealed his neglect by saying to them, 'Come on you miserable young bastards. Somebody's got to cover the back.'

They went to a small unpretentious Sicilian restaurant in Soho's Wardour Street, where the excellence of the food was only exceeded by the friendliness and efficiency of the service. It was also reasonably cheap. They dined on minestrone, lasagne, stuffed breast of chicken and zabaglione. Between them they drank four large carafes of wine with the meal. The bottle of Rémy Martin went round twice with the coffee.

An argument between O'Brien and a surprisingly belligerent Dewlip as to who would pay for the next round of brandies, was interrupted by a waiter calling Smith to the phone.

He returned to the table calling for the bill. 'Sorry to break it up. Gredek wants to see me.'

It was just on ten p.m. when Smith and O'Brien got back to the Yard. He had hauled the protesting O'Brien out of the car at the top end of the Mall and made him walk around the perimeter of St James's Park. He knew he needed to sober up as much as O'Brien did. And Gredek wasn't going anywhere.

Smith did not need reminding of Swarbrick's words but protocol demanded he make the approach through Fairchild. A staff officer told him Fairchild was at the Home Office, with Swarbrick and Commissioner Rachette, briefing the Secretary of

State on the battle of Appleshaw Cottage for the next day's Parliamentary debate.

He hesitated over the telephone. It was high-powered stuff, Commissioner, Home Secretary, Parliamentary debates ... should he wait for Swarbrick to return? After all, it was not his responsibility. But suppose Gredek wanted to talk? He knew there comes a time when a suspect will, just out of the boredom of confinement and thoughts upon the uncertainty of his future, suddenly decide to make that future a certainty, even if the certainty is a long term of imprisonment. But that only happened with the nervous, the guilt-ridden, the sensitive ... Gredek was none of these. Nevertheless ... why did he want to see him?

Oh fuck 'em all, he thought, you're getting windy in your old age, Smith. He got through to the duty officer at the Home Office.

He was horrified at the suggestion he interrupt a Secretary of State's conference over a police matter. 'You may say,' Smith laid on a tone of impending doom, 'it could have a most important bearing upon their discussions.' It had the desired effect.

'What is it, Smith?' Swarbrick's voice bore no trace of annoyance, only weary resignation.

'Gredek wants to see me. I don't know what for.'

'Then go and see him, boyo.' It was almost as if Swarbrick had never imposed his previous restriction. 'And take somebody with you, it may be he wants to take the pants off you again.' The line clicked out. Smith had no anger at the snide remark, only vague puzzlement.

Chapter XVIII

Apart from the service of meals and routine checks by the duty officer, Smith found no record of visitors shown against Gredek's name in the Detention Book at Cannon Row. The night-duty men had taken over half an hour ago and would not know much but the name of the late-turn duty officer was familiar. He knew where he could find him, and telling O'Brien to wait, he walked across the road to the dive bar in the pub opposite.

'What are you drinking, Ernie?'

The bald head did not turn, but the eyes looked at him with amused benevolence from the mirror at the back of the bar.

'A pint will do it.'

Ernie Routledge had been Smith's detective inspector when he was but a junior detective sergeant. That had been eight years ago, when one day it was alleged Routledge had his hand stretched out behind him, towards a rich Hatton Garden dealer, in custody for receiving a fortune in stolen jewellery. The receiver refused to confirm the allegation, but then he would not deny it. Routledge went back to wearing a uniform and had been frozen in the rank of inspector ever since.

'I wondered if you would be shrewd enough to suss something, Owen.' The crumpled face bent over the glass.

'I don't know that I do suss anything, Ernie, it's just that I didn't expect it. I don't even know what he wants. Any ideas?'

Routledge eased himself from the stool and jerked his head towards the back of the bar. Smith picked up his drink and followed him.

They got themselves into a corner by the stairs.

'Your man didn't say a word all day, then when I made a check on him about nine, he demands to see you. Wouldn't say why, just insisted you come and see him.'

Routledge drained his glass and handed it to Smith. 'You can just get another one in, Owen, before they call time.'

Smith gave him a long look but did as he was told. He brought the glasses back to the corner. 'Anybody else see him beforehand?'

'Did you look in the book?'

Smith nodded, 'Yes, Ernie, I looked in the book.'

'Well?'

'Stop playing with me, Ernie, I'm not your junior sergeant now.'

Routledge grinned amiably into his beer. 'I knew you would be a good 'un, Owen,' he said it with almost paternalistic pride, 'but I'll tell you this, if that Calvanistic old bastard Craddock was still in charge of the enquiry you wouldn't have found me here tonight.' It was Craddock who had recommended his return to uniform, refusing to accept Routledge's protests of innocence.

'Still it's down to you now, Owen. Oh I know you've got Cyril Fairchild on top of you, and probably all the rest of them right up to the eighth floor. But you're doing it. Owen, listen.' He placed a confiding arm round Smith's shoulders and pulled him into the wall.

'About four this afternoon, the new Deputy, Swarbrick, and another man, I don't know him, come into the nick. I get the beckoning finger into the charge room. Swarbrick tells me to hand over the cell keys then I have to remain in the charge room and see no one else comes through. They were with your man for about two hours, and three hours after that he asks to see you.'

'I don't suppose you heard what was said?'

'No chance, Owen. The door of the cell passage was locked behind them.'

Smith considered the possibilities. 'The other man, any ideas on him?'

Routledge pulled out his lower lip, letting it snap back against his teeth with an audible sucking noise that Smith found somehow offensive. It reminded him of his earlier service with the man. He had had the same habit then.

'Not a copper. Probably one of the funny people from across the river.'

Smith knew he meant a member of the security services. And it pleased him, for it gave him an explanation. After all, it would not be unreasonable for security to want to have words with Gredek.

'Well, thanks a lot, Ernie. I owe you one.'

'You owe me nothing. I have done nothing and said nothing. I haven't seen you or spoken to you.' He finished his drink and turned to the stairs. 'They read the Act to me before they left, Owen!'

Smith gave him a few minutes to get clear then returned to the impatient O'Brien. He ordered him to have Gredek booked out to the interview room.

He watched carefully as he was brought in. There was no longer hatred in the eyes. The face had softened into a relaxed, almost contemptuous expression of confident assurance. Just as when Smith was writhing on the floor at Nevis Mews.

Gredek sniffed as the warmth of the room brought out the alcohol on their breath. 'Been having a victory celebration, Mr Smith?' He was now clad in one of the suits they had brought from the basement at Agar Crescent.

'You wanted to see me.' Smith made it sound flatly disinterested.

'I apologize if I have interrupted your festivities, but I have decided to make a full and frank confession. Always assuming you are sober enough to take it down.'

From behind Gredek's back O'Brien's face lit up and he rubbed his hands together joyfully.

Smith kept his voice cold. 'Why?'

There was a silence, a thin feral glance at Smith's face, then, 'As I told you before I am a soldier.'

Smith looked at the now solemn, impassive face. 'I'm glad you didn't say it was your conscience.' He handed Gredek the cautionary card and pulled open the door of the Clutterbuck cabinet.

This was the outcome of years of discussion between numerous judicial and Home Office committees as to the most effective means of recording confessions of prisoners in police custody to ensure the confessions were not obtained under duress, threat, or promise of favoured treatment. The cabinet, named after the chairman of the last committee, Mr Justice Clutterbuck, was smaller and lower than a telephone booth. It allowed only the prisoner to squeeze inside and seat himself on a small stool in front of a microphone. The cabinet could only be locked by the prisoner from inside and the microphone only became live when the door was locked. The microphone itself was connected by landline to one of several recording centres manned by unknown civil servants, who in due course transcribed the tape and returned a typed certified copy of the confession direct to the Court authority concerned in the hearing of the case. Thus with the locked door, and the fact that only the prisoner could squeeze into the cabinet, suggestions that the police forced a confession were overcome. The same circumstances prevented any howls of protest and feigned anguish, inserted on the tape by a trouble-making prisoner, being believed.

The police, of course, could and did make their own simultaneous recording but it had no validity as evidence.

Gredek entered the cabinet, as most prisoners did, reluctantly. Criminals had named it by their epithet for an informer, as the 'grass chamber'.

Self-assurance returned as he slid the bolt on the inside and the red light came on above the microphone. He had to wait for a green light, indicating readiness at the recording centre before speaking. In two minutes the green snapped on and through the glass panel they saw Gredek pick up the cautionary card. His voice was carried into the room by an external speaker.

'I Richard Gredek wish to make a statement. I am not in fear of any threat held over me and nothing by way of promise or favour has been offered to induce me to make any confession. I have not been subjected to any assault of a physical or mental nature. I fully understand that whatever I say may be given in evidence.'

In accordance with the directions on this card, he signed it as having read and understood the contents.

Beside the microphone was a metal slot into which Gredek inserted the card, which was automatically timed and dated before being fed through to a heavy safe clamped to the side of the cabinet. The card could only be retrieved by the Civil

Service department holding the key. The whole complex formula had to be strictly complied with before any confession subsequently made could be admitted in evidence.

With his head thrown back and arms folded, Gredek cast recollective eyes at the ceiling and, enunciating each word with slow clarity, began to speak again into the microphone.

'During last April, a man named Wardoe visited my depot at Andover. He produced credentials showing him to be a civil servant attached to Ordnance Corps H.Q. He said he was on a touring holiday and as he was in the district and the depot was his administrative responsibility, he thought he would pay us a courtesy call.

'He invited me to lunch at a pub in Andover and during lunch made it clear he was a homosexual. Well, as they say, it takes one to know one. I am also a homosexual but not a catamite – a half effeminate submissive – like Wardoe, although he occasionally made aggressive overtures it was not his true role and he only tried it once with me.

'We became interested in each other and an affair developed. Wardoe made frequent visits to Andover. On rare occasions I would meet him in Hampstead.

'He was intrigued by the fact that as a child I was brought out of Hungary by my mother just after the suppression of the counter-revolution in 1956. My father was a party member and remained behind. My mother's flight was without his knowledge or agreement. He died shortly afterwards. The cause of death was said to be a heart attack but you can draw your own conclusions! I grew up with ambitions to become a great soldier but, because of my father's political history, I was refused a commission. I therefore joined as a ranker.

'My own political philosophy is of a rightist nature but early studies in an attempt to understand my father's views gave me considerable knowledge of the jargon and dialectic of the left. It became apparent to me that Wardoe was a committed anarcho-communist of the most primitive type.

'More for my own amusement than any other reason, I led him to believe my political beliefs were the same, if not even more extreme than his own. One weekend he met me at Waterloo Station and took me to the Alhambra Radio shop in Nevis Mews, Camden Town.

'I was introduced to Comrade Brent, and also to Solan, who ran the business, but as I was to discover, it was just a front for what was then a nebulous group of revolutionary extremists. Each cell leader had his own unit of peripatetic young cryptos, all except Wardoe. With his civil-service background, he was afraid of security checking up on him.

'I soon realized Wardoe's visit to Andover was no accident. He had, if you please, recruited me as a military expert. Had I not been so intrigued by the set-up I would have been annoyed, but I was getting a great deal of interest and enjoyment out of them and their dialectical arguments and stupid grandiose plans.

'I had to be careful with Comrade Canada or young Craddock as he was. He thought Wardoe's affection for me had clouded his judgment, which was quite true. Perhaps I overdid the dialectic on the political side, but he could not question my efficiency as military, would it be too grandiose of me to say – adviser?

'During the summer, Wardoe arrived at one meeting in a state of excitement. Some captured I.R.A. weapons were being sent to England and he had to arrange a suitable depot for storage. He had allocated them to me at Andover.

'When the arms arrived from Belfast, I was called in to discuss with Brent and Wardoe how best to secure possession of the arms for use by the Soldiers of the People, as they had now begun to call themselves. Wardoe was sure the weapons were simply there for storage and would soon be forgotten.

'I thought of going to the security services and telling them what was happening, but I was uncertain how they would view my initial involvement.

'About this time Liam Mulqueen was addressing a B.F.M. rally in Winchester. I had greatly admired the general ever since his victory in Northern Ireland. When he became politically active after his shoddy treatment, I was greatly attracted by the aims and objects of the B.F.M.

'I decided to approach him and seek his advice. To cut a long story short, I was granted an interview, after having told my story to a man named Menderfield, who seemed to act as the general's aide.

'The general was greatly intrigued, he said to Menderfield,

"With these people loose on the streets, it could not only give us the balance of power, we could have an absolute majority."

'The general asked how far I was prepared to go, and without wishing to sound banal I told him I was at his service. He assured me whatever I was called upon to do on behalf of the B.F.M. it would not be forgotten. Nothing specific was discussed, indeed, I was left with Menderfield, who grilled me very thoroughly.

'Two days later, I received a phone call from Menderfield to meet him at a pub on the A30 just outside Camberley. At the rendezvous, we went on to a large country house about three miles from the pub.

'We met the general in a summer-house by a small lake. He said it would be greatly to the advantage of the B.F.M. if I continued my association with the S.O.P. and fell in with their every plan. Indeed, I should assist and incite them where necessary to the most extreme action.

'To this end, I was given two "letter-boxes" for written communication. One was at the back of a weighing-machine on the east-bound platform of the Victoria line at Euston. The other under the left-hand corner of a bench at the bus shelter just outside the camp. I was told never to attempt telephonic communication with the general or any of his associates, as their phones were monitored by the security services.

'At a meeting attended by all the cell leaders, including a single representative from each of the two interlocking cells – they were masked incidentally – discussions took place to decide on violent revolutionary action against significant capitalist targets.

'Now ever since we had acquired the captured weapons, Wardoe became increasingly obsessed with a plan involving a full-strength armed invasion of the Stock Exchange at the height of its business. Those inside were to be ruthlessly slaughtered except for a manageable number of hostages. The building would be held until, according to Wardoe, a popular people's uprising overwhelmed the Government. He would quote Bakunin, saying, "the passion for destruction is also a creative urge."

'The change in Wardoe at this time was quite remarkable. From being a cunning, scheming, subservient character he became possessed with a fervour and dedication amounting to fanaticism. He saw himself possessing not only the violent revolutionary activism of Bakunin but also the far reaching intellectualism of Kropotkin and Proudhon. He produced reams of paper on the establishment of egalitarian and libertarian communes modified and adapted to modern conditions, concepts and philosophy. All to arise out of an attack on the Stock Exchange, his Bastille, Winter Palace and Dublin General Post Office rolled into one.

'This then was what Wardoe proposed to the Committee. To my surprise it was discussed and examined as though it was a viable proposition. Young Craddock looked on it with favour. Fortunately, Brent and one of the visitors saw the flaws and when I finally got through to them that it was contrary to every concept of urban guerrilla warfare to sacrifice everything in a single open attack, the scheme was finished. Particularly when Wardoe produced leaflets he said were to be distributed in the poorer industrial areas to coincide with the attack and bring people to our support. He had had them printed without the committee's approval by an underground press and it was a gross breach of security. He was severely criticized and censured. All the leaflets were destroyed together with his papers on the plan.

'Wardoe however was very upset; he became quite sullen and morose. His fanaticism was replaced by smouldering resentment, mainly of me.

'On the Friday night before the march on the Sunday in the course of which your commissioner, Steype, was kidnapped, I was in the sergeants' mess at Andover when I received a telephone call from Menderfield. I was to meet him urgently at the rendezvous on the A30 road.

'When we met, he told me the General was in receipt of information, from a highly placed senior police officer, that Wardoe had been in touch with the Commissioner, Steype, and had somehow convinced him a large quantity of arms were in the hands of a terrorist group.

'The police source was certain nothing was known of the precise details but the Commissioner had agreed to meet Wardoe outside his club in St James's on Sunday night, when Wardoe would produce complete evidence. Beyond mentioning it to the general's informant, the Commissioner had not taken any action prior to meeting Wardoe, in case it turned out to be a complete nonsense.

'Menderfield said the general's orders were to silence both Wardoe and the Commissioner. The S.O.P. should be induced to see it as an operation of necessity and as a means of taking their campaign into the heart of the enemy camp. I saw no difficulty in convincing them of that object.

'I went straight to Nevis Mews. Ian Craddock was there. I told him Wardoe had admitted to me, in a jealous rage, he had betrayed us to the Commissioner of Police and we had until Sunday to prevent everyone being arrested.

'Comrade Brent came in on Saturday morning. No, I don't know his real name. I had no difficulty in convincing both him and Craddock of Wardoe's guilt. His recent behaviour was enough.

'Craddock put forward the plan to kidnap the Commissioner during the counter-demo against the B.F.M. He was the group's intelligence officer on police policy, personnel, and methods. He was aware of the Commissioner's habits. It was agreed I would deal with Wardoe. Craddock with four of his soldiers would attend to the Commissioner.

'After I had dealt with Wardoe, I returned to Nevis Mews and in due course Craddock arrived in the van with Steype. As a precaution we removed his clothing to ensure he was not carrying any concealed radio or transponder. We left him secured to one of the pillars in the workshop for a few hours.

'Craddock and I drank some wine and smoked a couple of joints. Craddock told me he had kicked the hard stuff some time ago but he took a bit of grass now and again, to cool his mind. Had his puritanical comrades known they would have been very angry at such a bourgeois habit. This time, however, he became sullen and moody. Later on, when we went in to check on Steype's condition, Craddock began vilifying him as a fascist oppressor of the people, he became quite frenzied.

'I told him to go into the office and cool off. I tried to engage Steype in conversation but he ignored me completely. I was intrigued by the man and what he represented. I found his dignity in a very undignified situation sexually stimulating. I made an affectionate overture and he spat in my face. I simply buggered him on the spot.

190

'I then told Craddock he could have him. At my suggestion we strung him up by the ankles on the hoist. I gave Craddock my razor and said if he thought the man to be a police pig he should deal with him as a pig.

'Craddock stripped down to his underpants – residual bourgeois morality, I suppose. He reached out with the razor two or three times and just as I thought he had lost his nerve, he screamed "Mother" and started slashing.

'He stood there quite fascinated by the consequences, trance-like. I turned on the hose to swill the mess away. I then had to turn the hose on Craddock before he responded.

'We decided to put the body in an old wooden crate, it was not quite large enough so I removed Steype's head with an old cleaver. I believe I made a mistake and left the cleaver in the workshop.

'Then Craddock came up with the marvellous idea of dumping the body inside the Yard. Right inside the man's office. I was more than willing, especially when Craddock proved how easily it could be done. He even had keys for one of the side doors.

'We put the body in the crate; by then it was around two-thirty in the morning. Craddock decided to wait for another hour before we moved. On the pretext of going for coffee and sandwiches at an all-night coffee stall, I took the van to Euston and left a report of the occurrence and our intentions in the letter box.

'Craddock had brought in one of his soldiers to drive us and the crate to the Yard. We got in at the side entrance without difficulty, the driver was told to leave the area for thirty minutes, then return to a pick-up point at Queen Anne's Gate.

'Inside the Yard door we found a small trolley and wheeled the crate to a service lift which took us to the seventh or eighth floor; I cannot remember which. We had a circuitous journey along different corridors but Craddock knew where he was going.

'Once in the office we got the body out. I wrote the S.O.P. message on the chest; I thought the general could get some propaganda out of it. Craddock was pleased with the idea. It would be an initial statement of S.O.P. intentions.

'The thought of what we had done and where we were had brought us both to a state of elation and excitement. Craddock

191

discovered the uniform in a cupboard and proposed dressing the body in it and propping it in the chair behind the desk. I spiked the head on the helmet. When we finished, Craddock was laughing hysterically. I had to shake him to his senses.

'As we left the office Craddock put up the DO NOT DISTURB sign. He had a note already typed with the idea of leaving it in the office of the head of the C.I.D. He had some personal reason for wanting him to find the body.

'This meant stopping at a lower floor, but it was all accomplished without difficulty. I left Craddock just inside the side entrance, picked up the van at Queen Anne's Gate and went back for Craddock. We were safely back in Nevis Mews within the hour.

'I had a few hours' sleep then left the mews around midday intending to return to the depot with excuses to cover my absence. I checked the "letterbox" at Euston and found a message requiring me to meet Menderfield in the restaurant at the main-line station. He was waiting for me at the bar . . . He wanted another leak repaired.

'It seemed our presentation of the Commissioner's corpse had met with extreme disapproval from the senior police officer who was the general's secret ally and sympathizer. He had been led to believe there would simply be a complete and inexplicable disappearance. The man was now demanding written confirmation from the general that the position, as head of a national police service, the general had promised to institute on obtaining political power, would be his. A failure to comply would result in him aligning enquiries into Steype's murder towards myself, and, as the general feared, towards the B.F.M. The general was not prepared to be blackmailed.

'I pointed out I would already be in some difficulty in explaining my absence from the depot. Menderfield said I should be prepared to sever all connection with the Army for the time being.

'He gave me £1,250 and a Zeon night sight. He had arranged for the erection of a telephone engineers' shelter from where I could cover the street approaches to Scotland Yard. He provided a photograph and description of the target. It was the Deputy Commissioner, Hammertoe.

'As you are aware, I accomplished the mission. The S.O.P.

were quite impressed by my initiative on their behalf. Brent took it upon himself to issue a communiqué to the press, although he was angry at young Craddock's method of disposing of Steype's body. He called it "an example of irresponsible bourgeois flamboyance." But he had to accept Craddock's answer pointing out the suspicion and mistrust the crime had directed towards and within the police themselves.

'Over the next few days the operational committee discussed furture targets with proposals for hit-and-run attacks on the head offices of multi-national companies. Then came announcements of the B.F.M. protest march on the Ministry of Defence. I was asked to prepare plans for an attack on the column creating a maximum of terror with a minimum of risk.

'My report on this intention led to a meeting with General Mulqueen and Menderfield at an apartment in the Barbican. The general seriously considered sacrificing some of his leading marchers, his first thoughts being of milking a great deal of sympathy out of the martyrdom of his members. However, Menderfield was of the opinion such a step might have a retrograde effect on the movement's image of omnipotence and invulnerability and indeed might frighten off public attendance and support at future demonstrations. And at the election.

'I brought, or, more accurately, bought, Ackerman into the plot, using the general's money. Thinking ahead for explanations to excuse missing such a target as massed columns of marchers, I decided to use an R.P.G. launcher. Any inaccuracy could be put down to bad combustion in the propellant, at least to the uninitiated. I therefore needed a reliable man not only to assist me in loading and handling the weapon but to support such a story.

'It was necessary for me to tell Ackerman we were, in fact, secretly working for the general and the B.F.M. I had little difficulty in getting the committee to accept him with his obvious proletarian origins, but I did have problems over my choice of weapon. They thought a machine-gun would be more efficient.

'However, when they saw the rocket launcher could be broken down into two small sections and with projectiles fit into the gutted carrying cases of two portable police transmitters, they saw how necessary it was, particularly when we planned to reach our firing point by using police uniforms.

'The target of opportunity came with the sight of all those people milling around at the windows of the Treasury building. I did not know who they were and at the time I did not care.

'After the attack, we used a fake police van parked at the back of the Abbey in Great College Street, for our get-away. There was a general police chase in that direction and we simply joined in.

'Craddock said nothing all the way back to Nevis Mews, but he did not take his eyes from me for one second. As soon as we got in, I decided to strike first. I immediately accused Craddock of arriving late, and queried the propriety of his orders changing the target. The others were astonished to learn we had not hit the B.F.M. march.

'Craddock protested, saying it was I who deliberately aimed at the Treasury building, but Ackerman backed my story. When it came out later who the victims were, and that his father was amongst those in the room, his known hatred of his father and the police service was enough to confirm his guilt.

'The rest you know. I do not wish to say any more, only that I am sorry for those who died but I am convinced it was necessary to secure the establishment of strong and firm government to save the country. Only the Britain First Movement can and will provide that salvation. Britain First!'

Throughout Gredek's confession Smith felt as if he was in Court listening to a skilled advocate opening for the Crown. It was too effortless, so apparently extemporaneous ... and he knew such apparent spontaneity only came from thorough preparation.

Gredek held up the 'Conclusion of statement' card to indicate he had nothing more to say.

Smith picked up the external microphone. 'Bearing in mind the terms under which you have made your statement, I wish you to add a description of the man named Menderfield, and such details of the interior of the Barbican apartment and the country house near Camberley that would serve to corroborate your statement to have seen this person and visited those premises.'

Strictly speaking, he was only allowed to put questions to clear up ambiguities in the statement. But as far as he was concerned these were ambiguities. The lawyers could argue about it later.

He reluctantly asked Gredek to sign the 'Conclusion of statement' card and insert it in the timing safe.

Gredek let himself out of the cabinet, and stretched his cramped limbs. 'Well, Mr Smith, I trust you got everything you wanted?'

'Am I the only one that wanted it, Gredek?'

Only the eyes were alive in the blank impassive face. 'You must be the judge of that, Mr Smith.'

Chapter XIX

As O'Brien was saying next day, 'It's time we had a pop at the bloody general,' so the same proposal was raised in more formal terms with Police Commissioner Rachette.

Smith would have preferred to have 'had a pop' first at the mysterious Menderfield, about whom so little was known; even the Special Branch file contained only his surname and a quote 'said to be an administrative assistant on B.F.M. secretariat.' There was no photograph, only a vague description of a well-built man in his late thirties, a description now enhanced by further detail supplied by Gredek, but nothing to determine the man's history.

Rachette's discussions with Swarbrick, Hicks and Fairchild dealt mainly with securing an interview with the general and Menderfield, under the most advantageous conditions for interrogation, and clearly the ideal place would be at Scotland Yard itself.

This, however, would mean inviting them to attend without divulging the reasons and as Rachette said, 'after all I am not asking them to take tea with me.'

Fairchild pointed out even if the general and Menderfield did attend without the formality of explanation, they would no doubt alert the Press and other media, and attend in the full glare of all the publicity they could get. And with a pettifoggery of lawyers behind them.

In the end it was decided to do the only thing they could. Simply make sure the man was at home, knock on the door, bowl straight in and play it by ear.

Hicks was not prepared to play away from home, and it was decided Fairchild and Smith would inspect the General.

The manservant who admitted Fairchild and Smith to the eighteenth-floor suite in the huge complex of luxury apartments in that part of the City of London known as the Barbican, could not have been more of an ex-soldier had he presented arms as they passed through into a wide-windowed living-room.

'The Gin'ril will be wid yez in a few minutes, gintlemen. In the meantime I am required to see to your refreshments.' He stood poised over decanters and bottles with a glass in his left hand, awaiting orders to load and fire.

'No, thank you,' Fairchild raised an apologetic palm, 'later perhaps, er Mr . . . ?' He smiled enquiringly.

'Lucas, sor.' He replaced the glass, his face showing puzzlement, and even disappointment at Fairchild's refusal. He repeated his name, 'Lucas,' and turned to the door. 'If there is nothing else, gintlemen?'

'By the way, is Mr Menderfield with the general?' Fairchild enquired.

Lucas submitted a reproachful inclination of the head that said in his master's affairs there was only sublime ignorance, with no remembered past and no forseeable future. Only an immediate and non-attributable present.

'That I wouldn't know, sor,' he shook his close-cropped head and it took on the rounded solidity of a cannon ball. 'No sor, that I wouldn't know.' Lucas solemnly closed the door.

Smith had been taking stock of the room. There by the picture window was the antique brass telescope. On the book-lined wall were six of the titles mentioned by Gredek. The rich dark-red leather furniture, the Matisse above the Adam fireplace, the thick creamy-blue Chinese carpet, the heavy square brass-bound occasional table with a nineteenth-century map of Africa under the protective glass top. All were as mentioned by Gredek in answer to his questions.

'I am sorry to have kept you waiting.' The figure in the doorway was even more impressive than it was on a public platform. Smith saw that the blazing eyes were not enhanced by artificial means. They moved steadily from Fairchild to himself, and devoured every detail. The general would remember them twenty years from now ... if he lived that long.

'Please,' he approached, both hands gesturing towards the chairs, 'sit down and tell me what I can do to help you.'

'Before reaching matters that concern you personally, sir, may I ask if Mr Menderfield is with you?' asked Fairchild.

'No, he is not,' the reply was curt with a trace of 'and mind your own business.'

'Can you assist us as to his whereabouts?' Fairchild persisted.

'Beyond saying that he is abroad on matters ... on confidential matters, concerning the Britain First Movement and the election, I am not prepared to comment on his movements, for obvious reasons.'

'I am afraid the reasons are not obvious, sir,' replied Fairchild, 'at least to me.'

'Then sir, as a politically uncommitted police officer your lack of perception in such matters is perhaps to be commended, but as you must be aware, the demands upon me at the present moment are too heavy to provide time for esoteric explanations.'

Smith was tempted to say 'Bullshit' but instead he uttered another single word, 'Gredek!'

'I beg your pardon?' The balzing eyes were shaded under lowering brows.

'Staff Sergeant Richard Gredek, Royal Army Ordnance Corps, do you know him?'

The smile was politely pitying, 'I know many N.C.O.s in the British army, and even more N.C.O.s know me. I hope I will not incriminate myself if I say that to the best of my recollection, the name means nothing.'

Smith took out a photograph and passed it to the general. He gave it an uninterested glance and handed it back.

'No, I can't say it means anything to me. You must appreciate, and I have no wish to be snobbish or superior, that as a senior officer in the army, one may see N.C.O.s without having occasion to remember them.'

Fairchild intervened and said, 'Then sir, we must return to Mr Menderfield. Will you tell us what his position is on your staff and how long you have known him?'

The winter sun slid below the window and perched on the western horizon, magnified by the atmosphere into a menacing red giant. The shadows deepened in the room and in the general's eyes. Light-sensitive cells brought power into concealed panels that began to glow around the walls.

The door opened and Lucas, summoned by some means Smith could not see within the general's reach, entered and stood to attention by the decanters.

The general gave them a courteous order. 'I am sure you will join me. It seems an appropriate time.'

Silently and unbidden, gold velvet curtains slid across the darkening glass. Smith had no doubt every word mentioned in the room was being recorded on tape. 'Scotch and water please,' he said.

Fairchild joined the general in a dry sherry and murmured an appreciation of its quality. Mulqueen settled back in his chair. 'Deputy Assistant Commissioner,' he began, then with an amused and quizzical curl of the lips added, 'My goodness, you chaps, if you will forgive me for saying so, do have the most portentous titles.'

'I respond without offence to Fairchild,' said the latter quietly, 'and if we could continue with Mr Menderfield's background?'

The general sipped his sherry. 'His background, as you call it, was in one of the more obscure branches of the Civil Service. He became interested in the aims and objects of Britain First, resigned, and offered his services to the movement through Lionel Landon. I interviewed him and found him admirably qualified to fill the post of my personal assistant. I am not prepared to discuss his full range of duties other than to say they are quite lawful and mainly concern the administration and day-to-day running of the movement.'

'I am afraid we may differ about the legality of certain of his actions,' said Fairchild grimly.

'Legality and morality are not necessarily synonymous,' the blue eyes were challenging, 'neither are law and justice, nevertheless I would be surprised and disappointed if Menderfield has done anything illegal.'

'How about conspiracy and incitement to murder?' asked Smith.

The general rose to his feet and reaching for the decanter leaned across and topped up Fairchild's glass. He then filled his own to the brim and carried it to eye-level where he held it for a long moment, as if to demonstrate the steadiness of his hand. He sipped slowly and said, 'I presume you will be more specific?'

'Specifically the murders of Sir Maxwell Steype, Arthur Hammertoe, and three other police officers, the late Home Secretary, various Members of Parliament and assorted civil servants.' Obtaining no immediate reaction, Smith continued, 'We have a man in custody, the man Gredek, he has made a statement confessing to these murders, saying they were committed either directly at your command or indirectly through your instructions to Menderfield.'

'And you believe this nonsense?' Mulqueen's voice carried just the right amount of incredulity.

'He has given a very accurate description of this room where he says he discussed with you and Menderfield the action that resulted in the Treasury massacre.'

'My dear man, in the past three months there must have been at least two hundred people in and out of this apartment, journalists, T.V. people, members of the movement, trade-union officials, any one of whom could have passed on a description of the room.'

'He also mentions a country house near Camberley.'

The general laughed, 'Dammit man, I gave a television interview at Sperrin Point six months ago. The interior of the house and the grounds were shown on every television screen in the country. This fellow is really having you on, y'know.'

Fairchild restored some gravity and seriousness to the matter. 'General, you do realize Gredek has made a very lengthy statement in which he reiterates over and over again his meetings with you and Menderfield at which these murders were discussed and he implicates both of you on almost every page.'

He paused as though to let the weight of his words sink in.

He went on, 'Indeed, I have to tell you there is evidence to suspect your complicity in these crimes and for that reason inform you, you need not say anything unless you wish to do so as whatever you say may be given in evidence.'

The general rose to his feet and towered over Fairchild. 'You are insulting, sir, you abuse my hospitality and worst of all you insult my intelligence.' Instinctively Fairchild also got to his feet as if to reduce the velocity of the words falling upon him.

'I have presided at enough courts martial to know a confession is only evidence against the person making it. You come to my home with your tawdry bluff expecting me to crumble at the behest of some maniac who abuses my name, you caution me not to speak as if I were a common criminal. I will speak sir, and, by God, you may have occasion to regret my words.'

Without turning, but knowing nevertheless, he was there, he said, 'Lucas, show these ... persons out.'

As Smith went past him, he gave the general a wry smile and said, 'The Crown may decide to let him out and call him as a prosecution witness. Think on that one, General.'

He did not have to think on it. The words came straight back at Smith. 'Then to all his other crimes, you will have to add that of perjury.'

Fairchild accepted the abrupt termination of the interview philosophically. As they went down in the lift he said in cheerful tones, 'Opening round, Smithie, opening round. A little bit of sparring, a little bit of feeling out. When I saw we were not going to get anywhere with him I deliberately threw the caution at him hoping he would react as he did. Much better for him to throw us out than for us to retire with our tails between our legs, voluntarily.'

Smith gave a non-committal grunt in reply. He had not been entirely in favour of interviewing the general on his home ground. He had reckoned the general would be shrewd enough and tough enough not to be panicked by the fact he had been named in Gredek's statement. If the Attorney General were to consider using Gredek for the Crown it would mean filing a *nolle prosequi* or offering no evidence and letting him out completely. Even then, would the word of a Hungarian-born homosexual army deserter convict the general? It might if they got a jury of card-carrying party members somewhere to the left of Joe Stalin.

Better to have waited until they had more evidence. But what evidence ...? Where was it to come from? Well, better to have waited anyway until ... until they found Menderfield. And just how obscure was the Civil Service department he had sprung from?

He saw Craddock at his home that night. He had been putting it off since Gredek made his confession, but tomorrow Gredek was appearing at Bow Street Magistrates Court and would be committed for trial at the Old Bailey. He had asked for only one witness to give formal evidence ... Smith, in order that his confession should be placed on record.

Gredek had also asked for restrictions on Press reports to be lifted, so by late tomorrow afternoon it would all be out. Ian Craddock's cry of 'Mother' would echo round the world, and the blood of Sir Maxwell Steype drip from the pages of every paper.

There would be no rehabilitation, no rebirth for Ian Craddock. The neurotic mother-loving father-hating youth. A Freudian monster. Why had he written the coded letter? Remorse? Revenge upon his Comrade Soldiers? Or did he see the possibility of killing his father from the grave as he led police against Gredek and the heavily armed soldiers of Nevis Mews? He knew his old man, and despite his age and rank he would be at the front in that kind of action.

It was these thoughts that took Smith to Craddock's door and into his living-room. He related the details of Gredek's confession, leaving nothing out, offering no hope of rehabilitating the name of his son.

Craddock took it quite calmly, 'And do you believe him, Owen?'

'Yes.' He could not keep a defensive hardness from his face. 'It sounds true and it fits.'

'Oh aye, the bit about Ian sounds true – and it fits, but the confession as a whole. Do you think it is all true?'

The confession had lain on his stomach like an undigested meal; now Craddock was prodding his guts. 'How the hell do I know. We have to accept it ... you know that. All the others are dead, we only have Gredek. Leopold knows nothing. He was a hole Gredek crawled into.' He realized his words and added without smiling, 'In every sense.' He wished he didn't sound so plaintive.

A low rising moan from upstairs was followed by a tapping on the ceiling. Craddock excused himself and shortly his gruff voice sounded on the landing.

'Easy, woman. I've got you now, just take your time.'

Stifled gasps of pain followed heavy dragging movements, a choked scream. The bodily functions of Craddock's pain-racked, bed-ridden wife required frequent attention. Smith wondered why he didn't get somebody in to look after her. He must be able to afford it. Perhaps not in the early days, but now he had the rank and his son was off his hands . . .

Did a life that ran from pit boy to soldier to Deputy Assistant Commissioner require such dour rejection of the family entity? Or was he, were they, expiating some secret parental sin. 'He screamed – "Mother," and started slashing.' Gredek's words.

'Aye well. So you believe him then?' Craddock was suddenly back in the room, wiping his hands on a small towel. Smith turned in his chair; he had intended offering sympathetic words. They were obviously not wanted.

'At the moment I don't disbelieve him.'

'Oh . . . you are getting subtle, Owen. Subtle and devious. A sure sign of being fitted for higher rank.'

He resented Craddock's heavy sarcasm but said nothing.

'Did it occur to you, Owen, Gredek might be even more subtle, even more devious? Did it occur to you what will happen to Mulqueen and the B.F.M. when Gredek's statement comes out? The whole great enterprise will melt away, the people who were finding new pride, new discipline and new responsibility with Mulqueen . . . they will be broken . . . shattered. They will turn on him and tear down everything he has built.'

He held his fists clenched together under Smith's face, supplicating, yet somehow threatening. 'Dae ye no see it, Owen? Dae ye no see it . . .? Gredek was the leader, the dedicated leader, the Trotsky of 1917, the Commissar for War, the creator of a Red Army in this country. He sacrificed a few of his soldiers and he may even sacrifice himself. But there is a Lenin behind him. And a Stalin waiting in the darkness of the day after tomorrow. Gredek was never with the general. Dae ye hear me . . . never!'

Smith stared at the lined face, at the pocket of spittle gathering in the corner of the mouth. The lead in his stomach liquefied . . . the back hall office, the keys, Ian Craddock . . . Hammertoe.

'It was you . . . you were the general's man. Not Hammertoe. He found out . . . you had him killed by the B.F.M.'

Craddock's hands fell loosely to his side. His head fell back and he turned closed, blind eyes to the ceiling.

'Ach, Owen . . . Owen.' He flapped a weary hand and went across to the sideboard. He held a bottle of malt whisky up to the light. 'I don't seem so well stocked as I used to be.' He pushed a half-filled glass into Smith's reluctant hand.

'I always said you were good, Owen. You could paint pictures in the dark.' He sank into a leather chair by the fire. 'But this time ... you have been putting a jigsaw together and you are forcing the wrong pieces into the wrong place.'

He drank deeply and let the hand bearing the glass fall into his lap. 'I got myself in the position no good policeman should ever be. I got myself in the middle.' He looked up, challenging, 'Yes, Owen, I was the general's man.' Then with quiet menace, 'And I still am.'

Smith said nothing but he felt the chill of his nakedness in Nevis Mews.

Craddock saw it and laughed, 'Dinna fash yoursel, Owen. Nobody's going to jump out of the woodwork on top of ye.' He motioned Smith to a chair.

'Sit down for God's sake. You are making me nervous, standing there ready for anything. There is only a man, old before his time, and a dying woman in this house.'

Smith found himself smiling at his fears. For some reason the carpet-slippers on Craddock's feet made him feel safe.

Craddock turned a sad face into the heat of the fire, the flames reflecting in his eyes.

'The B.F.M. was better served by intelligence sources on left-wing activists than Special Branch, or the security services. We heard that a cell somewhere in north London had acquired a cache of arms, so when Steype told me he had this approach from Wardoe ...' He turned and saw Smith's widening eyes.

'Yes, it was me he told. He wouldn't confide in Hammertoe, they hated each other's guts. It's true, as Gredek says, Steype thought it was nonsense, but I told him there might be something in it and advised him to meet Wardoe.' Craddock held up a solemn hand.

'Believe me, I never thought for a moment they would kill Steype. Once he had the information I was going to wipe up the whole bunch ... But there was Ian ... I knew he was tied up with some militants; I wasn't sure if it was the same crowd ... I didn't think it was. I knew he was doing a bit of industrial agitation and in with the rent-a-mob organizers. But I couldn't take the risk.' His face went back to the flames.

'About this time he was ringing home every night to speak to his mother. Her condition had been getting progressively worse, but she hadn't taken to her bed at the time.' He eyed the ceiling, then settled his face again on the fire, seemingly lost in the red coal canyons. Smith got up quietly and poured the last few drops from the bottle into Craddock's glass.

'So when he rang up, I told him if he was mixed up with someone named Wardoe he had better get himself out of it for his mother's sake.'

'Then why did they go for Steype?' Craddock stilled Smith's words with an angry glance.

'They got it out of Wardoe. Don't you see, as soon as they put it to him, that nasty little queer would throw it in their faces like a spiteful bitch. He thought they would panic and run when he mentioned Steype's name, or more probably, from what you told me, he tried to blackmail them into going through with his stock-exchange attack.'

'And Hammertoe, why did they kill Hammertoe?'

'Arthur? Poor old Arthur.' Craddock leaned forward into the fire, his hand flexing against the heat as if trying to pluck something from the flames.

'I could have saved Arthur ... That clever wee lad, Dewlip, he found the traces of cuttlefish in the back hall office while you were at the post-mortem on Steype. Then he bumped into Hammertoe as he was coming along the corridor and told him all about it, to let him know just what a clever wee lad he was. Arthur sent for me. I thought it was about the row we had over the use of the conference room. I apologized for my behaviour. Then he told me how he had met Ian in the foyer during the previous week. He was Ian's godfather, ye know.'

Smith hadn't known, but nodded his head in agreement rather than interrupt the flow of words.

'I could see Arthur was worried. He knew Ian was on the floor financially, although he knew nothing about the political path the boy had taken. Rather than hand him a few quid out in the open he took him into the back hall office. They had a talk about this and that. Ian told him he was doing voluntary social work.'

The cackling laugh faded as Craddock wiped his mouth and chin with a soiled handkerchief. He spat hugely into the fire; the mucus globule caught on the bars of the grate and lay hissing and steaming in a welter of black ash. The sound seemed to fill the room.

'Arthur, Arthur, you poor old bastard.' Craddock spoke to the fire, then turning heat-reddened eyes on Smith, said with a brisk incredulity, 'He went for a piss, you know. Left Ian in the office ...'

Smith saw what was coming but allowed his face to ask the question.

'When he returned Ian was standing by the key cabinet, just standing there with his back to the cabinet. Arthur remembered the sliding glass panel was pushed back. It should have been closed and locked when the office was unattended, but as he had pushed Inspector Colby out of the office when he went in with Ian, he didn't give it much thought.'

'Ian did, though,' said Smith softly.

'Aye, he did that.' Smith wondered if the sadness in Craddock's voice was for his son or Hammertoe. Perhaps it was for both of them. 'He knew the discovery of Steype's body would lead to the building being torn apart for clues. He knew that the cuttlefish would crumble all over the carpet. He knew Hammertoe would remember ...' Craddock's voice trailed away as his face again sought something distant in the burning coals. 'I told Arthur there was nothing to worry about. The boy was doing fine. I believed it myself, or I deluded myself into believing it, at least for the first few days.'

Smith remembered. He remembered the shelter on the green. The smell of urine from men who had waited in the cold ... the other thicker smell. Hash, Neaterkin had said.

Gredek needed no photograph to put a bullet into Hammertoe's skull. Hammertoe had been identified by the pointing finger of Ian Craddock, who crouched beside Gredek in the shelter, hoping it was not too late to erase Hammertoe's memory for ever.

'What are you going to do?' Smith broke the long silence.

The crouched figure by the fire straightened back into the chair. 'Weel now ... I'm not going to repeat all that inside a Clutterbuck cabinet, if that's what you're thinking.'

'It might help the cause you believe in so much, if you made a statement to counteract Gredek's confession.'

This time there was real humour in Craddock's laugh. 'Are

you trying to con me into making a statement, Owen? Are you really trying to con me?'

Smith felt embarrassed, he rose uneasily to his feet. 'It's up to you.' He tried to sound cold and indifferent.

'You know it wouldn't change a damn thing. My association with the movement, my illegal association with the movement. And my son, my murdering, parricidal son ... Oh, yes, he saw me in that window at the Treasury building. Another truth among the Gredek lies. He did give the order to shoot into the room. He knew I was in there.'

Craddock came to his feet, and again the fists pounded the air in front of Smith's chest.

'He wanted me dead ...'

Smith took gentle hold of the trembling arms. 'Yes, I thought that might have been the way of it.'

Craddock tore himself away, resentful of the sympathy.

'Come on now, don't be so bloody stupid.' Smith tried rough cajolery, and knew it was a mistake as soon as the words left his mouth. Craddock looked at him with hard contempt.

'Dae ye think you're talking to some frightened wee bank clerk who has been caught with his hand in the till. Don't you worry about me, Owen ... Oh, I've been depressed and I've been worried. But panic, suicide – awa hame, Owen. I'll make up my mind in a couple of days and then I'll come in and see you.' He grasped Smith's arm in a gesture of reconciliation. 'You may be right. Maybe I'll make a statement after all.'

Smith knew he was being brushed off with a lie, but for the moment there was nothing he could do about it.

He had to stop the car before reaching the density of main road traffic. His mind was not capable of rejecting the persistent images and controlling the car on the busy road, now treacherous under thick falling sleet, churning into a half-frozen brown and white slush.

'Gredek equals Trotsky, therefore Ian Craddock equals Lenin and "X" equals Stalin.' Smith felt his scorn turn to anger at the implication he was so naïve as to accept such a stupid equation. Who the hell did old Craddock think he was talking to? Did he really believe that crap?

'It's political bullshit. The kind of rubbish the general would

207

spout from a public platform. Good for a headline in every paper. The old reliable political formula – when the coaxing, kidding and promising wears thin: Get out the big hammer and put the frighteners in.'

But Craddock did believe it. No doubt about that . . . but then Craddock was the general's man. Craddock was reaching back into his past for a stability he had once known. A patriarchy of dutiful wife and obedient children. When a man's professional standing was not threatened by social or domestic revolution. When a thief was a thief and not an inadequate social casualty seeking an outlet for a repressed libido. Craddock wanted the assurance of order today and the certainty of the big 'O' for Order tomorrow. Smith wished he could really dislike the old sod.

It all came back to Gredek stepping out of the shadows at Nevis Mews . . . stepping out of the shadows . . . ? Ackerman.

Out of the miasma swirling in his mind, a particle of matter solidified and grew like a tumour. And it brought pain, greater anger . . . and fear.

For two hours he sat in the car, until anger subdued fear, but the pain remained, throbbing high inside the front of his head.

With the weather and the passing of midnight, the traffic had all but disappeared. He pushed open the car door against a wedge of snow and brushed clear the windows and bonnet. The snow fell away in heavy lumps, fast becoming brittle and sharp under the increasing cold. Swirling snow still fell, light dry flakes, covering even the dirty slush in the middle of the road in a clean white sheet.

The wheels spun several times, then gripped on the nearside. The car crabbed into the road and straightened out. Smith was going back to the Yard to wait for Swarbrick – not Fairchild – Swarbrick . . . and possibly Rachette.

He slept fitfully through the early hours on the large armchair in his office. By seven he was awake, his decisions made. The pain had left his head as clarity of thought and action settled the turmoil of his mind. There was phlegm and a slight ache in the back of his throat but it disappeared after hot coffee from the first trolley of the day.

The lock on the door of Commander Bastwick's shower

yielded to his strip of celluloid and he made prolonged and luxurious use of the hot water. Like all dedicated and unmarried C.I.D. officers, his office knew more of him than the flat where he lived. He kept there a complete change of fresh clothing. The new shirt had a stiff crispness pleasing to his well-scrubbed skin. The cleaners had done a good job on the dark-blue pin-stripe. The crêpe-soled suedes were thrown into the bottom of his cupboard and the highly polished Oxfords dusted off with a yellow rag.

Smith adjusted the tip of white handkerchief in the breast pocket and centred the knot in his tie. He was ready for his day in Court, but first ...

They arrived together just before eight-thirty. Smith sat upright and stiff on the bench outside the Commissioner's suite. He rose politely as Rachette and his deputy came along the corridor. Swarbrick eyed the neatness of his dress with wary approval.

'You waiting to see me, Smith?' There was curiosity and suspicion in the question.

Smith kept his voice soft and respectful, 'Yes, sir. Just as Gredek was waiting for me.'

If Rachette heard, it made no impression. 'Won't this keep until later, Smith, there are several urgent matters I have to discuss with the Brigadier.'

Swarbrick smoothly interposed his hand in front of Smith's face. 'I believe, Commissioner, Mr Smith quite properly wishes clarification on the form the court proceedings will take this morning. I haven't had the opportunity of putting him in the picture.'

Rachette snapped his lips impatiently and wheeled towards his office. 'Do please be brief.'

The deputy watched the door close, then jerked his head in the direction of his own office. As Smith entered he closed the door gently and stood with his back pressed against it. His hands were behind his back, flat against the panel, his legs angled forward, and spread as if to barricade the door against intrusion. The pelt of black hair shone as the drooping head speculated upon the carpet between Smith's feet. The head slowly raised.

'What are you up to, Smith?'

Smith drew a forefinger across his throat. 'Up to here.'

'A significant gesture. I trust it doesn't mean you are going to metaphorically bleed all over my carpet.'

He ignored the words. 'I don't mind being used. I recognized a long time ago I was an instrument, a tool in this job to be used. But not to be ... abused ... not to be manipulated.'

Swarbrick was unimpressed. 'The subtlety of the distinction escapes me, Smith. What do you want?'

'I want to know what sort of deal you made with Gredek.'

The reaction was slight, a mere twitching of the formless nose. Swarbrick pushed himself away from the door and went to his desk. He glanced through the small pile of papers awaiting his decisions. An Interpol message flimsy retained his attention for a few minutes, then he put it back on the desk.

'Unlike Special Branch, you don't have a great deal to do with security in the greater meaning of the word. Do you, Smith?' The question was rhetorical, he did not expect an answer. 'It is like working in a compartment in a long-distance train. Other people are working in different compartments along the train, but they are only concerned with what is happening in their own compartment. They are quite happy with the knowledge they will, in due course, all reach their destination together. Only the ticket collector goes along the corridor from compartment to compartment. And on this trip, Smith, you are just a passenger in a second-class compartment.'

He dredged the words from the gathering mucus in the back of his throat. 'But this particular passenger has decided to go along the corridor for a shit.'

'You haven't got a ticket, Smith. You are in danger of being thrown off the train ... and in view of your bowel movement, it will not be standing at a station.'

Swarbrick added quietly, 'You see, I know all about your muted conversation with Routledge in the pub.' He then became slightly conciliatory, like a hanging judge passing a life sentence. 'Perhaps your displeasure is understandable at the knowledge I visited your prisoner with someone who is not a police officer, but I would have thought at your rank there was a realization that matters of national security must be conducted with some discretion.'

Smith felt the sweat on his forehead and the pain was

210

returning to his head. It only increased his determination. 'Right now I am not concerned about that particular visit and that particular deal.' He drew back his lips at the throbbing pain.

'Don't snarl unless you intend to bite.'

Smith went for the throat. 'It is the first visit and the first deal that interests me. The one that was made at Nevis Mews before I got there.' The black head looked up from the papers.

'I was stupid enough, egotistical enough, to assume I was the only one to figure out the Andalucian link with the Alhambra radio shop. I knew Brightside, Woulover and the funny people from across the river were buzzing around everything we did like wasps in a jam-jar. I thought they were playing their usual silly inconsequential games. After we found the list, they played over Wardoe's records as if it was a promenade concert. They indexed and cross-referenced every article in the room. They broke young Craddock's letter before even his old man grasped the significance. All they had to do was check the Foreign Office lists of British casualties in the Spanish civil war. The misquoted date and place took them right to the bloody door long before I ever got there . . . But by then it had nothing to do with the police. The funny people took it over.'

Smith glowered into the steady narrowed eyes, the cold mask of a face rock-hard, but again the twitch in the corner of a nostril. He waited for a challenge, a threat, a denial; but Swarbrick said nothing.

'They knew I would get there sometime. That's why Gredek was waiting for me. He never saw me go into the mews, he was waiting for me. I thought perhaps I had slipped up. Not seen him, but damn it, I know I wasn't followed into the mews.'

'So what was the deal, Mr Swarbrick?' He deliberately applied the civilian connotation. The steady eyes did not even blink, but a touch of colour appeared on the high cheek bones.

'As I see it, Gredek deserted after the Steype – Wardoe killings. He couldn't run his depot and his S.O.P. at the same time, especially as they were now at war. But he needed access to the depot. He needed Ackerman to supply an enlarging army, so he got hold of him just after my visit to the depot and fooled him into thinking he was secretly working for the General and the B.F.M. It was an ideal story for Ackerman. The fool probably thought he might become a Staff Sergeant someday; that would tempt him more than money. I will even give him credit for thinking he was serving his country.'

The pain tightened across his temples. Deep inside there was a spasm of uncertainty.

You are over-simplifying, Smith. He remembered the cold, contemptuous put-down and flexed quivering stomach muscles against a rising panic.

'But the crunch came for Gredek when the funny people got hold of him. Is that what gave them the idea? When he told them how he had recruited Ackerman? If Gredek could fool Ackerman, why couldn't he fool the country if his story was prepared by experts!'

He gulped heavily for air and looked for some reaction in the set figure before him. There was none, only an impassive disdain.

'I buggered it up, didn't I?' His contempt was not entirely for himself. 'I was supposed to take Ackerman alive. The poor fat little bastard was presented to me on a plate, but I broke the dish. He was expected to spill the lot, wasn't he? All the bullshit Gredek fed into him about working for the B.F.M. The natural, believeable support to the mixture of truth and lies manufactured for Gredek.'

He felt the weight of Swarbrick's authority boring into him. Smith resisted it and ploughed on. 'We were to keep Ackerman all nicely locked away for a few days while Gredek established his Soldiers of the People in Appleshaw Cottage, where clever Willie Woulover found them. What did he really do? See them from the window of his compartment as the train went by?'

The collar of his new shirt was beginning to chafe his neck. The room had become very warm. He pulled the tie open and loosened his collar-button. Was Swarbrick assessing it as a sign of weakness? In his mind he cursed the heat, the pain behind his eyes, and now the ache returning to his throat. What a time to start a cold. An eye watering, head splitting, nose running cold. He coughed into his handkerchief then drew it across his sweating face. He tried to keep his voice steady.

'They had to be wiped out, didn't they? They didn't have Gredek's status? His family connections? After all, you couldn't row them all into the act. I wonder what Gredek told them when he ducked out before the shooting started. "No surrender, Comrades. You have nothing to lose but your lives"?'

He loosened his tie still further, the stiffness had gone from the collar. It now felt limp and cold like a damp rag round his neck. His words had a nasal impediment.

'You lost Ackerman. You couldn't afford to lose Gredek. He had to be convincingly arrested. It would show out if he just gave himself up. He was told to get Leopold to apply for a passport knowing it would lead me to him.'

Smith let his tongue search the corners of his mouth for moisture. His throat was drying on him. The jug of water on the bookcase had a tempting cool clarity. But to ask for a glass of water meant a return to disciplined courtesy. He gathered what saliva he could from the recesses of his mouth and swallowed. A ball of emery paper seemed to turn over behind his larynx.

An intercom buzzed angrily on Swarbrick's desk. He fingered the control. 'How much longer are you going to be, Morgan?' There was impatient petulance in Rachette's demand.

'Mr Smith is still with me, Commissioner. He has a high temperature and is hallucinating.'

'Have you sent for the doctor?'

'No, I think his condition requires another form of therapy. It should respond to treatment. You will recall we considered the possibility.'

Smith was at the door. The handle turned in his sweaty palm; it was locked. It took him some time to turn round. Swarbrick was standing by the bookcase pouring water into a glass. He held it out to him. His expression was solemn, sad even, but not unfriendly.

'You really are remarkable, Smith. You have an intuitive facility for getting yourself into situations from which you suddenly want to retreat but you always leave it too late. Your ability to arrive at an abstract conclusion consistent with the truth is, of course, documented on your personal file. But this time . . .' Smith gulped down the water greedily. He stood with his shoulders sagging, panting a little, as if gathering strength. He retained the glass, grasping it deep in his hand like a grenade.

'This time,' Swarbrick went on, 'you have excelled yourself. You have also committed yourself irrevocably. There definitely is no retreat. No loose knots. The gun has been correctly loaded, fully cocked, and pointed right at you. But it's your finger on the trigger. Pull it and you blow yourself away.'

He returned to the chair behind his desk and picked up the Interpol message. 'Your visit to Mulqueen seems to have provoked some reaction. Mr Menderfield was killed last night in Zurich. Hit-and-run accident.' He initialled the message and marked it 'No Further Action'.

'No doubt the general reached a certain but erroneous conclusion as a result of your interview. Unfortunately for Mr Menderfield, the general does not have your depth of perception.'

Feeling he had gained an equality of terms, Smith refilled his glass. He made no request to do so. He was beginning to feel slightly less feverish.

'Menderfield,' he said, 'was just a bag-carrier – another bit of detail to give added veracity to Gredek's story, like the descriptions of the house in the country and the flat.'

'He carried some very valuable bags.' Swarbrick did not look up from the papers he was studying. He seemed able to carry on a conversation and at the same time absorb the material before him. 'He was Lionel Landon's man more than the general's. A sort of financial secretary to the Movement – Landon, of course, being the banker. And his bank little more than a money laundry for syndicated crime interests in the States, buying into legitimate business in Europe. The three million in bullion from the airport robbery last year? That went through the Landon Bank, as does most of the cash proceeds from major crimes both here and abroad.' He looked up at Smith's deepening frown. 'Oh, you didn't realize that? Fairchild will be pleased to know his Commercial Fraud Squad is beyond your powers of omniscience.'

The bantering, condescending Welsh accent had disappeared, the mocking 'boyo' no longer used.

'Let us suppose a deal, as you call it, was made with Gredek. A deal that was only conceived when Ian Craddock's letter led you, and others before you, to Nevis Mews. That advantage was taken of the situation to produce a solution to a problem that had long eluded ... certain parties – an end to what they saw as a far greater, more dangerous evil, than the Soldiers of the People.'

Swarbrick slapped his palms on the top of his desk and rose to his feet. He strode the carpet as he spoke. 'There are many differences, many distinctions between revolution and civil war, apart from the ethnic, political or ideological issues that divide the factions. The main difference, the essential difference, is that in revolution –' he swept the flat of his hand across his body like a sabre cut '– the factions are stratified, the social layer below wants to get on top. Or the layer that was on top wants to get back on top.'

He stopped suddenly and gave an apologetic shrug. 'I'm sorry, Smith. One sometimes forgets one is not lecturing to a class of rather immature cadets. But the point I wanted to make is that what we will be faced with if the Britain First Movement gains power, as they will unless we stop them, is not revolution, but civil war. Not the bottom lot trying to get on top, but –' he slashed the air downwards from shoulder to hip '– one complete cross-section of the population ranged against the other.'

Smith felt the salt in the perspiration stinging his eyes. He reached for the water jug and swore savagely. 'My God! You *are* going to use Gredek's confession . . . Just how long did you have him learning his lines before I dragged him out of Agar Crescent? This greasy imitation Che Guevara. And what's in it for him? Don't tell me, it would sound too trite. This must be the biggest fit-up since the crucifixion of Christ.'

'Don't preach at me, Smith. Hypocrisy does not become you.' Swarbrick massaged the back of his neck. The gesture held an indication of weariness. Again he took to pacing the floor.

'Suppose we actually were at war? Would not the introduction of a deception plan, a subterfuge, a deliberately planted lie, that so confused the enemy, we won the battle . . . Would that not be a commendable act? A story to be retold with pride? Why is the lie that defames one man, and in so doing prevents a war, prevents the self-destruction of our country, why is that lie so despicable?'

'Perhaps because you know it is a lie. Perhaps, because the war may never happen.'

'Oh, it will happen. In this age of violence and impotence . . . and war was always a good remedy for impotence . . . In this age of greed and envy, an envy that in some primitive, mysterious way, is of the war in which we think our fathers found some fulfilment, a greater manhood. However much we despise or pretend to despise them, and their war, in our country there is now a generation in search of a war of their own. Give some of

215

them ... give most of them, a gun and a cause and watch them kill one another. The psychologists used to say everybody should have the opportunity of acting out their own fantasies in controlled conditons, but now there are no controls, only causes, and men who represent the causes. Destroy them and you destroy the cause. We cannot afford the luxury, or even find the excuse for a patriotic war against a foreign enemy – so we will go hunting for an enemy within ourselves.'

He stopped pacing. Smith found himself wondering how old the man was. He subconsciously hoped he was older than himself. He could then more readily accept his words.

'The undefined lines of civil war are being drawn in the minds of the people. The cities, the streets and the houses are divided. The battle cry on both sides will be "Destroy to Create".'

Swarbrick gave a wry grin, 'And the general would win his war, if we allowed him to have it. After all, you and I will be on his side. We who are disciplined, responsible and believe in order. We may not be Rightists, Smith, but we like things to be right.'

He fished around in his pocket for the key and unlocked the office door. Smith made no move. 'So why do it?' he asked. 'Why destroy him?'

'What will we win? There will be an Appleshaw Cottage at every street corner in the country and they will not be full of murdering extremists this time.' Swarbrick turned to the window and stood uncharacteristically with hands in his pockets. 'What was that catch-phrase Mulqueen was so fond of? Freedom and responsibility are what some people will die for. Liberty and licence are what others will kill for ... Well, there will be a lot of dying and a lot of killing and nobody will be able to tell the difference.'

He swung on his heel and faced Smith. 'And afterwards, what have we got for a country? Spain, circa 1939? Admittedly, we have not got a great deal at present, and these argumentative idiots sitting on their leather benches down the street are damnably expensive, I know, but I think we should hang on to them. They will be cheaper in the long run.'

Smith found his anger fading. The spirit had gone out of him. Get it over with. Too many people leaning on him. Craddock? He owed him nothing. Another who had manipulated him. Get it over with and get to bed and sleep ... And what about Hammertoe?

He repeated it aloud. 'And what about Hammertoe? Did you have to use Hammertoe? Destroy his name?'

'His wife pre-deceased him years ago. There is no other family. It was logical and necessary. He was the type. He was of the B.F.M. even if he was not in the B.F.M. No one will suffer.'

'What he represented will suffer.'

Swarbrick came forward slowly. 'Would you rather it was Craddock and what he still represents? We cannot prove he was the General's man. Can you, Smith?'

He just stood and said nothing. There was nothing he could say. Deceit was a bloodless device. They always gave fraudsmen lighter sentences because they never hurt people ... physically, directly. The victim got little sympathy; *caveat emptor*, let the buyer beware. The fever shook him like a goat in the mouth of a tiger. Swarbrick was looking at him compassionately ...? Pityingly ...? Contemptuously ...?

He grasped his shoulders to still the trembling; his mind in a fishbowl, disembodied, suspended above the room; endowed with a clarity obliquely magnified, distorted. Where was he in all this? What was he ...? A knife, a surgeon's knife to excise an evil growth? No, it was not as clinical as that, not as clean. An antibody, a white cell rushing blindly forward to destroy an infection? The detached clarity of his vision refused him such comfort. Gredek was the antibody. Refined and synthesized out of an opposing bacillus ... He was merely the needle penetrating the skin into the bloodstream. A needle thrust home by weight of the enormity of which he was part, of which Swarbrick, Rachette, and all the others were a part. And beyond them all, a finite entity, but somehow elusive, always beyond reach as if in an expanding universe. Old archaic words came to his mind: Objects of police, prevention of crime, detection of offenders, preservation of public tranquillity ... Tranquillity ... what a marvellous word. Tranquillity.

'Smith.' In the far distance someone called his name, and again louder, nearer. 'Smith!' Swarbrick was holding his elbow; he became aware he was swaying on his feet, and of the strength in Swarbrick's supporting arm. He allowed himself to be guided into a chair. 'You are in a bad way, Smith. That is as nasty a bout of flu as I have seen. You've been sitting about in the cold far too long. Here, take this.' Swarbrick held out a glass of cloudy grey liquid.

'No, I'll be all right.' He tried to get to his feet to prove the point but Swarbrick pushed him back. 'It is soluble aspirin, Smith,' he said patiently as if to a reluctant child. 'Double the normal dose, I admit, but I need you on your feet for the next five or six hours. Now drink it.'

He took the glass. Suicide or salvation? Certainly not salvation, surrender perhaps. He held the glass up to his mouth to allow the last bitter dregs to enter his system.

Swarbrick took his overcoat from the wardrobe, and as he struggled into the sleeves something of the mocking lilt returned to his voice. 'Come on, boyo, let's go to Court and get Gredek's confession into the news. We'll take my car.'

Swarbrick leant across his desk and pressed the intercom button, 'Commissioner! Smith is feeling a great deal better; however, I must go with him to Court. I'm afraid these other matters will have to wait.'

Rachette's reply was curt, 'I presume you know best.'

The car swept past Horse Guards towards Admiralty Arch, with Swarbrick at the wheel. He had dismissed his driver, he knew there was more to come from Smith and it came. 'I am not going into this blind. What was the deal with Gredek? If you let him out it will stink to high heaven.'

'Oh, Gredek will hang! Or at least, he will appear to hang. New and more refined procedures will be adopted. After all we haven't hanged anyone for nearly twenty years. When Gredek is placed on the trap, the witnesses will be some distance away behind a glass screen. The trap will be sprung by remote control. He will be recovered intact from beneath, and will afterwards depart these shores in an easterly direction.'

'And the guarantees? How does he know there won't be a double-cross?'

Swarbrick ground his teeth in annoyance. The words came out reluctantly. 'The man who accompanied me to see Gredek at Cannon Row, the one your chum Routledge no doubt mentioned, was a diplomat from a nation who have a certain antipathy to the form of dictatorship Mulqueen and his Britain

First Movement would establish. He has been of considerable assistance to us in convincing Gredek to ... would "act" be the right word? ... as he has done in exchange for his life.

'Not that his masters are averse to a good old-fashioned class struggle taking place, but, as Mulqueen would win, it would be against their interests to allow it to happen. They much prefer to bide their time and let us destroy Mulqueen ourselves. They feel their chances will be better if the status quo continues. Anyway, the gentleman concerned was able to show Gredek a copy of a suitably impressive document we earlier handed to his embassy, guaranteeing Gredek's delivery to them in due course.'

Smith coughed dryly into cupped hands. Swarbrick offered him a fresh handkerchief from his pocket and said, 'Subject always to reliable performance during the trial period.'

Chapter XX

The overnight snow had, as usual, turned to thick, dirty, foot-freezing slush, as London slowly dissipated the accumulated heat of the two million people who daily swarmed into the offices, stores and markets of its centre.

In Bow Street, a jostling herd of reporters, photographers and T.V. technicians kicked and cursed as they struggled for positions of advantage at the barriers of a small security enclosure. A few of their more fortunate colleagues had already passed into the Court buildings, but it was their fate to wait in the cold for the arrival of the strongly escorted prison van.

The public, penned even farther back, was a mixture of the merely curious and the politically opposed. The trim menacing aloofness of the Britain Firsters contrasting with the simmering volatile fluency of the Left. Yet apart from the cross-fire of visual hatred, both parties maintained an uneasy and uncertain quiet, not entirely imposed by the massive police presence surrounding them.

There had been rumours, whispers and much speculation during the last twenty-four hours. Where one side thought it had an exploitable villain and the other a viable martyr, now doubt and uncertainty left both to wait in icy alliance for a capricious truth.

The scene had been played, in a shortened version, before a much smaller and less appreciative audience, eight days previously. Then Gredek had been unobtrusively taken before the Court for formal remand. Now, with unheard-of legal alacrity, he was to appear again to be committed to stand his trial at the

Central Criminal Court, built upon the site of Newgate Prison at a place called Old Bailey.

In the yard of Bow Street Police Station, the distant baying of two-tone sirens brought an alert stiffening to the police guarding the perimeter. One side of the yard was buttressed by the back wall of the Court building where a door gave access to the courts and the cells beneath.

Smith stood with O'Brien in the far corner. Near them, Swarbrick was in polite conversation with the Divisional Commander, who was explaining the extent of his security arrangements.

As the van and escorting vehicles pulled in and the siren crescendo fell to a moaning whine, Smith saw the door open and the white-haired gaoler emerge from the Court building. He was in smiling, jovial conversation with someone just behind him. Smith caught sight of a grease-stained, grey homburg hat.

Although Craddock was officially on sick leave, he was still a Deputy Assistant Commissioner and would have no difficulty in passing through the security of the Court.

'What the hell is he doing here?' The fever erupted again at the shock of seeing Craddock. He knew the man's masochistic pride. Was he going to sit in Court and listen to it all coming out? He could do it, he could sit there with cold contemptuous eyes looking up at him in the witness box ... The prison van swung round in front of the door and blocked Smith's view. He moved across to the left side.

Craddock was now standing away from the gaoler, the tail of his tartan scarf thrown across his shoulder, his hands deep in the side pockets of the well-worn Crombie coat. The grin, the fixed humourless grin, etched into his face pulling his lips back from his teeth.

The officer handcuffed to Gredek was easing his prisoner down from the back of the van as Smith started forward, breaking into a hesitant run. The slush moved under his feet and he went down scrabbling on his hands and his knee, the agonizing knee, twisted under the weight of his body. He saw the gun was already out of Craddock's pocket. It looked huge, even in Craddock's hand, a monstrous .45 Webley, a souvenir of his distant war.

Then a slithering light-footed figure hurtled over his head as he dragged forward. Gredek's escort stood in stupefied awe at the sight of the rising gun in the hand of such a senior officer, but Gredek saw the intention behind the frozen eyes and kicked at the gun-barrel as Swarbrick lunged between them.

The bullet struck high on Swarbrick's shoulder and in the reverberation of the shot, Smith heard the thud as it struck bone. Swarbrick spun round to take the second bullet in the middle of his back. He fell forward between the handcuffed wrists of Gredek and his escort and swung there for a moment, then slid into the cold dirt between their feet.

For a small second of time Craddock looked down at him, puzzled resentment melting his face. Around him, indecisive horror stayed the many hands of those that knew him. He took a step backwards and began to lift his gun.

The young smooth-faced policeman did not know him, and his pistol thrust out in a firm two-handed grip. Smith, crouching on his knees, tried to reach him with restraining fingers. The young officer fired twice into Craddock's chest. Craddock looked at him with enormous outrage, then as if he still controlled his muscles, he sat down and rolled slowly over on his side.

In the silence, the young officer looked around for approval. Finding none, he slowly holstered his pistol and took an indecisive step towards the body of his victim. Then he stopped and with a reddening face walked over to his Inspector, who saw the concern in his face and gave him the comfort of a reassuring arm.

Smith limped forward and picked up Craddock's gun. He faced Gredek, the gun hanging loosely in his hand. Their eyes met and locked in a conflict of wills against a babble of shouts and orders ... until Gredek turned his head downwards to the bodies at his feet and pulled against the restraining handcuff.

Neither he, nor any who heard, understood Smith's words: 'Do you think either of them knew the bloody difference?'

He passed the gun to O'Brien and went through the door into the Court. Behind him, Swarbrick's truth and Craddock's truth lay dead in the dirt. Now he had to find his own truth, and he wondered if he knew the right way.

PRODUCTION
EDITO-SERVICE S.A., GENEVA

PRINTED IN ITALY